MY
CUBA

A Novel

L & L Meier

Beachwood Publishing LLC
bwpub2020@gmail.com

ISBN: 978-1-7353137-0-2 - Paperback
eISBN: 978-1-7353137-1-9 - ePub
eISBN: 978-1-7353137-2-6 - mobi

Library of Congress Control Number: 2020913585

Printed in the United States of America   0 8 2 0 2 0

♾ This paper meets the requirements of ANSI/NISO Z39.48-1992 (Permanence of Paper)

Cover by Delaney-Designs
Spanish translation of Fidel Castro's Speeches by L Meier

To the Memory of

Doctor Luis Manuel Barreras, esteemed father and father-in-law

Ofelia Perfecta, mother, and mother-in-law

Ofelia Mercedes, sister, and sister-in-law

Enrique Barreras, uncle

Ana Magdalena, aunt

Yoya, aunt

Teo, cousin, and Cuban patriot

Gulf of Mexico

US

Miami •

Key West •

Straits of Florida

Havana ★ Guanabo
Hershey Matanzas
Rancho Fontana

Aspiro
Pinar del Río •

Bay of Pigs

Isle of Youth

CUBA

├─────────────┤
100 miles

CARRIBEAN
OCEAN

ATLANTIC
OCEAN

THE
BAHAMAS

Camaguey

Sierra Maestra
Mountains

Landing of
Granma Yacht

Santiago de Cuba   Guantanamo
U.S. Naval Base

Illustrated map by L. Meier ©2020

Killing

MY

CUBA

PREFACE

How many times have you read a novel and wondered how the author derived the characters' names? Fortune reigned for us with impressive family nicknames on deck—Wichi, Cuco, Nena, Charo, Yoya, and Teo. Wichi's wife was Ofelia, but her persona demanded a true appellation—Ofelia Perfecta. We allowed him to abridge it to OP—easy to pronounce, plus it piqued his mother-in-law, María Teresa, whose family dared not degrade their status with a moniker. Her brother, Nicolás, bore a name reminiscent of European aristocracy.

As for the children, the coauthor became Lizzi, because it was easier to develop the story, thinking of her in the third person. Our editor advised a fictional epithet for her older sibling since she had the same name as the mother. Luisito kept his true name.

We portray family members in both real and fictional scenes, and their behavior is consistent with each one's personality.

Many non-family fictional characters sprang from actual individuals who played significant roles in the lives of Wichi, his wife, and children.

Writing the book was a labor of love and a project in our golden years. By reading *Killing My Cuba*, we hope you will learn and laugh and love and cry and crave Cuban cuisine.

ONE

Two Births and One Prediction

Havana, Cuba
December 18, 1949

The 1950 brown Coronet sped west on San Rafael Street. Doctor Luis Barreras swerved in the Christmas holiday traffic and came to a screeching halt at the Galiano crossing. El Encanto, the enchanted department store, stood on the corner, its display windows adorned by artificial trees with white-colored lights, icicles, and ornaments. He wiped the sweat off his brow and thought how unrealistic these wintry scenes were since Havana's temperature was eighty-five degrees Fahrenheit. OP loved to shop there, but now she was at the hospital about to deliver their second child.

The light changed as the Santa Claus in the window waved a mechanical arm. The doctor recalled hearing his two-year-old daughter, Didi, laugh when the jolly man said, "Feliz Navidad." While he headed for the next intersection, a woman ran across the street after a little girl. He slammed on the pedal and prayed not to hit them. His brakes squealed, white smoke rose from the tires, and they imprinted black rubber lines on the pavement. She froze, holding the child as the sedan rushed toward them. It jolted, turned, slid sideways, and ended three feet short of the pair. He got out of the car, examined the couple, and breathed a sigh of relief that they were okay. *What a day so far.* First, the emergent call to see a patient in Old Havana. Next, his wife goes into labor, and now he came close to injuring two people. He zoomed away and hoped to reach the hospital before the baby was born. It was a balancing act to run a laboratory, practice hematology and general medicine, and be a good husband and father. He wanted to stay on OP's good side and missing the baby's birth would not help matters. Fortunately La Clínica en Vedado wasn't far. He stopped near the entrance and bolted out of the car.

An orderly pushing a wheelchair shouted, "Doctor Barreras, big emergency?"

"My wife's in the delivery room. Maybe I'm not too late."

"Good luck. Hope it's a boy."

Flying past the front desk, he thrust his hands between the elevator doors just in time before they shut. An older lady and a trembling little girl stood against the back wall. The third-floor button was lit. The child tugged on his white coat and asked if he was a doctor. He smiled and told her he was. "I'm afraid of elevators," she said. "They're not big enough."

"Me too." He suspected she had claustrophobia as he did. He preferred the stairs if several people were in the elevator, but today the necessity to arrive on time in the obstetrical suite outweighed fear. The bell dinged as they went past the second level—his goal within reach. The top-floor chimed. Then came a jolt, and the doors remained closed. *Oh, no, not now.* His chest tightened; he banged on the door and yelled for aid.

"Doctor, please help my granddaughter," said the woman. "She's not breathing well."

His inward focus melted as he stared at the little girl who had grown pale and was now panting. He took a large shawl from the lady's tote, put the cloth on the floor, and laid the child on it. He dropped to his knees, locked eyes with the girl, and told her she'd be all right. After he covered her nose and mouth with a brown paper sandwich bag, she took slow breaths, and within five minutes her respiration and color returned to normal. He heard a scraping sound; a crowbar separated the doors. Hands pulled them open, and a man stuck his head inside the lift. "Is everyone well?"

"The child had a scare, but she's fine." He hugged her. "You'll be okay now."

"Thank you, Doctor," said the grandmother.

He darted out the elevator, sprinted around the corner, stumbled over a broom, and crashed into the wall. Two nurses strolled nearby. The blonde said to the other, "Who's that tall and clumsy and handsome young doctor?"

He winked. "Where are the surgical gowns?" She pointed to the utility cart next to him. He lifted the cover, found a pile of folded gowns, grabbed one, tied it behind his neck and back, and sprinted to the end of the corridor. A sign showed three delivery rooms—Sala de Partos 1, 2, 3. He paused for a moment. *Which one? Can't afford to be wrong.* Didi was born in room 3, so this had to be his lucky number. He made a beeline toward the third door. He pushed it open, rushed in, turned to the right, and stopped at the sight of two legs spread apart in the stirrups. A protuberant abdomen hid the patient's face. Silence deafened the room.

The obstetrician removed his mask. "Hola, Doctor Barreras, you may recognize this patient—Ofelia Perfecta. She's having your baby."

"Whew, glad I'm in the right place."

"Wichi, is that you?" OP said. "Where have you been?"

"Who's she referring to?" the nurse asked.

"That's me, my sister couldn't say Luisi, so she named me *WeeChee*." She smiled. He rushed to OP's side. "Complicated emergency—couldn't get away any sooner. Lo siento."

"You're sorry. Can't you see I'm the emergency? I've been in painful labor and had to endure a wild taxi ride to get here." He said not to worry, he was with her, and soon they'd have their son. "Don't be so cocky, thinking it's a boy." He mentioned he'd go peek to check on progress.

As he moved toward her feet, she grabbed his arm. "NO, you're not peeking anywhere. You stay up here with me so we hear the news together whether it's a boy or girl."

"One more big push," said the OB. "We're almost there. I can see the head."

Next arrived the long-awaited sound of the baby's first cry. Wichi looked at the clock on the wall: 5:00 p.m., December 18, 1949. "Tell me, is it a boy?"

"No bebito, Doctor Barreras, but you have a healthy baby girl. I believe she's a nine-pounder."

OP raised her head. "Let me have her." The nurse examined the infant and placed the newborn on her mother's chest. "She's beautiful, my early Christmas present."

"Mira, que gordita, how chubby she is," Wichi said. "Have you thought of her name?"

"Isabella—let's call her Lizzi. What do you think?" He stroked his daughter's head and said Lizzi Barreras was a good name. OP remained in recovery for a short time after they carried the baby to the newborn nursery. Wichi took off the surgical gown and pushed her to the maternity ward. They entered the room and discovered a new mom snoring. "I wanted a private accommodation," OP said. "What happened?"

"They didn't have any." He helped her from the wheelchair to the bed, adjusted her pillow, and sat beside her. "Well, now we have two lovely daughters."

She nodded. "I thought I'd have this baby by myself." He told her besides the emergency, he got stuck in the hospital elevator. She clasped his hand. "I'm glad you made it." Her eyes began to close. He kissed her and said he'd come tomorrow, then sauntered out of the room.

Wichi chose to celebrate the birth of another daughter. It was happy hour at Valencio's Bar on Línea Street, a short drive away, and a rare scotch was perfect for the occasion. He parked the car and ambled along the sidewalk whistling "Bésame Mucho," his favorite tune. He pulled open the door and peered into the tavern, jammed full of patrons. *Is everybody in Havana celebrating their newborns?* One bar stool was empty, so he hurried to it.

The bartender turned to him. "What'll you have, Señor?"

"Scotch on the rocks." He scanned the crowd—men, near his age, puffing habanos. Based on their jovial state, they were relishing happy hour prices.

"Here you are."

Wichi held the glass and took a sip. *Aah, good whiskey.* A ruddy, white-bearded man in the adjacent seat looked at him. "You celebrating something?"

"Sí, I just had a new baby girl."

He handed him a cigar. "Congratulations. I'll drink to your daughter, but she ought to wriggle back where she came from instead of entering this stinking place."

"What the hell did you say?"

"Sorry, I didn't mean to insult the birth of your child."

"So, what's 'this stinking place'?"

"Cuba. I know too much." He shook his head.

"What is it you know?"

"Another birth arrives—a new decade begins—and the outcome looks lousy."

"Hmm, people are having fun, shopping, and celebrating."

"It's the government, Señor. President Socarrás's administration is inept, and crooked Batista's out there waiting—I'd better talk lower." Wichi glanced both directions at the men seated along the bar. No one paid notice. "So how well do you know politics?" the man asked.

"Not much, I look after my family and practice medicine."

"Since you have a new daughter, it's best you learn a few facts about our country."

"Go on, you have my attention."

"Remember 1933, Batista led a coup, controlled the military—and Cuba—for seven years, and then was elected president in 1940. He emptied the treasury in '44 when President Grau San Martín took office, and now Batista lives like a king in the US."

"But he's not in power at the present."

"He still pulls the strings, even got elected senator in absentia last year. He'll weasel his way back onto center stage, and that'll spell disaster for Cuba." The man stroked his beard and looked Wichi straight in the eye. "Imagine

Cuba, a shimmering school of fish, with Batista the barracuda lurking, then attacking, again and again."

"Whoa, you're giving me goosebumps."

"Oh, but there's more: the water turns crimson and draws a more ominous predator who comes to devour."

Wichi took a deep breath, his shoulders slumped. "You think this will happen?"

"Ha, I'm sure of it. When the next decade is over, you will relive this day and the words of Elías Verdadero."

"Hmm, not enamored with your prediction. Let's toast to good times ahead."

The man lifted his glass. "We'll drink, but first tell me your name."

"Wichi Barreras."

"Okay, Wichi Barreras—to Cuba—we shall love it or leave it." They toasted and shook hands. Elías got off the bar stool, turned, and disappeared into the smoky room.

TWO

Pig and a Date

Havana, Cuba
December 23, 1954
Five Years Later

A hard bump and Wichi was airborne off the truck seat. His head hit the ceiling. "Rey, take it easy on the potholes. You'll have to repair a broken axle, plus I don't need a concussion to spoil Christmas Eve." This Nochebuena was special. His wish for a son had come true. Luisito was now a year and a half old and liked lechón asado. Rey said the best hogs for the traditional roast pig dinner were raised at Pepe Fontana's farm, twenty miles southwest from Havana.

"Sorry, Doctor, these country roads aren't well-maintained, and I haven't been this way in ten years."

Wichi picked up a crinkled pamphlet off the seat titled: "Batista, No Más." He asked, "What's this?"

Rey's eyes widened. "Guys in my apartment building circulate these anti-Batista flyers."

Wichi read how much they loathed Batista. Rey said they despised the dictator because he took over the presidency by force in the 1952 election and did away with the constitution. The protests had increased since July 26 last year, when a group of communist youths and members of an opposition political party rebelled against Batista. "I believe they attacked the Moncada military barracks in Santiago and were led by Fidel Castro," Wichi said. He grabbed the seat as the truck veered to avoid a tire in the road. "But if I recall correctly, the raid was a bust, and Fidel wasn't in the group that stormed the garrison." Rey agreed and said following the fiasco Castro went into hiding and later surrendered under the protection of an Archbishop in Santiago. "And they jailed him," Wichi added. Rey nodded and turned sharply to miss another pothole. Wichi had heard Castro wanted to retaliate because he lost in a previous rigged election and was now planning a revolution while in prison. He asked Rey his thoughts.

"Batista is corrupt. I don't like what he did."

"You're a good man and a son to me. Just be careful with this political stuff. I don't want you to get hurt." Rey thanked him and nodded. Wichi felt at ease in his presence. After caring for his dying father, he sponsored Rey through trade school and set him up in an automotive shop nearby. The young man also maintained the professional office building where Wichi practiced, and he kept the Coronet running as if it were brand-new. The pair reminisced the Barreras family's move from the Vedado apartment in the city to the Biltmore neighborhood. "It's a farther drive for me," Wichi said, "but I enjoy raising the family in the suburbs near the ocean."

"My father's old truck came in handy hauling the furniture. It was fun except for the time I braked to miss the dog, and we almost lost your desk."

Wichi laughed and slapped him on the shoulder. "What's that whiff of cologne? Didn't know you had to smell good to catch a pig."

"I have to come clean, Doctor. The pork will be scrumptious, but I have an ulterior motive to bring you to Rancho Fontana."

"Ah, the farmer must have a daughter."

"Sí, Sarita, the love of my life. We planned to get married, but then my family moved to Havana." Wichi questioned why the relationship ended, and why Rey now wished to go back to the ranch. "We left when I was seventeen," Rey said, "and Sarita didn't respond to my letters. Later I discovered her mother died and she took it hard."

Wichi cocked an eye. "Could a spark still burn?"

"Maybe, but ten years have passed."

"Don't let time hinder you. My wife and I courted for eight years before getting married."

"You gotta be kidding?"

"Well, it wasn't our choosing. A possessive mother-in-law didn't want to share her daughter with a socially inferior man from a poor family of eight children in Camagüey." He said that troubles escalated when she learned he moved his new wife into an apartment that fit his budget. Problem was, they carried the corpse of the previous tenant out the back as he and OP entered the front. Rey couldn't help but laugh.

"Are you in her good graces now?"

"Afraid not. She remains a thorn in our marriage and family. Differences between my wife and me are enough, but she magnifies them."

"Sorry to hear that. If Sarita likes me half as much as Pepe does, we should do well."

Rey stomped on the brakes and slowed down. "What's that ahead?" Two police cars with flashing lights blocked the road. He maneuvered the truck closer and stopped. The confrontation between a dozen sugarcane workers standing on the shoulder and two policeman pointing guns at them baffled Wichi. Another policeman held a man face-down on the pavement, the cop's boots pressed against his back. The guy screamed obscenities. After cuffing him they jerked the hombre to his feet, his hair soaked in blood. The workers waived their blades in the air and chanted, "Macheteros sí, Batista no." They rushed toward the cops. An officer fired a shot over their heads.

The prisoner shouted for them to stop. "Time's not right for you to die. We'll get these pigs later."

Rey pushed open the door and jumped out. Wichi tried to catch him but missed. "Where are you going?" he said.

"I went to school with that fella they beat. He's no criminal."

"Get back in, Rey. You're asking for trouble."

He headed for the man as they shoved him into the police car. "Let him go. He doesn't deserve this."

One policeman grabbed Rey, gave him a hard jab to the face, pushed him to the ground, and followed with a kick in the flank. Wichi got out of the truck and rushed to the scene. Another officer stood in his way. "Señor, you asking for the same treatment?"

"I'm Doctor Barreras, a hematologist from Havana. This man is my mechanic. Please stop hurting him."

The cop stared at Wichi and said, "Hmm, you look familiar, I've been in your office. You treated my father for leukemia several years ago. Because of that, I'll let you and your man go. Leave and forget what you saw—if you know what I mean."

Wichi hurried over and helped Rey back to the truck. "Can

you drive?" He nodded and sat behind the wheel. Wichi closed the door and watched as the workers lowered their blades, then turned and lumbered to the fields. Rey moaned and reached for the ignition. "Sure you're okay?"

"Sí, I'll get us out of here." His hands trembled as he cranked the engine and sped away. "Thanks, Doctor, for saving my life. I couldn't sit here and let those bastards . . ."

"Don't worry, you did what was humane." Neither one had much to say for the next several miles until they spotted the RANCHO FONTANA sign in the distance. "Stop before we get to the gate and let me examine your forehead." Rey halted the truck on the shoulder, and Wichi checked him — nothing cracked, just a small cut above the left eye. He eased up the gravel driveway to the house where a man stood on the steps and waved. The beefy, middle-aged rancher took off his straw hat to greet them. His weathered face revealed long hours working in the hot sun.

Rey stepped out and greeted him. "Hola, Señor Pepe, Cómo estás?"

"Bien, missed seeing you." He pointed to Rey's eye. "A little cut there, been fighting over women?"

"There's only one woman I'd fight over." Rey glanced toward the house. The farmer patted his shoulder and they laughed. He accompanied Pepe to the truck. "Please meet my employer and good friend, Doctor Luis Barreras." They shook hands and exchanged greetings. Pepe offered a tour of the farm.

Wichi winked at the young man. "No need to come with us. I'll call you later."

"Sounds good," Rey said. "There's a familiar swing waiting on the porch."

Pepe escorted Wichi in the direction away from the house. He said his family had owned the ranch for years, not a huge place but self-sufficient. Farms had always intrigued Wichi, and he guessed rural blood flowed in his veins. He caught a whiff of the aroma from the tobacco curing barn nearby. Pepe provided a basket for him to gather eggs from the chicken yard. He picked bell peppers and a few garlic cloves from the garden. A cow mooed in the barn. Pepe looked at Wichi and extended his hand. "Oh no, sorry, but no one taught me that." Pepe tittered and said not to worry, Sarita did the milking. Wichi inquired how the two managed the ranch. He said he was fortunate to have Ignacio, his trusted hired hand, to help run the place and take care of the horses. "Horses—put me on one, and I'm in heaven."

The farmer smiled and kept walking. "First let's find your pig."

Rey rocked in the porch swing with eyes transfixed on the horizon. He finger-combed his hair, once, then a few more times, with thoughts glued on images of the enchanting Sarita. A soft female voice from behind said, "Rey, you're here."

He turned toward her. "Sarita, good to see you." He stared at her long and wavy brown hair, stunning figure, and the most gorgeous green eyes imaginable. "You haven't changed—lovely as ever."

"You're always the flirt, and handsome to boot." She smiled and joined him on the swing. "How have you been? Rey, you're hurt."

"It's nothing and a long story."

"Ours is a long story."

"True, Sarita, all those years and no word from you. I didn't think you loved me anymore."

"You're wrong. I still loved you, but after Mamá died I couldn't leave Papá alone." He leaned over and kissed her. She paused and took a deep breath. "I've missed you. How's the big city?"

He mentioned he had a good life and enjoyed working as a mechanic in his own shop. He clasped her hand and apologized for not reaching out during the years following her mother's passing. "I'm glad you didn't hate me."

"Rey, I've never hated you. We had special times together."

Pepe's voice roared from the barn. *Caramba*, he had to go. He walked away, peeked back, and said, "The doctor's here for lechón. Me—another reason."

"Rey, por favor." She flashed a coquettish smile. "Go on, I'll be waiting."

He dashed toward the sty. A luscious pig snorted and slopped in the mud. "Doctor, this one looks too big for your family."

"No problem," Pepe said. "The doctor can have the loin, and I'll take the rest to my cousins." He offered to butcher and prepare the lechón asado.

"Bueno," said the doctor, "my wife can't boil water, and Modesta, our new cook and housekeeper, doesn't come until January." He turned to Rey. "Is it possible for you to pick up the pig and bring it to my house tomorrow?"

Without hesitation he grinned and replied, "Sí, I don't

need an excuse to return to Rancho Fontana." He darted back to the farmhouse; the doctor and Pepe strolled to the stables.

The police incident still preyed on Wichi's mind. He described what happened to Pepe, who wasn't surprised. He said that many plantation owners made macheteros cut sugar cane for long hours in sweltering heat with little pay. Foremen beat the defiant cutters, and if any insurgency occurred, police arrived on the scene. "I saw eyes filled with hate for Batista," Wichi said.

Pepe nodded. "He uses his guns to keep workers under control, for a price I suspect."

"Rey recognized the guy they arrested," Wichi said. The farmer was sure the man belonged to a militant group that planned to overthrow Batista. "It looks like revolutionary factions are forming." Pepe agreed. "Sorry I brought up politics," Wichi said. "You told me you had horses."

"Five, and plan to buy more." Wichi complimented the rancher on his red barn and immaculate stalls. He said that horses had been in his blood since birth. Pepe introduced Camagüey, his prized brown stallion. Awe transformed Wichi's face as he stroked the mane of the magnificent animal. Pepe smiled. "Are you interested in riding him?"

"Sí." His eyes blazed with excitement. The farmer bridled and saddled the horse. "Aren't you riding too?"

"No, I promised my cousin a sack of feed, but I'll return soon."

Wichi mounted the splendid steed with real cowboy know-how. After a deep breath and a firm grip on the reins, he clicked and nudged the horse's flanks. The stallion reared his head, and they galloped away. The wind lifted the animal's mane as they sprinted across pastures and wove around patches of tall grass standing in the fields. Trotting along the creek, the stallion stopped dead in his tracks. Wichi flew forward, out of the saddle, and over his head. He hit the ground, arms first, slid on his belly, and ended up with a mouthful of dirt—not hurt, just irked. He spat, wiped his mouth, and cursed. *Can't believe the horse spooked and threw me.* He got up, brushed the dust off his pants, spotted the stallion race across the pasture, and hoped he made it to the barn before Pepe returned.

Swinging with Sarita on the porch delighted Rey. He placed his foot against the warped floorboard and gave a push. They held hands, smiled at each other, and reminisced old times. She beamed and said, "Do you remember those walks beside the creek?" He recalled well the time she slipped on the rock and fell into the swimming hole. He jumped in and rescued her, and they went skinny dipping. She batted her eyelashes. "It was our first time together."

"Wonderful in the water," he said.

She blushed. "Shame on you."

The sound of hoof beats interrupted the moment as Camagüey charged toward the barn. Terror gripped Rey when he saw the empty saddle. He needed to find the doctor. Sarita stabled the stallion while he hurried to the field. He spotted his friend walking the dirt road and mumbling to himself. As he got closer, the doctor's clothes appeared dirty and his hair ruffled. He made a fist and swore.

"What happened?"

"Camagüey threw me. I can sense it when a horse is prone to spooking, but I misjudged him." They trudged to the front of the house. Sarita joined them and whispered in Rey's ear if his friend was hurt. He shook his head and said the only thing injured was his pride. The doctor looked furtively in several directions and asked if Pepe had returned. A few moments passed, and his vehicle appeared in the driveway. He brushed off his clothes and smoothed his hair.

The farmer got out of the truck. "Enjoy your ride in the country?"

"Sí, he's an impressive horse, had a great ride."

Rey gulped. He and Sarita shared glances and suppressed their smiles. His eyes focused on her. "I'll return tomorrow afternoon for the pig." A thought flashed through his mind. "Care to have Nochebuena with my family?"

Her face brightened. "Is it okay, Papá?"

"Sí, mi amor."

Rey smiled. "See you tomorrow." He and Wichi got into the truck.

Pepe walked over to the window and shook the doctor's hand. "You'll soon have mouthwatering lechón on the table." He thanked the farmer and said goodbye while Rey waved at Sarita.

They drove along the road past the gate. "Need a map for your return trip?"

"No way, Doctor."

THREE

Garlic and the Good Night

Havana, Cuba
December 24, 1954

Rey awoke before light the next morning. As he lay in bed, thinking of Sarita's bedazzling emerald eyes, he imagined a warm embrace and a kiss. Seven o'clock, the alarm rang and interrupted his fantasy. He stumbled into the bathroom and looked in the mirror. *Ugh.* After splashing water on his face, he brushed his teeth, put on his mechanic clothes, and returned to the sink. Something needed to happen with his ugly mug before leaving to see her. He placed his nose to his armpit and took a good whiff—the odor of a wet dog.

That morning at work, his mind stayed focused on Sarita. By noon, the crew had finished. "Amigos, it's Nochebuena, Christmas Eve, let's close the place. I have a hot date and need a shower and a dab of cologne."

The men burst out laughing. One mechanic pulled the floor jack from under a car. "Man, you gotta be kidding."

A buddy grabbed a shop towel and wiped his hands. "Cologne, ha. Nothin' will replace the stink of motor oil."

"Get out of here, guys. Feliz Navidad."

Pepe had Ignacio help carry the pig to the kitchen and place the meat on an aluminum pan. After salting the pork, he punched holes in the skin with a knife and poured in mojo marinade. His wife, gone these past nine years, used to mix the sour oranges, garlic, salt, and olive oil. When his ranch hand wasn't looking, he wiped away a tear.

Sarita walked into the kitchen. "What can I do?"

"Make more mojo."

"I'll reek of garlic tonight."

"No, you won't. When you're finished, rub your fingers with lemon juice as Mamá used to do." Sarita asked if he planned to stay home alone. "My brother invited me to celebrate Nochebuena with his family, and I'm taking part of the lechón for dinner."

She cleaned her hands and said it was time for a shampoo. "I want to make sure Rey knows the aroma belongs to the pig and not me."

Pepe snickered, sat in his favorite chair, and waited an hour for the mojo to flavor the meat. Ignacio helped him place it on the roasting pit. After several hours the lechón gained a golden tone and crackled skin. Pepe carved the hog and prepared the loin. A sample of his prized pork tasted delicious. This should be the best lechón the doctor ever ate.

Rey returned to the apartment, showered, shaved, and scrubbed his hands with extra soap. Only the best shirt and a pair of khaki pants were acceptable for this occasion. A little spiking of the hair with greasy pomade and vintage cologne dabbed on the chin should do the trick. The first stop on his quest for Sarita's gift was Woolworth. He entered the building and instantly realized the merchandise was too cheap for the girl of his dreams. While walking along the sidewalk, he spied Fin de Siglo, an upscale department store, and hurried through the revolving door. An employee waited to assist and pointed the way to the jewelry counter. Rey looked through the glass display. *Caramba, these prices are out of sight.* The salesclerk appeared as he rubbed the back of his head. "May I help you, Señor?"

"Sí, please show me that pearl choker." She handed over the necklace—the perfect present imaginable around Sarita's neck. Not even thinking, he blurted out, "I'll take it."

The lady inquired if he wanted to know the cost. He nodded. She inspected the strand. "Five pesos." He bit his lip, knowing that price represented over a half day's work. But without hesitation, he reached into his pocket, pulled out the money, and told the woman to wrap the gift with Christmas paper. "Sí, Señor."

The store clock showed 3:30, and he'd likely not get to the ranch on time. He raced home, cleaned the front seat of the truck, took out the trash on the floor, and sprayed cologne in the cab.

Beyond the city limits, the temperature had dropped, but Rey still felt the heat. He was running behind schedule and must be careful not to hit a pothole and get a flat. The gift-wrapped box rested in the seat. Fontana's gate lay ahead, and he drove up the gravel road toward the porch. *Hmm, why is another vehicle parked in front of the house?* Sarita and a man climbed out of the cab, so he stopped the truck and watched. She gave him a hug; they smiled and laughed. Rey slapped the steering wheel. "Dammit, Sarita, what are you doing?" Thoughts stirred in his mind to turn around and leave. *No, she owes me an explanation.*

The man drove out of the driveway and yelled, "Feliz Navidad." Rey engaged the gears, churned a few rocks, and stopped at the porch. He got out and slammed the door, and with narrowed eyes he stared at Sarita. Didn't matter to him that she had on a sexy tank top and tight white pants.

"How many guys are you seeing?"

She blinked her eyes. "Whaat? Rey, you have it wrong. That was Ignacio."

"Ignacio who?"

"Our hired hand—married with a wife and three children. Didn't you see him yesterday with Papá?"

"No, I was with you. Why were you two hugging and laughing?"

"It's Nochebuena, the good night, for heaven's sake. The man has worked here ten years, and we couldn't manage the farm without him." Rey lowered his head—wrong impression. Sarita placed her hand on his cheek, lifted his chin, and looked him in the eye. "Rey, are you jealous?" A grin covered his face. She smiled and grabbed his arm. "Come inside the house."

He followed her up the steps and stopped. "Un momento, I forgot something in the truck." He returned with the gift and opened the front door. Sarita stood in the kitchen and wrapped foil around the pork loin. "The pig smells delicious," he said. She turned and smiled. He winked. "Ven aquí, come here."

"What do you want? We have to leave soon."

"Not yet." He walked toward her with the gift behind his back.

"What are you hiding?"

"You'll see. Close your eyes and hold out your hands." As she waited there, he marveled at her beauty. He handed her the box and said, "Open it."

She held the present and blinked. "What is it?" He shrugged. She unwrapped the Fin de Siglo package and pulled the tissue back, revealing the pearl necklace. "Rey, you shouldn't have. I LOVE IT." She set the box on the desk and threw her arms around his neck and kissed him. He caught his balance, held on to her, and said she hadn't even worn it. Sarita lifted her long brown hair to the side. "I want you to place it on my neck." His breath warmed her skin as he fastened it. She faced him; her cheeks flushed. The pearl strand looked stunning, and he pulled her close. Hidden feelings resurfaced––ones he'd suppressed for years.

The embrace lasted forever. He gazed into her eyes. "During these years I have never stopped loving you." His finger outlined her lips. "Mi amor, you're the loveliest woman I've ever seen."

"I'm glad you came back," she said. "Can we make up for lost time?" She held his hand and led him to her room. "I have something to show you." On the nightstand lay a stack of letters. "I've kept them, every one you wrote. I'm so sorry I didn't answer." Tears flooded her eyes. "Each night thoughts of you helped me fall asleep."

Rey drew Sarita into a tight embrace; her emerald eyes sparkled with passion. She sat at the edge of the bed, pulled him beside her, and stroked his face. He kissed her lips, her cheeks—then flinched. "What if your father returns?"

"He won't, mi amor, he's at my cousin's." She yanked him back and kissed his neck. "You smell so sexy."

"OH, NO." He jumped up and clasped his head with both hands. "The smell—the lechón——the doctor."

She pulled on his arm. "Let the pig wait."

"I can't, my love. I promised to deliver it to my boss before dinner."

He rushed to the kitchen, grabbed the loin, and took it to the truck. After opening the passenger door, he helped Sarita inside and placed a soft kiss on her cheek. They sped along the driveway, she slid over to his side and put her arm behind his neck, and they kissed again. He smiled and hummed "Aquellos Ojos Verdes," his favorite tune. "Those Green Eyes" seated next to him made his day.

Wichi paced the living room, going from one window to another, worried if Rey had encountered a roadblock. He rambled into the kitchen, picked up a spoon, and sampled the "Moors and Christians." *Umm, the black beans and white rice are tasty.* He forked a fried plantain before taking a whiff of the garlic aroma from the yuca con mojo simmering in olive oil. The garlicky Cuban potato had always been one of his favorite dishes. "We're fortunate Olga's not just my secretary but an outstanding cook," he said to OP.

A sneer arced in his direction. "Don't forget, I made the pineapple and avocado salad. Where's the lechón you promised?"

He searched for an answer. "Uh, Rey and Sarita are coming." The truck horn sounded their arrival, and he rushed to the driveway. "You have the pig?"

"Sí, Doctor."

"Por favor, take the meat to the kitchen. OP has the serving dish ready."

Sarita stood in the foyer, and Wichi complimented the pearl choker on her neck. A surprise Christmas gift, she told him, from Rey who returned and put his arms around her waist. "You have great taste in selecting jewelry," Wichi said, "and finding this lovely señorita."

"Gracias, Doctor, I have to agree with you—she's my sweetheart." Rey said they must leave for Nochebuena dinner with his family.

The two men embraced. Wichi hugged Sarita, handed Rey an envelope, and escorted the couple to the door. "Feliz Navidad." He waved and smiled as they walked away clasping hands. He remembered the plate of chicharones on the buffet and rushed to crunch the tasty morsels. Soon he called out, "Let's eat, I'm filling up on pork skins." OP brought a bottle of wine, and they sat at the dining room table with Luisito and the girls. He looked over the delectable feast. "Now this is a real Nochebuena dinner."

After several helpings of just about everything, Wichi leaned back in his chair, loosened his belt a notch, and took another sip of red wine. It was time for a good smoke, so he headed to the study while OP put the children to bed and then left for midnight Mass. He sat in his comfy chair behind the desk, opened the cigar box, and pulled out his favorite— H. Upmann. The aroma of the fine tobacco evoked a pleasant feeling. He snipped the end of the habano, struck the match, placed the tip above the flame, and rolled the cigar around for proper lighting. Relaxing in the seat, he drew a puff and blew the smoke upward. As he watched the cloud dissipate, he reflected on his family—complete with two beautiful daughters and a son. A smile settled on his face, and he puffed again. This time the billow took on an eerie crocodile shape—*strange*. He pondered a few moments before making the association—the island of Cuba. He gazed as the image persisted, then evaporated, leaving an omen that lingered in his brain—the prediction he'd heard five years earlier—from a stranger named Elías Verdadero.

FOUR

Birthday, Brother, and Batista

Havana, Cuba
December 18, 1956

"I'll murder that Batista bastard," said the man seated at the table near the sidewalk. The girl with him put her hand over his mouth and said he was going to get them shot.

Wichi sipped his espresso cup and scanned the customers sitting in the outdoor café. Most were young, likely students at the University of Havana. He supposed they had nothing to do since a group in November closed the school in protest of the Batista government. While he waited next door to the bakery, he looked forward to a few moments of tranquility. They promised to have Lizzi's birthday cake finished in thirty minutes. Ten o'clock showed on his watch, and he needed to stop at the office and pick up medication for a patient. He crossed his arms and passed the time but noticed the crowd had become agitated.

"You're right, man," blared a bearded student sitting nearby. "Get rid of Batista before he kills Fidel and Che."

Wichi recalled recent headlines when Castro and Che Guevara landed near Santiago on the Granma yacht and barely escaped to the Sierra Maestra mountains. A girl seated at another table stood and shouted, "It was you revolutionary guys and a few of our faculty who shut down the university." A tall, blond male beside her rose and shook his fist. "Yeah, and you blamed it on Batista."

People began talking and arguing among themselves, and soon the noise level turned into a roar. A student leaned over to Wichi. "Hey, Señor, where do you stand in this?"

"No idea, I'm waiting for the baker to finish a cake."

"Leave now, things will get nasty." Just then a long-haired, stocky guy walked over and punched the blond man. A coffee cup whizzed by the table and crashed on the floor.

Wichi jumped to his feet—time to go. He hustled past a girl hit by a flying saucer and saw blood dripping from her face. He stopped and wadded a few napkins in his hand. "Miss, I'm a doctor, hold pressure on the wound." She thanked him and moved inside the café. Pandemonium exploded, with at least a dozen people fighting. As he scuttled toward the bakery, a gunshot sounded, sirens pierced the air, and three police cars appeared on the scene. A man pursued by a cop ran along the street. The two rounded the corner and disappeared, with several more shots fired. Three officers herded the students against the wall and began questioning them.

Wichi grasped the door handle when he felt a firm grip on the shoulder. He winced, turned, and a policeman stood in his face. "What do you know of this anti-government uprising?"

"Nada."

"Are you one of the university troublemakers?"

"No, I'm Dr. Barreras, here to pick up my daughter's birthday cake at the bakery, and then on to my office in Vedado."

The officer demanded proof and marched him inside the

store. The baker verified he was a customer, and the cop apologized. "Students have threatened to attack the Presidential Palace, and we're on alert." Wichi accepted the explanation, and the policeman left. He admired the birthday cake—a work of art. Lizzi got her winter theme of silver bells and holly and small, outfitted dolls that skied along the edges of the icing snow. She'd love the big red "7" perched in the middle. The riot at the café left him shaken, but his nerves calmed enough to make a quick stop at his nearby office. *Glad OP didn't come to the bakery.*

Lizzi peeked from behind the kitchen door and watched her little brother sneak into the dining room. She knew Luisito was going for her cake, and like a cat eyeing the mouse, she prepared to catch him in the act. As he ran his fingers through the icing, she sprang on him and surprised the frosting thief with a sharp slap on the wrist. "Get your grungy hands off my cake. I'm calling Mami."

Luisito didn't appear the least bit worried. He looked at her and grinned. "Yum, yum."

"Mami, come here." No answer. She rushed into the kitchen.

"Just a moment, it's mealtime for Apollo, Apache, and Diana."

"Your boxers can wait. I want you to see what Luisito has done."

She followed Lizzi and found his lips and fingers white with frosting. "Leave your sister's cake alone. Now, run along, and behave."

"That's no punishment. He'll do it again."

She stood there fuming when Didi called, "Lizzi, come get dressed. You don't want to greet your guests in shorts."

The doorbell rang. Lizzi and Mami welcomed Patsy and Señora Purcey, her first guests. Patsy jumped inside and greeted Lizzi. "Feliz cumpleaños."

"Gracias," she said. "Hola, cómo está, Señora Purcey?"

"Bieeen, cómo estaaas. How y'all doing?"

"Muy bien, Dottie. Please enter."

"Graaaciuus, OP."

Lizzi looked over at her smiling father standing across the room. She knew it was hard for him to keep from laughing when Señora Purcey sang her words. He said that southern Americans spoke that way. Patsy handed her an oversized box with a pink bow and tugged her into the living room to open the present. "Let me guess—a doll, maybe comic books?" She ripped off the wrapping paper, showing three layers of candy bars. "Hershey chocolates, thanks, and I love your Hershey, Penn-something story."

"Hershey, Pennsylvania, where they're made. We visited there, and I ate so many candy kisses, they came out of my ears."

She chuckled and pulled Patsy's arm. "Let's go see my cake. The frosting is white as your ponytail."

The bell rang again, and Mami opened the door. "Hola, Pilar, glad you could come to the party."

Lizzi came to the entrance and greeted her teammate. "You look darling in that pink sundress and purple headband. I'm happy we have on dresses instead of our competition swimsuits." Pilar returned a half-smile. A tall man wearing a black suit and dark sunglasses handed Lizzi a gift wrapped in green glitter and a gold bow.

"Girls," Mami said, "go to the backyard. Modesta has lemonade for you."

Wichi walked to the door as the man stepped toward the black limo parked in front of the house. For sure he was the body-guard and driver. The earlier events of the day echoed in his mind, and he guessed that anyone related to Batista needed protection, especially Pilar's father since he was Batista's cousin. "Please join the party."

"No, I'm on duty," said the man. "I'll be in the car until it's over."

Wichi returned to the festivities, grabbed a drink, and sat on the stone patio to watch the girls play pin the tail on the donkey. Lizzi blindfolded Patsy, spun her, and she staggered toward the burro. They laughed at the tail on the donkey's ear.

A loud pop came from inside the house. "Qué caray." Wichi said. Twice again it happened—the shots at the café and Batista's relative here in his home—the radicals had come after her. He shouted, "Girls, get low." He ran to Pilar and pulled her behind a tree.

The door slid open; the bodyguard flashed his pistol and made a sweeping motion across the lawn with the weapon. "Where's Pilar?" Wichi motioned him to the palm. The man rushed over to the sobbing girl and secured her behind his back. He continued to survey the yard with his finger on the trigger.

Lizzi and her friends cried. Wichi told them to stay put, and he hastened into the house. He stalked by the kitchen and heard another pop. This time it didn't sound so ominous. Peering into the room, he witnessed Luisito puncture another balloon with the donkey pin. He took a deep breath—afraid to laugh considering the gravity of the situation. He rushed outside and explained to the bodyguard and the girls what happened. The man grabbed Pilar, and they ran to the front. Wichi and Lizzi followed. "Pilar, don't go. The party's not over."

"Sorry, I have to leave. My present is on the table."

The limousine sped away and Lizzi sat on the curb, sniffling. Wichi helped her up, handed a handkerchief, and they went to the bedroom. She cried and sat on the mattress for several minutes. Wichi hugged her and said she had other guests and a delicious cake still waiting.

She wiped her eyes. "You're right, Papi, I have seven candles ready for me."

"Bet you can't blow them out."

"Bet I can." She raced to the dining room.

FIVE

Medals and More Medals

Biltmore Neighborhood
March 1957

"Presidential Palace Attacked." Wichi caught the headline as he unfolded the Saturday morning paper and showed it to OP. She cringed and let a plate of food fall to the kitchen floor. "Is Batista dead?" she asked. Modesta grabbed a dustpan and broom to clean up the mess.

"Apparently not, let me keep reading. It says he was not in his office when a group stormed the building, and before the attackers could reach him, the guards shot them."

OP pulled up a chair. "Who did it?"

He glanced at the list and learned they were members of a revolutionary student organization. "It was only three months ago on Lizzi's birthday that those undergraduates almost got me arrested at the bakery." OP asked why he hadn't told her that before now. "I've tried to spare you and the children the ugly details of Batista's corrupt government."

She read more of the paper. "Oh, no, they killed José Antonio Echeverría. I know his family. The article says he and other students took over Radio Reloj and broadcast Batista was dead, but the message didn't get over the air."

"Unfortunate." Wichi shook his head. "He'll retaliate with a bloodbath, and we're in for more violence and killing." After the last gulp of espresso, he suggested she quit teaching kindergarten near the Palace. OP agreed, but said her goal was to finish the school year. "Until now Batista's regime hasn't bothered us," he replied, "but it may soon spread to the suburbs. He reminded her to not mention political problems to the children. She concurred.

Lizzi poked her head into the kitchen. "Mami, time to leave, I can't wait to swim with the angelfish."

"I'll be ready in a moment. Go get the Martin girls."

Lizzi knocked on her neighbor's door and Señora Martin answered. "Buenos días, sweetie, come inside. Rosie's in her room and Graciela's tying her pigtails." She ran upstairs and saw the housekeeper finish the last braid.

Rosie grabbed her blue dolphin inflatable and asked Lizzi if she could bring it. "Mami won't mind because you're my best friend. We'll squeeze him into the car." The two girls sped down the stairs, with Rosie dragging the float. Lizzi inquired where her sister was. Rosie said she was preparing lunch, her job because she was older. They stopped by the kitchen and found Margie packing a basket full of sandwiches. Lizzi patted her stomach. "Those look yummy. I'll get Didi to make some for me."

"Come along, Lizzi," Señora Martin said. "I want to show something to OP before you leave." She handed her mother the latest edition of the Biltmore neighborhood directory. Mami had the biggest grin Lizzi had ever seen. Señora Martin asked her and Didi to look at the front page. "They printed this picture of your family and wrote a caption."

Doctor Luis Barreras, his lovely wife, Ofelia Perfecta, and their children, Didi, Lizzi, and Luisito. Also present is the family dog, Apollo, a boxer with a face that attracts few friends.

Everyone laughed, and Didi said the photographer didn't know how to make Apollo smile.

Mami called for Luisito, "Hurry and jump into the back seat. Your friend's birthday party starts at ten."

"OP, can you drive with that dolphin sticking out of the window?"

"Sí, Margo, I'll be okay since Biltmore club is only a mile away."

"Aren't we fortunate to have this gathering place on the ocean where the children can swim and play on the beach?"

"The club was a major reason Wichi moved out here—for our family activities and horseback riding."

"Mami, you told us we had to leave, and we're still sitting here," Didi said.

"You'd better go, OP. Thanks for taking my girls."

They waved goodbye and rambled toward Biltmore. Lizzi shoved the float aside and clapped her hands when she caught sight of the huge waves in the ocean. She thought of the two most wonderful places on earth—her home and this club.

Mami stopped at the entrance. "Lizzi, don't forget your swim training." The girls dashed out of the car. "Have fun. I'll pick you up at two o'clock sharp."

Everybody ran to the beach, found an empty hut, and put their belongings in it. Didi and Margie sunbathed nearby. Lizzi and Rosie rushed to the water. Lizzi swam toward the pier, looking for yellow angelfish while her friend paddled after her on the float. The two got a short distance when she remembered swim practice. "We have to go back to shore. I can't be late, or Coach Tutu will make me do extra laps." Rosie wanted to stay on the dolphin. "See you later." Lizzi headed to the hut and grabbed her bag, Didi told her she was going to meet Julito on the boardwalk. Lizzi yelled back at Margie that Rosie was still riding the waves. "I'll return in an hour," she said and hurried to ask the coach how she should train today.

"Have to prepare you for our inter-club meet next Saturday," Coach Tutu said. He reminded her of the Big Five competition in Guanabo in June. "For this session do twenty-five freestyle laps. Concentrate on fluid strokes without leaving a wake behind."

"Bueno, I'll try."

"Don't try, do it."

Lizzi nodded, knowing the coach was a stickler for perfection. He climbed up onto the wooden lifeguard chair. His dark, leathery skin made him look like a dried-up lizard. She finished swimming, pulled up to the edge, and sat there catching her breath when Didi yelled from the pier, "Rosie is drowning!" Lizzi stared at the ocean and spotted her friend thrashing in the waves, the float deflated. Coach Tutu curved his hand above his eyes and squinted at the sea. He jumped off the chair and sprinted toward the pier. He made a shallow dive, and his long, thin arms cut through the surf, one rapid stroke after another until he reached her. A motorboat couldn't have gone any faster. Lizzi stumbled as she ran across the sand. Her heart raced while the coach pulled Rosie from the ocean.

Margie dashed to the shore and stood there bawling. "Oh, God, don't let my sister die." Coach laid her on the sand. Placing his arms around her stomach, he squeezed her body. Water spurted from her throat. He swung her over, lifted her chin, and began mouth-to-mouth resuscitation. Coach Tutu worked hard to get her breathing again. "Come on, Rosie," said her sister. She lay motionless. Lizzi held Margie, and she screamed, "She's dead." The coach turned Rosie to the side and pounded her back with his fist. She gurgled and spat more water. She coughed again, blinked her eyes, and gasped for air. Margie hugged her. "Thank God, you're alive."

She inhaled. "My dolphin went flat. The waves covered my eyes."

"That's okay," Margie said and caressed her cheek.

Didi came running and cuddled her little friend. "I'm glad

I saw you," she said, "otherwise you may have drowned."
She wrapped a towel around Rosie's shoulders.

Coach announced his two o'clock practice. Rosie hugged
him, and he ordered her to get swim lessons. Lizzi realized
her mother may have arrived and told the others to gather
their belongings and hurry to the front entrance. Just as they
got there, Mami drove up to the curb, and in they climbed.
"Niñas, how was the beach, and where's the blue dolphin?"

"A long story." Didi said.

The following Saturday, Lizzi strutted into the kitchen wearing her swimsuit, ready for the meet at the club. Papi chewed
the last slice of mango, looked up, and tickled her. "Let's go,"
he said, "I have to get my gold medalist to the competition on
time." She twisted and giggled. On the way to Biltmore, he
gave her a pep talk and said he'd be at the end of the lane to
make sure she swam the fastest. He kissed her, dropped her
off by the entrance, and left to park the car.

Swimmers gathered and warmed up. Lizzi approached
Pilar as she stretched both arms and adjusted her swim cap.
The competitor bragged she'd win today. Lizzi replied, "You
tell me that every meet."

"My father said it is time I win the gold."

"We'll see."

Coach Tutu blew the whistle. The girls jumped into the water
and took several practice laps before the 25-meter freestyle
event. He called for the swimmers to take their places on the
blocks. Lizzi looked at Papi waiting and got a thumbs-up.

"On your mark, get set, go!" The official fired the gun;

Lizzi dove into the pool, using the strokes the coach had pounded into her head. Pilar was behind on her left, soon they were even. Lizzi extended her arms; her legs kicked harder with every move. *Faster, faster,* she couldn't let up, *just focus on the finish.* She gasped for air as she touched the wall. Did she win? Papi knew the answer.

He pulled her out of the water and handed a towel. "It's a close one; we must wait for the call."

Moments dragged on before the officials' decision. When they announced Lizzi won the gold medal, she jumped for joy. "I did it, I beat Pilar." She noticed Papi looking toward the judges' table. He asked who the soldier was wearing dark sunglasses and arguing with the officials. She cupped her hands to his ear and said, "Pilar's father."

Papi's forehead creased. "It's weird—he's dressed in full army attire at a swim competition."

While Lizzi marveled at his rows and rows of medals, Coach Tutu approached them with waggling eyebrows. "Captain Joaquin Lopez has challenged Lizzi's win, saying she dove off ahead of the gun. I trust he isn't using his military rank to change the outcome."

Lizzi saw Papi raise his hands and knew he wasn't happy. More soldiers appeared on the scene. She hoped they didn't take back her gold medal. Papi said he couldn't believe Pilar's father called in the troops for a swim meet dispute. Coach Tutu shook his head while they sat and listened to the Captain shout at the judges. He grabbed a skinny official by the collar. "You're blind—the Barreras girl dove in ahead of my daughter. Never forget, I can be your best friend or worst enemy." The man trembled and staggered away.

"I'm scared, Papi, he mentioned my name."

He placed his arm around her. "Don't worry, mi niña."
Her whole face lit up when the judges said the title was hers.
The crowd cheered. The Captain clicked his heels and put on
his hat, grabbed his daughter and marched out of the club.

Papi hugged Lizzi. "Vamos, let's get your gold." Coach
Tutu congratulated her.

"Gracias, I'm glad to win, but I feel sorry for Pilar. Maybe
her father will give her one of his medals."

Wichi rose early on a June morning to read the news. Revolutionary violence flared following the Presidential Palace attack in March. He lifted the paper from the driveway and spotted Mani Martin reading his copy of the suburban publication. "Any good news, neighbor?"

"Posiblemente." Mani walked over, and they shook hands.

"We need it," Wichi said. "Batista's been on a revenge spree since they tried to kill him. He went after people not involved in the revolt, and someone assassinated an opposition leader."

Mani looked at him and nodded. "Sí, and the rebels have responded by burning buildings, setting fires to sugar cane fields, and torching tobacco sheds."

"So, give me the 'posiblemente' good news, my friend."

"At the office yesterday, I heard that five groups opposing Batista have signed a document demanding he step down peacefully if the people vote him out."

"That's great. How's it going to happen?"

"Not sure, but they say the alternative is a vicious cycle of more killings on both sides."

"Let's hope these groups prevail, and that today I don't encounter any problems driving Lizzi to her swim meet."

On the road to the Big Five competition in Guanabo, they stopped at a service station. The little town on the northern coast wasn't far, but he couldn't afford to run out of gas. The attendant warned him of insurgents in the vicinity. Wichi wanted to know more. The guy pointed to a large building smoldering in the distance. "Rebels set fire to that warehouse containing millions of dollars' worth of sugar."

"Wow, that's a lot of money."

Lizzi arrived with plenty of time and saw Pilar standing by her father dressed in his military garb. She leaned to Papi. "I hope he doesn't cause trouble."

"Best to ignore him and win medals." She nodded and strode to the pool. With arms extended she shook her hands in the air. Coach Tutu gave last-minute advice and went to his chair. As the contenders took their positions, Lizzi prepared her mind — *ready, set, focus*. She looked at her competitors. Pilar was on the right. *Good* — that was her best side. Swimmers dove in at the sound of the gun. At first, she moved ahead. *Concentrate. Stop gazing at Pilar and kick harder.* This was the moment—Lizzi's heart pounded and muscles burned as she planned to go for the win. She dug deep in the water and made a loud splash with both hands against the wall to end the race. She turned; Pilar trailed an arm's length. Papi smiled, and that meant the gold was hers. He helped her out of the pool and hugged and kissed the first-place winner.

Coach Tutu handed a towel. "Lizzi, that was flawless swimming. Keep working hard and you'll gain many more gold medals."

Papi took her aside. "I'm glad you won decisively so the Captain didn't have to take out his guns."

"Me too."

As Pilar received her silver medal, Captain Lopez's guard

appeared. "Capitán, we have to leave at once. They've bombed downtown Havana." A soldier swooped up Pilar, and the entourage fled Guanabo.

Papi grabbed Lizzi's hand. "That sounds dangerous, let's go too."

On the road home, blue skies gave way to a blazing orange sunset. Lizzi smiled. "I'm so happy with my medals. Someday I may have as many as Pilar's father."

"That's funny. It's easy to see how you won yours, but I wonder the number of men the captain executed to get his medals."

"What do you mean by 'executed,' Papi?"

"Nothing, mi amor, just lie back and rest. You deserve it."

SIX

Halloween Hobos

Biltmore Neighborhood
Halloween 1957

"An old witch lived in a haunted house and spent her days stirring a rusty cauldron," OP said as she squinted at Didi and Lizzi, then Luisito. He scooted across the bed and inched next to her. "The woman had black penetrating eyes and a green wrinkled face with whiskers and a hawk-like, pointed nose. A terrifying sight to behold, she grabbed her cat and . . ." A lizard darted across the floor, dragging a cobweb from under the dresser. Lizzi chased him until he disappeared under Didi's bed. She lifted the bed skirt, pulled out one of her medals, and asked how it got there. "It's not important," OP said. "Pay attention to the story, we're getting to the good part." She cleared her throat. "The witch's favorite time to snatch juicy children for her stew was Halloween night. She rode out of the spooky house on her broom and flew searching for kids trick or treating. The ugly green woman swooped and snatched a child if . . ."

Luisito yelped and Lizzi poked him in the ribs. "You're just a little chicken."

"Enough, nobody's listening to me. Go play, I have to get back to my project." She hustled the three into the hall and picked up multicolored cloths on the way to the sewing room. The boxers followed and soon snored while the American sewing machine whirled until the last patch found its place on Lizzi's shirt. As OP held up the masterpiece, Diana awakened and barked. She guessed her creations met the dog's approval. The vagabond attire was perfect for the annual Halloween parade at the Biltmore club. Although the children loved roller skating on Friday evenings, one of the club's top activities of the year was the October event. She wanted the girls to win a prize wearing the hobo clothes. She laid the work on the kitchen table and called her daughters to come in for lemonade. "I finished your Halloween costumes."

The two dashed inside the house and gulped the drinks. Didi glared at the apparel and sneered. "You don't expect me to wear that?" She held the costume in front. "Aargh. A hobo, boring and ugly. That's not me."

"No way these outfits can win the contest," Lizzi said.

OP snatched the garments and scowled at them. "I've decided you both will be twin Halloween hobos." Didi stormed out of the kitchen, slammed the bedroom door, and wailed through the walls. Lizzi pleaded to let her dress as something other than a beggar. "Not another word, end of discussion."

Lizzi lowered her head. "Mami, I'll be a hobo this year, but next time I want to be a princess. Patsy Purcey is a swan with satin and feathers."

"Okay, in the future you can be whatever you want."

The howling from the bedroom ceased, and Didi returned. Her bloodshot eyes blinked away the tears. "I'll wear the hobo clothes, but not because I like them." She picked up the outfit

and plodded back to her room. Lizzi grabbed her costume and
followed. Soon they returned dressed as Halloween hobos.

Lizzi asked who was taking them to the club. "Your father," she said. "He's having dinner there with Señor Martin. I'm staying here to prepare for the trick or treaters."

Wichi walked into the room. "Vamos."

A white sheet with two eyeholes darted from behind the sofa and shouted, "Boo."

The evening sky had darkened. Wichi, the vagabonds, and ghost waited beside the car for Patsy to arrive. Dottie Purcey stopped in the driveway and stuck her head out the window. "Hi, ya'll. My goodness, what cute hobos." Out of the vehicle stepped a white swan. Lizzi ran to her side and snuggled amidst the feathers. The potpourri of costumed youngsters jumped into the Coronet, and they headed for the club.

Wichi pulled into the front entrance, and the girls waved at Rosie and Margie outfitted as twin witches. "They're better than twin hobos," Didi said. Ahead of them Pilar's driver stopped and escorted her to the door. She wore a regal outfit—a golden tiara and a skirt strewn with jewels. Wichi let the children out of the automobile and wished them good luck in the contest.

He parked the car and ambled to the terrace by the beach. Lights flickered from pumpkin lantern centerpieces. Moseying around the dining area, he plucked a stuffed mushroom off the waiter's tray. Many tables had reserved cards leaning on glass goblets, and he grabbed a vacant table for two nearest the water. The calm ocean reflected moonbeams flickering on its surface. He signaled a waiter, ordered scotch on the rocks, and sipped the drink. As he swirled the glass, the ice cubes mirrored the moon's glow. He gazed at the yellow sphere, in part obscured by dark wispy clouds. It was a perfect evening for dining alfresco. He flinched at a tap on his shoulder. "Wichi, cómo estás? Hope I didn't startle you."

He turned. "Mani, hola. No problem. Guess this Halloween moon had me mesmerized."

He got up and they shook hands. "What'll you have to drink?" Mani sat and ordered a daiquiri. While they talked, a whistle blew. The contestants paraded around the terrace edging the beach. Wichi marveled at the assortment of witches and cowgirls and clowns—even an Elvis Presley. "Glad I'm not a judge," he told Mani. Rosie waved at her father as she strutted by. Wichi pointed at Luisito. "There's my boy, he's a ghost." The crowd murmured in awe at Patsy floating by in a swan-like fashion. Mani's eyes widened at the girl dressed as Queen Isabella. Wichi said she was Pilar Lopez, the daughter of one of Batista's captains.

"Wow, that costume cost a fortune," Mani said. Wichi winked at his girls staring ahead, unhappy with their home-made hobo outfits. After the procession the contestants sat at decorated tables by the pool. The server had just delivered Wichi's shrimp platter when a raucous noise sounded at the entrance. Several armed soldiers walked alongside a military man approaching the dining section. Wichi whispered to Mani that he was Pilar's father.

The waiter apologized to the captain. "There's no outside seating, but we have inside tables."

"There's one," he said and pointed to the table next to Wichi and Mani.

The man trembled. "Capitán, that one is reserved."

A guard got in his face and yelled, "Give it to him."

Wichi leaned over to his neighbor. "Better watch what we say." Mani agreed.

Captain Lopez removed his pistol holster, gave it to a guard, and sat with his entourage. "Bring us whiskey with ice."

While the waiters served coconut ice cream for dessert, Wichi watched as two soldiers rushed to Lopez's table and saluted. One tried to keep his voice low, but he heard the news that insurrectionists burned sugar fields near Havana. "It's my night off, and I'm here to watch my daughter win first place in the contest," the captain said. "You take care of it—dismissed." The soldiers left, and Lopez turned to his guard. "That coward Castro hiding in the Sierra mountains is behind the disruptions."

The man nodded. "Sí, Batista wants Fidel's head on a platter."

With a smile Lopez said, "We'll get that bastard." He straightened his jacket and brushed his sleeve across the medals.

Wichi leaned toward Mani's ears. "We're in for rough times—lots of killing for sure." Mani wiped his forehead with a napkin.

The master of ceremonies tapped on the microphone. "Ladies and Gentlemen, we have winners for our annual Halloween costume parade. Pedro Salinas, dressed as Elvis Presley, wins first place for the boys." The audience roared and clapped while The King received his bag of treats. The man then said, "I'll now unseal the envelope for the girls' best-in-costume."

Captain Lopez leaned back in his seat, took a puff on a cigar, and elbowed his cohort. "That's Pilar."

The MC tore open the paper. "And the winner is—Patsy Purcey—the white swan." People applauded the young girl gliding across the stage to receive her prize. Lopez banged his fist on the table; plates rattled, and glasses fell to the floor and shattered. He jumped up, grabbed his holster, and buckled it on his waist. He stormed over to the announcer, clutched his shirt, and pulled him forward. The man's face drained as he stood there shaking.

"You and the so-called judges are impaired; my daughter's costume came from the top designer in Havana, and she deserves first place." He grabbed the mic and threw it. The audience shrieked when it hit the floor and the speakers boomed. He stormed out, kicking and breaking a chair along the way. One soldier escorted Pilar as the cortege marched out of the club. People stared in bewilderment, and waiters scurried to clean up the mess.

Lizzi and the other children rushed to the table. "Papi, what happened?"

"Pilar's father got mad because she didn't win. It's time to go now."

The girls raced back to the parking lot. Before leaving, Didi told the Martin girls to meet in her yard. "Not a boring dinner," Wichi said, "and enough excitement to last until next Halloween." Mani chuckled.

ᘓᘏ

Lizzi gathered the others in a circle. "Shout trick or treat." Rosie asked if she knew what it meant. "I kinda do. Doesn't matter though, it gets you candy."

"Let's go to Señora Lucas's house first," Patsy said. "She has the creepiest decorations."

Quivering skeletons surrounded dozens of tombstones in the yard. Everyone wove through a stringy maze of hanging spider webs, and a black cat darted ahead. As the group approached the house, they huddled and listened to loud shrills. A witch came out with a black robe and long white hair to her knees. Lizzi's voice quavered as she tried to say trick or treat. The witch's dark eyebrows above her green face and pointed nose moved when she cackled. "What do we have here? Fine looking trick or treaters perfect for my supper. Who wants to jump into my cauldron?" A tingle rushed along Lizzi's spine. She stepped back and stumbled on Luisito crouched between her legs. "Mmm, since no one yearns to be part of my stew, I guess it's time for treats. Here's my bowl. Reach in and get chewing gum and sugar-crusted orange slices." Three shots cracked. Señora Lucas threw her hands into the air, and the container fell, scattering pieces of glass and candy on the floor. "That's gunfire, children, go home, NOW." Lizzi grabbed one of Luisito's arms, Didi, the other. They dashed off the porch and across the yard. She glanced at Margie and Rosie caught in cobwebs. Patsy cried as she ripped the swan outfit on a bush.

"Didi, shine the flashlight. It's dark," Lizzi said.

"I dropped it."

Lizzi tripped on a rock and tore a hole in her pant leg. Blood trickled from the cut on her knee. It hurt, but she ran anyway.

Didi scurried ahead with Luisito, and Lizzi limped behind. A
man stepped in front of her. He wore black clothes, and a mask
hid his face. Just enough light from the moon showed his dark
eyes staring at her. She froze. It had to be the gunman. *Is he
going to kill me?* She ran around him and fell, nose down. A
hand touched her shoulder, and she knew he was going to
murder her—on Halloween. She dared not look upward.

"Lizzi, Lizzi Barreras, is that you?" sounded a man's voice.
She rolled over to find out who called her name. A flashlight
shone in her face; she couldn't see the person. "It's Señor
Martin, your neighbor," he said. "Are you hurt?"

"I'm okay."

"No, you're not," Didi said as she and Luisito returned
and hugged her. Lizzi then burst out crying and told them
she saw the man who fired the shots, and he planned to shoot
her too.

"I don't think he intended to harm you," said Señor
Martin. He carried Lizzi to his driveway. "Tell your father
what occurred and have him come see me." She thanked him
and ran inside with the others.

Papi and Mami were sitting in the living room. "Papi,
something awful happened." He saw blood on Lizzi's knee
and asked how she got hurt. "There were loud noises," she
said. "Señora Lucas told us to run home. We ran and it was
dark and I fell after I saw a masked man."

"Wait a minute. 'Noises' and 'a masked man'?"

"Señora said a gun fired."

"A gun?" He said he'd heard nothing earlier that evening.
He looked over at Mami. She shook her head and said the
radio was on and remembered the dogs barked. He checked

YOUR ONE-STOP ENCYCLOPEDIA OF THE COLLECTED WISDOM FROM OVER 250 OF THE WORLD'S BEST DOCTORS

Discover the hidden health threats women face throughout their lives and how to beat these threats once and for all!

The Ultimate Women's Guide to Beating Disease 2022 *is the best ever, with all-new information to help you live healthier and happier in the year ahead!*

THANK YOU FOR PAYING THE ENCLOSED BILL PROMPTLY.

Lizzi's knee—just a scratch. "Everybody, clean your face and stay indoors. I'll find out what's happening."

"Papi, Señor Martin said to come to his house."

Wichi opened the door as thoughts raced through his mind: gunshots and a masked shooter—in Biltmore? *My children could have been hurt.* Sirens blared as three police cars whizzed by. An officer approached people gathered along the curb. Wichi joined them. One man caught the policeman's arm and wanted information. Another resident standing nearby demanded the details of an alleged killing. "Everybody off the street," the officer said. A woman inched closer, her lips trembled. The cop picked up his bull horn and bellowed, "Get back inside your houses." Wichi dashed through the hedge. Mani stood in the window and motioned him over. He opened the door, and Wichi darted inside.

"What's happening? he asked.

"A shooting, possibly a murder."

"Murder, are you sure?"

Mani said he walked outside and encountered a neighbor who yelled he'd seen a slaying. "He said it occurred outside the big house at the end of the block."

"Isn't that where Batista's officer lives?"

"Sí, the neighbor heard the shooter yell, 'Batista's men murdered my innocent cousin, and you're responsible.' He shot the soldier three times." Wichi gasped. Mani took in a deep breath. "The guy had an ax to grind with Batista and blamed the officer."

"Lizzi said she saw a man wearing a mask."

"Me too, but I scared him away with my flashlight."

"He could have . . ."

"No, I don't think he planned to harm Lizzi; he was trying to escape."

Wichi's temples tightened. "That was frightening. I'm worried for our neighborhood."

"Me too."

"Halloween in the suburbs just became a war zone."

SEVEN

Neighborly Surprises

Havana, Cuba
November 1957

Modesta caught the early-morning bus from Regla to Biltmore. She climbed the rusty metal steps, opened a dingy duffel bag, and handed the driver money, then plopped into the steely seat behind him. Passengers boarded, women carried crying babies on their hips, while others carted fruits and vegetables in baskets. The gears ground as black diesel exhaust spewed forth, and the vehicle moved onward. She glanced around and spotted her old friend. "Graciela, you way back there again, sweet lady?"

"Modi, you know I grow dizzy upfront. Riding this hot bus since six o'clock tells on you. Got to finish my rosary beads before I start work at the Martins'."

Modesta muttered as she slumped in her seat, "Forgive me, God, it's not in me to pray except from time to time when things go bad."

"Next stop, Miramar Heights," the operator hollered. He wheeled to the right and screeched the brakes. Travelers jerked forward. A man hit his face on the overhead bar and howled an obscenity. Mangoes and papayas and bananas fell to the floor. Modesta lunged ahead and caught herself on the driver's shoulders.

"Get your hands off me," he growled.

She punched him. "You, old turd, are a terrible bus driver." She clutched her bag, turned, and yelled, "Graciela, you okay?"

The gray head lifted. "Just a praying, Modi."

The coachman stood up and said, "Get off now." He kicked a few smashed papayas out the door. A man slipped on a banana in the aisle and stained his white pants. He cursed, gave the driver the finger, and stepped off the bus. The operator returned the gesture and grabbed a few quick puffs on a cigarette before sitting on the cracked vinyl seat cushion.

Modesta gripped the rail and leaned forward. "Better find yourself another job, you old fart."

He swung around with nostrils flared. "You bet, so I don't have to stare at your ugly face."

"Shut your lips."

"Bitch, hitting your trusty driver, shame on you."

"No shame in me. Get this thing moving. We got work to do."

"Ain't hurrying for you."

The doors closed and Modesta settled in the seat, twisted around, and saw Graciela's head bobbing, her prayer finished, and now a nap. Modi stared out the window. A woman ran toward the coach. She nudged the driver. "Mister, open up, my friend needs a ride."

"This bus is moving—not stopping for nobody."

"What if she was a good-looking, big breasted mulatta?"

Lickety-split, he stopped and opened the door and smiled. "Get on, you may sit behind me."

She handed a coin and sat by Modesta. "Come here, Concepción, and give me a hug. What you been doing?"

"Not too much." She lowered her voice and said, "Let's change seats, I have something important to tell you."

They moved to the rear next to Graciela, and the older lady awakened. "Hola muchachas, you sit here with Mama Graci." Concepción hugged her, and the three huddled.

"Did you hear what happened on Halloween night?"

"No, child, what?" Graciela made the sign of the cross. "Hate Halloween, devil's day, and didn't have to work."

"I was off too." Modesta lowered her voice. "Tell me, I'm dying to know."

"My employer, Lieutenant Colonel Cruz, the rich man, was shot and killed."

Graciela's mouth flew open. "Say it's not true."

"He was a big wig in Batista's government," Modesta said.

"Tell us more, sweetie." The old lady moved closer. Concepción said she'd just put the Lieutenant Colonel's baby to sleep and returned to her room when gunfire sounded outside the house. The chauffeur knocked on her door and yelled someone shot the boss. She looked through the window and saw him lying on the ground in a pool of blood. While they loaded him into the ambulance, the police swarmed the place and rounded up the servants for questioning. "Have they caught the killer?"

"No, but don't you breathe a word, or they'll arrest and shoot me for what I'm about to tell you."

Graciela placed a finger on her lips. Concepción said when

she got home the following morning, somebody grabbed her from behind, put their hand over her mouth, and said to keep quiet. Then she realized it was Uncle Calixto. He was in serious trouble because he killed Cruz. Graciela gasped and fidgeted with her rosary. Concepción held her hand and said she asked Calixto why he shot the man. He explained that his son, Carlitos, a machetero, cut sugar cane in the blazing heat with no water. The boy requested a drink, the foreman said no and told him to keep working. Carlitos begged again, and the guy whipped him.

Modesta shook her head. "This is terrible. He should have killed the bastard."

Concepción looked at her and said Carlitos didn't kill him, but the macheteros beat the overseer, and the owner called Batista's soldiers to stop the fight. Lieutenant Colonel Cruz's men arrived, fired into the workers, and murdered Calixto's boy in cold blood. He said Batista's officer had to pay for taking his only son. Modesta took Concepción's hand. "Your uncle is a dead man if they find him. Where is he?"

"Hiding in an abandoned warehouse close to town."

"Girl, don't think of going there. They'll get you too."

Graciela crossed herself. "I'll keep your secret." She turned to Modesta. "Modi, we're lucky, our families are right nice and not mean rich folks. No killing there."

Modesta clicked her tongue. "May be so, but I don't cater being bossed. Besides cooking, I put up with three boxers and three canaries. La Señora lets those fowls loose, and I got to clean up bird shit."

"Honey, everybody gets told what to do."

"I want to be giving orders instead of taking them."

"Modi, you deserve a rich man," said Concepción. "You're good-looking and strong as a bull."

"Man's more trouble than he's worth, besides, if they kill more of these Batistianos, and we get a new government, I'll work for them."

"Be careful what you say and wish for, girl." Graciela laid a hand on her shoulder.

"You sound like my mama."

"Next stop, Biltmore," the driver yelled as the bus came to a smooth halt. The three women collected their bags and went to the front. "Do you always talk this much?" he said. "Your tongue must be tired."

Modesta slapped him on the head. "Shut your mouth; I hope Saturday we have somebody else in this seat."

The short walk to the Cruz residence on the corner ended with two guards at the entrance. A police car blocked the driveway. Three policemen with German Shepherds patrolled the property. The ladies hugged, and Graciela held Concepción's hand. "You be careful."

"I will," she said and waved goodbye. After showing a piece of paper to the guard, she walked toward the house.

"Modi, I worry for this young'n. God help her."

She looked Graciela straight in the eye. "Now, old woman, no yakking about Calixto."

"Dios me libre, God forbid."

Modesta entered the doctor's kitchen by the side door and straightened her white cotton uniform. A long list of written chores waited for her on the red melamine counter:

1. Apache and Apollo need more food.

2. Give Diana one dog biscuit.

3. Clean Sashita's cage.

4. Let her out for a while.

5. The chicken is defrosting on the stove. My kindergarten superior has called a meeting, be home late.

Modesta walked into her quarters off the kitchen and plopped the bag onto the bed. She tied on an apron and looked in the mirror. Sure as hell, she'd not do everything on the list. She lumbered into the living room and unhooked the birdcage from the stand, then took it to the sink and cleaned it without letting the canary out. *I might as well work in a zoo.*

Lizzi came in for a glass of water and greeted her. "Are you planning to let Sashita out?"

"I will if you clean her poop."

"Sorry, I'm going outside to play with Rosie." A few moments later Lizzi stuck her head inside and yelled, "Didi, Luisito, come out, there's a huge truck parked in front of the house." Modesta rushed to the window and saw a flatbed vehicle with a large wooden box. A knock and a man announced a delivery for Doctor Luis Barreras.

She opened the door. "What's on the truck?" The man shrugged, looked at the clipboard, and told her a live animal. *For this house—no way.* He insisted on opening the box and leaving. Perspiration dripped from her face. She fanned herself and hustled to the street. The kids climbed onto the flatbed and stood around the large enclosure. Luisito peered through a hole and said it was a lion. "No, niño," she said. "It can't be." Using a crowbar, the man removed the back panel.

Lizzi stared into the crate. "It's a giant dog."

"Not another one." Didi turned and jumped off the truck.

"He's big enough to ride." Luisito said.

The animal shook his massive head and slobbered the boy's face. "He'll be my pony."

"Look at his smooth golden fur," Lizzi said and then kissed his dark square face. "I love his adorable brown eyes."

"I need a signature," the man said. "Where's the doctor?"

Modesta stood with her hands on her hips. "At work—I guess I have to do it." He gave her the invoice and a handwritten note. She read out loud, "Call him Dobin." She threw up her arms. *This must be a prank.* After cleaning the flatbed, the driver left. Lizzi grabbed the leash and wanted to take Dobin to the backyard. "Go right ahead," Modesta said, "he may need to do his business, and I'm going inside the house." The novela started at one o'clock, and Modi dare not miss her favorite soap opera, but she still had clothes to wash, cooking, and those damn bird cages to clean.

❧

At half past one, Wichi arrived home just as OP pulled up in her car. Modesta sat in the living room watching TV. He asked if everything was okay.

"Peek out back and see for yourself."

He laid his medical bag on the table and hurried to the patio door. The children and three boxers romped with a huge puppy. "Who sent him?" he yelled.

"I don't know," Lizzi said. "He was in a big box on a truck, and his name is Dobin."

He slid the door wide open, and OP pushed past him. "What a cute puppy. He's an English mastiff."

"Great, you're familiar with the breed, but who's responsible for sending him here?"

"I have no idea."

"And I'm determined to find out." After he asked Modesta the scoop on the dog, she reached into her apron pocket and handed him the note. He read the message. "Call him Dobin. Nicolás." He threw his hands in the air and returned outside, his blood boiling. "Your crazy uncle sent this animal without asking."

"How nice to remember us with this precious bundle."

"What do you mean 'precious bundle'? That son of a bitch has unloaded a horse on us. I'm calling him right now." Wichi stormed into the study, flipped through the address book, and dialed the number. It rang twice. "Nicolás?"

"Sí, Wichi, has Dobin arrived?"

"What's the idea of dumping this monster on me? Take him back."

"I'm afraid I can't. He'll trample the ten chihuahuas."

The phone clicked and proved what Wichi suspected for a

long time—OP's family belonged in Mazorra, the mental hospital. He proceeded to the yard and stared at the colossal puppy.

OP came out with a book, *Guide for Raising Dogs*, and found the feeding schedule for an eight-week-old mastiff. She put on her glasses and read, "Feed your puppy four times a day. A fully grown dog may eat three to five cups of food twice a day plus bones for his teeth. This breed can weigh up to two hundred pounds."

"A dog this size needs training, or he can't stay," Wichi said. OP volunteered to teach him. He led Dobin into the kitchen and spoke with Modesta. "I'm sorry, but he has to sleep on the floor in your room. There's no other place."

She frowned. "I'm scared of this animal and need more money if he sleeps near me."

"Okay, we'll talk later. These sweet eyes will melt your heart. Before long he'll think you're his mama."

"No chance."

EIGHT

Frenzy Flight

Miami, Florida
December 29, 1958
Thirteen Months Later

Melmont read the newspaper in the departure section at Miami International Airport. A prominent article featuring opposition against Batista caught his attention. Cubans said they wanted Batista out, and it didn't matter who replaced him. Melmont took a deep breath. This sounded dangerous since it paved the road for a revolution and possibly another dictator.

He wondered if the political climate warranted travel to Havana. While reading further, it bothered him that a candidate advocating a democratically-elected government won the November election, although officials declared Batista's puppet the winner. *Ballot fraud such as this never produces a good outcome.*

At seven o'clock, the overhead speaker announced final boarding for Havana Aviación's charter flight to Rancho Boyeros Airport. Melmont caught the last article that said Castro's rebels now controlled eastern Cuba and predicted Santa Clara should fall today to Che Guevara, an Argentinian Marxist revolutionary. He'd awaited this trip since spring and decided to ignore depressing news and enjoy a few relaxing days in Havana. He headed to the tarmac and boarded the plane. A woman in front shook her hips to background mambo music, and that uplifted his spirits. The attendant pointed him to an aisle seat on the left toward the rear, and then reminded everyone to read the card describing the DC-3. After takeoff clearance the two engines hummed as the airplane gained speed on the runway. Melmont relaxed in his seat, and the craft was airborne. Soon it pushed aside fluffy white clouds scattered in the blue sky.

"Good morning from the cockpit. On behalf of my co-pilot and stewardess, I welcome our twenty-one passengers to your four-day paradise vacation in Havana, Cuba. Coca-Colas and Cuba Libres are complimentary. We are now cruising at an altitude of ten thousand feet. Sit back and relax, and we will land within the hour."

A young girl sitting across the aisle from Melmont pressed her nose against the window. "Daddy, look how the water has different colors."

The passenger in front leaned her way. "You're right, Annie, it changes from aquamarine to a deep blue, and then to emerald green, depending on the depth." She described studying coral reefs in school and wanted to go snorkeling to see the marine life. "You'll get your chance since we have a day trip to Varadero beach. The travel guide said it had the bluest water and whitest sand in the Caribbean."

Annie pulled out her brochure and showed her dad a picture. "The Hotel Nacional is a scenic place, right across from Havana harbor."

The blond next to Annie's father removed her dark glasses and yawned. "This ride's bumpy, and it makes me nervous.

William, did you pack a good novel?" He told her it was in the luggage.

"Mom, you can read this: *Things to See and Do in Cuba*." Annie passed the book to her.

"I'd better not; I might get nauseous."

"Peggy, soon you'll be relaxing by the pool and wearing your new blue bikini."

She left for the lavatory. Melmont tapped William on the shoulder. "Excuse me, did I hear you're staying at the Hotel Nacional?" He said he was. "I'm there, too—Doctor Richard Melmont from Miami, Florida." They shook hands. William said his last name was Russel, and they were from Wisconsin. The girl jumped up, stood next to her father, and announced in two days she'd be twelve years old. Melmont told her that visiting Havana was a great birthday present. Peggy returned and William introduced her. After a brief conversation, Melmont observed her flat affect, and he suspected the purpose of the vacation was more than just a present for the daughter.

"First trip to Cuba?" William said. Melmont replied that he, his wife, and son came last year and loved the place so much that they planned this visit nine months ago. Six days ago his mother-in-law broke her hip, and they couldn't come, but insisted he make the trip. William inquired if he was bilingual. Melmont confessed to knowing only a few Spanish words such as "Donde está el baño?" and a few more phrases to keep him out of trouble. They shared a laugh for a moment until chattering in the cabin ceased.

A loud scream bellowed from a woman seated over the right wing. "An engine's on fire!"

"She's right," shouted the man behind her. "I see flames and smoke."

Passengers gasped and shrieked and stared out the windows. The speaker sounded, "Ladies and gentlemen, your captain speaking; we're twenty minutes from Havana and have encountered an emergency. Please return to your seats, fasten your seat belts, and stay calm."

"Damn right, an emergency," shouted a bald man in the front row. "An engine's burning."

"'Stay calm,' that's a joke," said an older guy.

Next the captain explained they had a fire in the right-wing engine. Another voice came over the speaker. "Everyone, please take your seats and let us handle this emergency. I'm your co-pilot, and we are following safety precautions. Now, relax and allow us to fly this plane to Havana."

Melmont listened to the conversation in the seat behind. "I don't want to leave this earth with a guilty conscience—I've been an unfaithful husband."

"You scoundrel, now you tell me right before we die." From the corner of his eye he caught the woman rolling up a newspaper and heard her whack the guy on the head. Melmont wiped the sweat off his brow as he observed the passengers and the chaos in the cabin. *These people are out of control.*

William caressed Peggy's pallid face and told her the pilot said everything would be okay. "Not with a fire," she cried. "We will die!" She began hyperventilating. Melmont offered an airsick bag to place over her nose and mouth. Several years had passed since medical school, and he hoped he could treat severe injuries if this plane crashed. He caught the arm of the stewardess as she attended to the frightened passengers.

"Miss, I'm Doctor Melmont, Mrs. Russel needs sedation. Please bring us motion sickness pills."

She nodded, rushed to the back, and returned with medication, cups, and water. He reached over William's shoulder and handed him a tablet. "Peggy, my love, in a few minutes you'll relax." Melmont looked along the aisle. A woman sporting a fancy hat squalled and shook her hands in the air. He gave her a pill before plopping back into his seat.

The man next to him raised his head and folded a book on his lap. The cover read: *Murder in Matanzas.* "You've been busy," he said.

"Yeah, unfortunately I'm not as relaxed as you."

"I flew planes in the air force and had a few engine fires. Name's Hart, Major James Hart."

"I'm Richard Melmont, a medical doctor. Blood doesn't bother me but dying in a ball of fire is another matter."

Hart grinned and they shook hands. He explained that when a fire breaks out in an engine, a warning bell goes off in the cockpit and alerts the pilot to close the fuel line. Then he discharges the extinguisher and puts out the blaze. Melmont wanted to know if they could land the plane with one engine. Hart said it's doable with the crew making proper adjustments.

"Will it be a crash landing?"

"I think he'll land okay, but they always prepare for the worst. Fire trucks and emergency vehicles await us, so don't be alarmed." Melmont gave a thumbs-up.

"I should have stayed home," said Peggy.

He leaned over to William. "She'll soon get groggy from the pill and relax."

"It's good that you're a doctor. My wife has issues, and her psychiatrist recommended this trip, but it may not have been a suitable idea."

"Try to keep her calm as possible; we'll make it to Havana."

"Daddy, I'm getting my things ready," Annie said. "I'll take Mom's hat when we get off the plane."

A loud, raspy voice sounded over the loudspeaker. "May I have your attention? This is your captain. We're cleared to land, but the fire has reignited. Everyone, stay buckled in your seats. We should be on the ground momentarily."

Melmont looked through the window across the cabin and saw black smoke trailing behind the engine. "Not a good sign, eh, Major?" Hart nodded and said that a quick landing was vital.

A sudden drop occurred, and the craft shook. People screamed, and someone yelled, "God help us, I don't wanna die."

"This is it," Peggy said. "We're going up in flames."

Annie rubbed her eyes and told her father she was scared. He grasped her hand. Melmont thought of his family back in the States. A lump welled in his throat. He was glad they weren't on this trip.

The stewardess announced, "Prepare for an emergency landing. Everyone, stay seated, lean forward, and lower your head. When we land and come to a stop, you will leave the aircraft as directed."

The DC-3 hit the runway with a massive impact and zig-zagged. Melmont glimpsed at sparks flying as metal scraped the concrete. Passengers shrilled while the plane careened and turned and slid tailfirst. The grinding decreased as it slowed and went sideways before stopping. A moment of deafening

silence prevailed, followed by mixtures of shouting and sobbing and praying. "Thank God, we made it," cried a man.

The woman behind said to her husband, "I forgive you for
cheating on me."

After the crew opened the door, the pilot's voice sounded
and explained how everyone should deplane. Fire trucks
surrounded and sprayed the engine. Red lights flashed atop
waiting ambulances. William led his wife to the exit. She
clutched her purse to her body. Annie followed. "You go first,
Doctor, I have your back," Hart said. Melmont stepped from
the plane and walked toward the bus with other passengers
and crew. He asked if anyone was injured.

The bald man from the front row smiled. "Nothing
serious, Doc, maybe a few hurt feelings."

The captain eased to Melmont's side. "Thanks, Doctor, for
your help." He gave an affirmative sign and glanced back at
the plane sitting edgewise on the airstrip. He entered the bus
and mopped his forehead. Passengers applauded their pilot
the moment he stepped aboard the transport.

"Please tell me everything will be okay," Peggy said.
William kissed her cheek and told her they were safe in
Havana.

"It was great to meet you," Melmont said to the major as
they got off at the terminal.

"Perhaps we'll see each other again—a Cuban bar?"

"Okay, next time under better circumstances."

In the arrival section, a young woman wearing a tight red skirt
and a tropical print blouse stood holding a sign: HOTEL

NACIONAL. "Bienvenidos a Cuba. I'm Raquel, your guide. Get ready to leave your troubles behind and enjoy Cuban sun and white sand, *plus* the hospitality of our grand hotel." They boarded the van and soon were traveling along Havana's coast. The guide pointed out the famous Malecón, the five-mile long concrete seawall, sidewalk, and street that separated Havana from the ocean. She said during high winds, waves splashed over the wall and gave free salt-water carwashes. "Cubans socialize and stroll the Malecón. It provides a fabulous and unforgettable sunset." The vehicle stopped, and Melmont beheld the world-renowned hotel perched on top of a hill overlooking Havana harbor and the azure sea.

"Make sure you have your luggage. I'll be in the lobby for day excursions and nightclub tickets," Raquel said. "Your travel package includes a return to the airport on January first." She paused and smiled. "Don't miss that ride."

"This is an incredible place," William said. Peggy complained the air smelled salty. Annie held onto her father and grinned. He hugged her and said he knew they'd make it. Melmont told Annie she was a brave young lady and to enjoy her visit. They walked up the steps to the entrance.

Melmont stopped for a moment inside the lobby and noticed two fierce-looking German Shepherds leashed by policemen patrolling the hotel. The dogs brushed by—a twinge of fear rushed through his body. Security wasn't this tight last year. Something was different now. The Miami newspaper article came to mind. An announcement shifted his thought. "Doctor Melmont, please come to the front desk." He registered and was given a room on the second floor. A prominent sign near the elevator caught his attention:

INTERNAL MEDICINE AND HEMATOLOGY SOCIETY

December 29, 1958 Meeting

3:00 p.m. Grand Ballroom

INTERESTING CASE
PRESENTATIONS & HEALTHCARE ISSUES

English Interpreters Available

Registration at Front Desk

It had been a long, emotional morning. Melmont's stomach grumbled. The café menu showed ham croquetas. He remembered those tasty appetizers, so he ordered two. The medical conference lingered on his mind. An opportunity existed for him to discuss his research project with Cuban doctors. After the snack he signed up for the meeting, then hoofed it upstairs to unpack. He considered calling his wife but decided against it—she'd worry. So far, the trip had more drama than he expected. Tomorrow promised humdrum moments under the Cuban sun.

NINE

Melodrama and Medicine

Biltmore Neighborhood
December 29, 1958

A blood-curdling scream awakened Wichi at six in the morning. He sat up, threw open the mosquito netting, and rushed to the bedroom door. "What in the world?" OP said. "That sound came from the kitchen."

"I will investigate. You stay here." He hesitated for a moment in the hallway, glad the girls had a sleepover with Rosie and Margie. The only defensive tool on hand was Luisito's stick horse. He tiptoed past the dining room and stopped short. Scuffling and growling and thumping sounded nearby. Next, a chair fell, and a woman's voice said, "You beast, trying to kill me?"

A thief, or a killer, he wondered? With his weapon raised, he dashed around the corner, froze, and stared downward. On the floor was Dobin with Modesta dressed in floral pajamas. Her left hand grasped the dog's collar while she shook a right finger at him. "You oversized hippo." The animal loved the roughhousing and paid no attention to the reprimands. She turned her head, and there stood Wichi in his skivvies, holding a toy horse and looking at them. She jumped to her feet. "Doctor," she said, covering her eyes.

"Oh, no—perdón, I'll be right back." He darted to the bedroom to put on his trousers.

OP grabbed him. "What's happening? Are we in danger?"

"No, it's Modesta."

"Is she hurt?"

"No, but something occurred between her and Dobin."

Luisito walked into the room half-asleep while Wichi pulled up his pants and OP slipped on her robe. She lifted the boy onto the bed, covered him, and joined Wichi on the way to the kitchen. Modesta stood by the patio door, pointing at the mastiff. "Go outside where you belong."

"Qué pasó, what happened?" Wichi asked.

"I'm out of here, Doctor. That monster climbed on my mattress and pressed his cold nose on my face, scaring the living daylights out of me. I can barely take these animals, and this horse-of-a-dog trying to sleep with me did it."

"Now, now Modesta, try to calm yourself. He didn't hurt you, did he?"

"If I'd died from a heart attack, it would have been your fault." OP said they were sorry, and Dobin wouldn't enter her quarters again. "I mean it when I say I'm gone from this place if that creature comes into my room."

"You have my word on it," Wichi said.

"Okay, Doctor, I'll hold you to it and stick around as long as you do what you say." He told her it was a deal and asked her to iron his guayabera. The white linen shirt had to be perfect for the medical meeting in the afternoon.

"Sí, Señor."

His smile faded when he and OP entered the bedroom and shut the door. This incident couldn't happen again, or they'd lose Modesta. While OP ran a comb through her black silky hair, she mentioned that Modesta wasn't the only domestic help in Havana. He reminded her they needed someone who cleaned the house *and* cooked, otherwise the family faced starvation. She swiveled on the dressing table seat and narrowed her eyes in his direction. "Wichi, you love to exaggerate."

"Not really, but we must solve the dog problem."

"Sí, Dobin has to stay in here," she said. "If he gets in bed with us, I won't yell."

"What do you mean *if* he gets in our bed? That will not happen."

Luisito threw back the bedspread. "Can Dobin sleep with me?"

It was nine o'clock, and the presentation at three still needed editing. Wichi closed the study door and began to concentrate on how to make his colleagues more aware of healthcare issues facing the country. The words had to be right. A knock interrupted. "Wichi, I need to talk to you."

"I'm busy, can it wait?"

"No." OP entered and wanted to know their plans for New Year's Eve. She needed an answer soon, and he promised to think of something. The children posed no problem with Modesta there to supervise while they counted grapes and waited for the New Year.

"Can't you see I'm working on this speech, and I'm short of time?"

"Don't forget," she said and left.

A glance at his wristwatch showed he was running late and hadn't completed the talk. The office should be quiet and give him the opportunity to finish the work without more melodrama. He dressed and faced the mirror. The guayabera and trousers looked good. He grabbed his satchel and headed for Vedado.

Olga greeted him at the office door. "Hola, Doctor. Cómo estás?"

"Bien, any activities this afternoon except my meeting?"

"Colonel García called and asked for an appointment at one o'clock."

"Is Albertito not well?"

"Didn't say, but it sounded important, so I put him on the schedule."

"Shouldn't be a problem," he said. She expressed appreciation for having the rest of the day off to buy grapes and shop for a dress. They wished each other a Happy New Year. She left, and he locked the door. It was strange that the colonel made an appointment without his son. He'd never done that in past visits. Wichi hoped nothing had happened to Albertito since his visit six months ago. He pulled the boy's medical records to refresh his memory. The anemia should have responded to the iron medication, and a new infection was unlikely. The idea crossed his mind that he should have presented Albertito's case today but too late now to consider it. As he polished the final sentence of the speech, a firm tap sounded. The clock on his desk showed 1:00 p.m. sharp—the colonel had arrived.

He opened the door to find Colonel García standing tall and thin and not groomed nor wearing his usual immaculate, blue uniform with epaulets. Instead, his black hair appeared ruffled, and he wore a loose-fitting, plaid shirt, baggy pants, and sandals.

"Buenas tardes, come in, how's Albertito?"

García took a furtive glance over the shoulder before he hurried into the office and snapped the door shut. "He's doing well since the iron pills—happy and playing baseball."

"That's wonderful. What can I do for you?"

"Are we by ourselves?" he said.

"Sí, but let's go to my private office." They entered the room. "Please have a seat." Wichi sensed a serious problem. For the past four years, the father never came alone or casually dressed.

"I can't afford to be seen here and won't stay long, so I'll get straight to the point." His dark eyes locked on Wichi. "You've been my son's doctor for many years, and I want you to continue seeing him."

"Of course, I will look after him. Why do you ask?"

"The government is changing, and I don't want anything to affect our relationship."

"Politics has nothing to do with my caring for Albertito and you."

"Thanks, Doctor, I needed to know that. His health comes first." Wichi detected more to the story. "Because I trust you, I'll give you information so you understand my position. If it leaks, I'm a dead man." He paced the floor and made a few glances out the window.

Wichi stood up and looked him in the eye. "Whatever you

tell me stays in this room." García explained he was a high-ranking member of Batista's security force, and it disturbed him to see so many innocent people jailed and killed. "Go on, Colonel."

"I've decided to help Fidel and the rebels overthrow Batista's regime in return for a position when they form a new administration. For your own sake, I won't give you any more details." He paused. "Doctor, I hope and pray what I'm doing is the right thing for me and my country." Wichi nodded and agreed the right political thing was elusive. García took to his feet. "I can't stay any longer." He extended his hand. "Thank you for being Albertito's doctor."

"Your secret and your son are secure with me."

"I'll be in touch." Wichi followed him to the door, locked it, and sat at his desk. He leaned back in the seat and wondered how much more suspense he could endure in one day. The clock showed 2:05 p.m., and he wanted to arrive early for the meeting.

On the way to the Hotel Nacional, he stopped for lunch at El Lechón, a café on the corner. Partygoers reveled along the sidewalks while increased numbers of policemen patrolled the area.

On arriving in the lobby, an attendant welcomed him. "Are you a guest?"

"I'm Doctor Barreras, here for the medical meeting."

The man led him to the ballroom, where Doctor Tony da Silva waited to greet him. "Hola amigo, thanks for coming today. Appreciate your willingness to help with the program."

"My pleasure, Tony, pleased to see you're still our president."

"The Society hasn't voted me out yet." Their faces crinkled in laughter. Wichi sat at a front table, took a sip of water, and glanced at the crowd—not an empty seat in the room. Tony approached. "I just noticed an American doctor has registered. Although he's not here now, I made sure he has an interpreter." Wichi was pleased to have foreigners attend the conference.

The technical crew finished adjusting the lights and speaker equipment. Tony took the microphone and welcomed the members and guests. He smiled at the large crowd present at their final meeting in 1958. The goal today was to present unusual cases and to discuss healthcare issues. "We'll begin the program with a well-respected Havana hematologist and my good friend, Dr. Luis Barreras."

Wichi stepped to the lectern. "Gracias, Tony. I'm honored to speak to my distinguished colleagues and proud to say that our country has an advanced health sector with state-of-the-art technology. Cuba has *the* lowest infant mortality rate in Latin America and ranks ahead of France, West Germany, Italy, Spain, and other European countries. Our physicians per capita rank third in Latin America, and we're ahead of England and Finland. This is great news and speaks well for our profession, but the downside is that we have rural regions where basic needs such as clean water, good hygiene, and proper diet don't exist." He urged the medical community to insist the government tackle these issues or face political consequence. Other speakers corroborated the information.

Tony returned to the front to continue with case presentations.

An internist from Miramar presented a young woman with fever. Preliminary test results showed everything was normal except for anemia and a blood smear with strange red blood cells. The woman's infection cleared, but the doctor couldn't make a diagnosis. He asked if anyone had seen a similar case. Wichi raised his hand. A physician from Vedado requested that he tell them more. Wichi stood and asked the doctor, "Did the family originate from Cuba?"

"No, they came from North Africa."

"The likely diagnosis is beta thalassemia," he said, "an inherited blood disorder causing anemia, more common in people from the Mediterranean region." He further explained there were three types, and the patient had the mild form. The internist thanked him for the information.

"Give us the details of your case, Doctor Barreras," shouted a member from the audience.

Wichi took to the podium. "My patient, a seven-year-old boy, came to me at the age of three with anemia and a blood picture comparable to the one presented. Both sets of grand-parents were from southern Italy. Further testing showed he has the intermediate form of beta thalassemia. I continue to follow him for mild anemia and his unrelated susceptibility for infections."

Following the last speaker, Wichi picked up his briefcase before leaving. The holiday weekend had arrived, and OP was on his case. He still had no clue where to go on New Year's Eve. Two men walked toward him before he reached the entrance. One he recognized as an interpreter. The other tall, thin, middle-aged man wore rimless spectacles on his pointed nose, so sharp it could cut cold butter. Freckles dotted his face and fair skin. This person had to be the American Tony mentioned. He sported a tropical shirt splashed with pineapples and banana designs. The bushy red hair from his chest poked through the unbuttoned upper part, and white pants rode above his ankles and oversized feet. By the time the two approached him, Wichi stifled a laugh.

"Doctor Barreras," the interpreter said, "allow me to introduce our American guest, Doctor Richard Melmont from Miami, Florida. I'm happy to translate your conversation."

They greeted each other. Melmont spoke first. "Doctor, I'm glad we meet. You impressed me with your diagnosis of beta thalassemia." Wichi thanked him. "After hearing you speak, I had to contact you in person. I practice internal medicine in Miami and do research in my laboratory."

"What kind of research?"

Melmont's face brightened. "I study the phenomenon that cancer created in my rats doesn't spread to their spleens. Have you noticed this finding?" Wichi paused for a moment, rubbed his forehead, and said several of his patients with widespread cancer had normal spleens. Melmont smiled. "I'd love to discuss this further. Do you have plans for dinner this evening?"

"I'm afraid I do."

"Another time then? I've got two extra tickets to the Tropicana Club."

Wichi gulped. "For New Year's Eve?"

"No, dinner and show are for tomorrow night, December 30. People booked the thirty-first, months in advance."

Wow, a holiday party and OP off my back. For years he'd

wanted to go to the Tropicana Club, but it was expensive and tough to enter without connections. He answered right away. "You honor me with your invitation. Are you here by yourself?" Melmont said he was alone; his wife and son couldn't be with him. "Thanks for inviting us. The Tropicana's reputation is world-famous, and I know we'll have a great time."

"Fantastic. See you tomorrow night at eight."

They both thanked the interpreter and said good-bye. Standing at the front entrance, Wichi craned his neck and peered over the sea of cars. While searching for the Coronet, he bumped into Tony, who congratulated him on the beta thalassemia diagnosis. He snickered to himself, then said to his friend, "Gracias, what a coincidence that I thought of that little boy and his father this very day." Tony declared he hit a home run on his assessment of Cuba's healthcare problem. They walked a few steps, and Wichi paused. "Our profession is behind the eight ball on this one."

"We don't control the government," Tony said.

"Sí, the question is—who will?"

"You sound as if you have inside information."

Wichi hesitated and realized he spoke too much. "Not particularly," he said, jingling the keys in his pocket. "Just spotted my car."

TEN

Tropicana and Trouble

December 30, 1958
Havana, Cuba

"Hola Havana—Dulce, your sweet companion on the air to-night. Are you ready to bring in the New Year this weekend? Can you mambo?" While driving on 25 Avenida headed toward the Tropicana club, Wichi turned up the radio. He smiled when the woman's sexy voice announced one of his favorites, "Sabor a Mí, A Taste of Me."

He hummed along with the sensuous melody and looked over at OP. She adjusted her strapless top with its glittering bird motif. He tapped her thigh. "Where did you buy that evening attire?"

"I made it, Wichi Barreras, and it took half the night to embroider the blouse and sew the skirt."

He squeezed her bare shoulder. "It was worth the effort, because you look gorgeous in that outfit."

"So you approve of my homemade clothes?" He winked and lowered the window. The balmy breeze complimented the magnificent moonlit sky and added romance to the evening. OP peered into the mirror. "The wind is messing up my hair."

"Take it easy and enjoy the ride."

"Does Doctor Melmont speak Spanish?"

"No, but I've taken care of the language barrier. I discovered that Marco and Eliza Perez, two physician colleagues, have tickets and will join us. Since both are bilingual, we have perfect interpreters." He turned into the winding coconut palm-lined boulevard and passed under the grand TROPICANA arch.

"It's spectacular," she said. "Do you think we'll see any famous people tonight?"

"Possible." He pulled in front of valet parking.

"Bienvenidos, welcome to the Tropicana." A hostess served piña coladas topped with decorative umbrellas. Doctor Melmont, sporting a blue bow tie, striped red and white shirt, and black pants, waited under multi-colored lights that illuminated the magical foyer. A huge pair of black and white saddle shoes covered his feet. OP caught Wichi's attention, pointed to the American, and cleared her throat.

He shot her a quick glare, and they approached their host. "Hola, Doctor Melmont, cómo estás?"

He plucked out a piece of paper with scribbled notes. "Bien, gracias. Por favor llámame Richard." Then he looked up and grinned.

"Bueno, good Spanish. Call me Wichi." Melmont pocketed the note, and they thumped each other on the back. "Esta es mi esposa, my wife, Ofelia Perfecta."

He said, "Ofe—Perfe."

"Just call her OP."

He took her hand, raised it to his face, and left a kiss; she smiled. "Gracias por la invitación. Sorry, my English—no good."

"No problem, my español—no bueno."

Marco and Eliza arrived in time to help with the translation. Wichi made the introductions. After the hostess escorted the group to their seats, he was ready to celebrate. "A round of Cuba Libres, por favor," he called to the waiter.

Melmont raised his glass and announced he had practiced a toast: "Salud, dinero, y amor—health and money and love." Everyone grinned, clinked their glasses, and savored the drink.

The flamboyant floor show featured famous "flesh goddesses" in tight, transparent leotards, who captivated the crowd as they danced inside a giant champagne goblet. Wichi leaned toward OP. "Have you ever seen such talent?"

"You're just gawking at those girls making sexy moves."

"None has an outfit to match yours." She fired a glare that could freeze a firecracker.

After the show Wichi's eyes widened as white-gloved waiters decked in crisp black suits served gold-rimmed goblets bubbling with French champagne. Butterfly jasmines overflowed from tall, fluted, crystal vases centered on tables covered with white linen cloths. The head camarero handed out silver-edged menus and recommended the chef's top entrée—lobster—fresh off the coast. Melmont pulled his collar aside. "Speaking of lobsters, look at me after spending the afternoon by the pool."

"Nothing beats our sun," said Wichi. "Hope they served Cuba Libres?"

"Sí. Why do I appear so happy?" Laughter erupted. They perused the menu, and everyone at the table chose the crustacean delicacy except OP, who ordered rigatoni Florentine.

Eliza raised her eyebrows. "Are you not having the lobster?"

"I don't want to see another living creature boiled alive and eaten."

"But you didn't have any problem eating that poor pig on Nochebuena," Wichi said.

Eliza dabbed the napkin on her lips, while OP gave him a sneer. The lobsters arrived on silver-domed platters. When the lid was lifted, Wichi inhaled the tantalizing aroma and remarked that the lobster was number one. Dinner concluded with a fabulous flan served among purple orchids. He sipped the last drop of coffee and announced, "I'm going to find a good cigar."

As he meandered through the crowd, a voluptuous cabaret girl carrying a tray stopped him. "Cigar, Señor?"

"Sí, H. Upmann por favor." She was so well-endowed he had a difficult time locating the habano partially covered by her overhanging anatomy. He reached for the twisted treasure beneath the cleavage.

"You picked a good one, Señor."

He gingerly removed the H. Upmann from its vantage point, rolled it between his fingers, and cut off the end. Then he lit it and drew a few puffs. "Do you realize what this cigar symbolizes?" After admitting she didn't know, he said it was the essence of Cuba.

"Señor, are you enjoying your evening at the Tropicana?"

"I'm having a great time, especially since I found your tray."

"I have a large selection," she said with a titillating smile.

"Indeed, you do."

"May I help you otherwise?"

"I need a few more cigars. How much are they?"

"Four pesos each but cheaper if you buy a box."

"I'll take it, just give me three singles for my pocket."

"Sí, Señor, the rest will be at the front desk. Don't forget to pick them up when you leave." He gave her four extra pesos and winked as he left for his table.

He sat and placed the habano on an ashtray. "What took you so long?" OP said.

"I bumped into a girl selling cigars. She had a magnificent tray, and I bought a box of H. Upmann at a good price."

"What do you mean 'a good price'? They're cheaper elsewhere."

"Cost isn't everything."

"Sí, Wichi, you don't fool me."

"Mambo! Música! Maestro!" The bandleader cued the bongos and drums and trumpets while Wichi enjoyed a smoke. Guests flocked to the floor and rocked to the beat of cha-cha-cha. Melmont asked Wichi permission to dance with OP. He nodded. Halfway through the song, the American had trouble keeping up with the Latin rhythm. She tried to guide him, but the large feet toppled her high heels. Wichi saw him stumbling and figured he'd better cut in to prevent further embarrassment. OP hobbled to the dinner table after the music ended.

"Ladies and gentlemen," the speaker said, "it's an honor to introduce our special guest for this evening. Please welcome Mister Nat King Cole."

As the applause diminished, the artist's soothing voice mesmerized the crowd. OP turned to Wichi. "I told you we'd see famous people."

"Shh, let me listen." Mister Cole sang "Mona Lisa" and many other hits. He thanked the audience, and for his final melody, he invited everyone to swing to "Bésame Mucho, Keep Kissing Me."

"We have to dance now," Wichi said. "It's one of our all-time favorites." OP got up but pointed to her feet. He took her in his arms, and as they glided across the room, he sensed a sublime, yet foretelling sensation related to this song. The dance ended with a gentle dip within inches of the floor.

"I thought you would drop me."

"No way, we don't need any disasters tonight." She ambled back to the table, and Wichi joined Marco and Melmont at the bar.

"I've been enjoying rum and Coke this evening," Melmont said, "and I don't understand what 'Cuba Libre' means."

"It translates 'free Cuba,'" Marco said. "We celebrated our independence from Spain in 1898."

He wondered why the drink was tastier in Cuba than at home. Wichi explained it was a genuine Cuban mix— American Coca-Cola and Cuban rum and a dash of lime. "Then let's toast to 'Cuba Libre' and the US and good friends," said Melmont. As Wichi raised the glass, he had a flashback of the last time he toasted to Cuba—1949—in a bar with a stranger who predicted the future.

"Are you okay?" Marco said. "Your blank stare had me worried—must be the rum."

Wichi blinked several times, then nodded and laughed. "Just a long day."

"Let's call it a night," Melmont said. Wichi told him the evening was fabulous. "Even if I stepped on OP's feet?" the American asked.

"It adds to the memories." Wichi patted him on the shoulder. "We'll take you to the hotel."

The attendant drove up with his car. Wichi gave a tip and said goodbye to Marco and Eliza. They passed through the Tropicana arch and OP looked back. "I want to come again."

"One gets in this place by being rich and famous and having connections. Last time I checked we weren't on the list." Traffic was heavy as he drove to the Nacional. Pedestrians filled the sidewalks; most were young people. Couples held hands; men waved beer bottles and sang. A guy darted ahead of the car. Wichi laid on the horn, hit the brakes, and nearly clobbered the smiling punk who gave him the finger. "What an idiot, trying to get himself killed before the New Year."

He stopped near the steps of the Nacional and looked around at Melmont, his head lowered and eyes closed. "Richard, estamos aquí, we're here."

He raised up and gazed out the window. "Hotel, huh? Bonito." Wichi agreed it was beautiful and then helped him from the back seat. Melmont threw open his arms and hugged OP standing by the car.

The men shook hands. "Gracias, Doctor Melmont, buena suerte, good luck."

Melmont reached into his pocket, pulled out a business card, pointed to it, and said, "Come to Miami, and we'll talk research." He gave it to Wichi and faltered toward the hotel entrance. Wichi beamed when he got back in the Coronet and remarked he understood English. OP shook her head and told him she didn't catch a single word. They headed home, and he took a sharp right at the next street.

"Why are we turning here?" A shortcut was the response. The street was dark and narrow. He slowed as two young men wandered into the road. They swaggered toward the sedan until he stopped. "What's going on?" she asked.

"These guys are blocking the way."

Four men joined the hooligans, and they rocked the car right and left. Wichi held on to the steering wheel while OP grabbed the door handle. One of the gang members came at them swinging a baseball bat. Time to act, so he pushed the accelerator, and the Coronet lunged forward and knocked the guy sideways. Suspecting they may have guns, he told OP to get low. The tires peeled as he glanced in the mirror. A thug lay on the pavement, and the others yelled and shook fists at him. Sweat covered his face. He hunched his shoulders and waited to hear gunfire. *What if a bullet stops the car or hits us?* He stared ahead, his foot pressed hard on the pedal, and the vehicle raced along the street. The automobile screeched as he swerved onto the main thoroughfare.

"Wichi, they could have killed us."

He kept driving and pondered. He'd taken that route many times before with no problems. *Why is tonight different?*

The corner marker showed 194—his street. Wichi pulled into the driveway and caught his breath, his shirt drenched. OP sniffled, took a handkerchief from her purse, and wiped her tear-streaked face. Her hands trembled on the door handle. She inhaled, got out of the Coronet, and tottered to the door.

"I'll come inside in a minute," he said.

His heart raced as a police car zipped by—an unusual occurrence in his neighborhood at this hour. Tonight the city had gone loco. After hustling indoors he paused in the hallway, went back, and locked the door. OP was sound asleep when he entered the bedroom. Wichi brushed his teeth, put on his pajamas, and paused—*Dammit, I forgot to pick up my box of cigars.*

ELEVEN

Unlucky Grapes

Biltmore Neighborhood
December 31, 1958

Wichi smothered his ears with pillows to lessen the squawking of birds in the backyard. After jumping out of bed, he opened the jalousie window to a strange phenomenon. A flock of blackbirds fluttered in the mango tree and pecked the fruit. His father had told him years ago these fowls were jinxed, but he'd forgo superstition on the last day of 1958. The warm shower grazed his face, and surreal images of last night swam in his mind. The party at the Tropicana—a dream, and the ride home—a nightmare. He whistled "Bésame Mucho" as he lathered his arms and legs. A beady-eyed lizard scurried along the windowsill, and he brushed the reptile aside. "Go eat mosquitos, two's a crowd." The gecko disappeared and he finished the bath in peace. The trousers worn last evening lay on the floor. While hanging them up, he found Melmont's business card in the pocket. He held it for a moment and imagined their paths crossing again, then slipped it into his wallet. He dressed and walked into the living room where OP orchestrated canary rituals. The interaction between his thirty-nine-year-old wife and her feathered offspring provided entertainment he couldn't afford to miss.

"My sweet Rosita and Sashita," she said, "you may fly around the house if you sing for your mama. It's New Year's Eve, and we must be happy little birdies."

Wichi cleared his throat. "Why do you shun Coquita? She's part of the family too?"

OP waved her finger at Coquita's cage in reprimand. "Bad girl, when are you going to behave?" The yellow bird cocked her head. He asked what crime she committed besides making caca on her left shoulder. She grimaced and flicked a gray dropping off her blouse. Coquita was punished because she pecked at her face the other day.

"The canary thought your pimple was birdseed."

"Qué gracioso, you're so funny."

"I'm confident she'll behave after she gets out of jail."

"Quit the nonsense, what are we doing tonight?" Wichi shrugged, told her he'd think of something, and reminded her they just spent a great evening at the Tropicana last night. "We always go somewhere on New Year's Eve," she said. "Make sure you get us home safely this time."

He looked at her and smiled. "Remember, 'we must be happy little birdies.'"

The squawking blackbirds continued to feast on the mangoes and irritate Wichi. He slid open the patio door and sent the dogs to the yard. "Scare away those blasted creatures devouring my prized fruit." The clock showed 12:30 p.m., time to leave for hospital rounds. On the way he thumbed through radio stations. *Where is Dulce?* The music they played made him yawn. Lively tunes were the usual on December thirty-first. He clicked off the knob and enjoyed the fresh breeze along Quinta Avenida. When he reached the Malecón, the sea pounded over the wall. A wave arched across the pavement and drenched the car. A thundering sound in the distance interrupted his pleasant thoughts. *Fireworks—people already celebrating New Year's Eve.*

In the parking lot a boom echoed as he met a nurse rushing from the building. Desperation masked her face. "That was an explosion," she said. "I'm out of here." He nodded and quickly hoofed it into the hospital. While walking the hall, he bumped into a young surgeon and asked if he'd been busy. A rough night he admitted. Besides emergency gallbladder surgery, he operated on several guys beaten up by men who called themselves revolutionaries. Wichi explained his close call with the goons and realized these two violent events may not be random. He patted the doctor on the shoulder and told him to go home and rest. After rounding on his patients, he stopped at the nurses' station to write orders on the charts.

Another loud noise resonated not far away. "New Year's Eve celebration has begun with a bang," said a cohort. Wichi paused writing a progress note. The sounds resembled explosions rather than people celebrating the holiday. A nurse held up a publication and mentioned Fidel Castro and Che Guevara planned to overthrow Batista and save Cuba from Yankee imperialism. She wasn't sure what that meant. He didn't have all the answers for her but said Castro's hatred for Batista originated in part because of American support.

"As for freeing us from Yankee imperialism, look around the hospital and you see much of our technology comes from the US." He told her it remained unclear who was being saved.

"Doctor, you have a reputation as a wise man," she replied.

"Thanks, I'll use it and go home."

He sprinted to the car, climbed in, and locked the door. At the end of the parking lot, a toothless old man blocked the exit, held a rifle across his chest, and yelled, "Viva La Revolución." He waved for the fellow to move. Another deafening boom pierced the silence and distracted the gunman. He wheeled the Coronet to the left, then sped through the gate and along the street. A chill seized him as he heard the rebel fire several shots. Now he knew a tsunami rolled toward Havana, soon to crash into the city. He hurried, taking the back roads to Biltmore, and pulled into the carport. He turned off the engine, took a deep breath, and wondered if his family was safe in the suburbs. *Maybe not.* Across the street stood Mister Crawley watering his philodendrons, and the sight lifted his spirit. He had taken a liking to the dapper, well-mannered Brit with snow-white hair and blue eyes the color of the Cuban sky. He spoke perfect Spanish and learned the language as a film director in Spain. The Englishman had the amusing habit of interjecting British slang into the conversation. Wichi moseyed over.

"Mister Crawley, cómo estás?"

"Jolly good." He turned off the hose, and they shook hands.

"Heard any bombs?"

"Only fireworks, but the chap who cuts my grass says Fidel Castro and his rebels are coming to Havana. He called the bloke a bloody savior."

"Saving us from whom?"

"I'll be gobsmacked if I know—must be those Americans

trying to take over Cuba." He paused and winked. "Those Yanks pilfered our colonies in 1776."

"So, you mean Cuba will fight the Yankees? That'll be a quick skirmish."

The pair belly laughed.

"We're staying at our gaff tonight, too bloody dangerous to go out. Come over at nine bells and let's celebrate together." Wichi thanked him and wanted to jump with joy. "Carina will have the full monty, including seafood paella. We'll count grapes for luck and ring in the New Year—a jolly good time for everyone." Wichi gave a two-handed handshake, hustled home, threw open the door, and yelled for OP.

She came around the corner. "Qué pasa?"

"Mister Crawley invited us over tonight for a New Year's Eve party." She clapped and said the perfect dress waited for the occasion.

The last rays of the tropical sun dissolved while Wichi stood at the front door. OP wound the clock on the sideboard. "Girls, your grapes are in a bowl on the dining room table. Behave and take care of Luisito." Wichi waved adiós to the children and reminded them to eat their grapes on time for good luck in 1959. He clasped OP's hand, and they ambled to the Crawleys'.

BONG! The clock chimed the first sound of midnight. Lizzi gulped a half-chewed green grape. She had barely swallowed it when BONG! the second ring. Didi still had one in her cheek. "Four seconds," Lizzi said. "Here it comes. Get ready." BONG!

The third strike sounded. Luisito scrambled on the floor and reached for fallen grapes. He pocketed more than he ate. "You've spilled yours," said Lizzi. "Put them back on the table." The fourth and fifth and sixth gongs clanged, and by this time the three were laughing while pointing fingers at each other's crammed mouths. "Didi, let me see your teeth?" She opened her lips and drooled green mush. She tried to toss a grape in Lizzi's mouth. It missed, but Luisito made a good catch. "I'm afraid we won't make it. Are you counting?"

"No, playing's more fun than munching," Didi said.

After the twelfth chime, Modesta entered the room. A flying grape smacked her head. "Niños, grapes everywhere––what are you doing?"

"Eating them."

"No, you weren't. You were throwing them." She pointed at Lizzi. "Fetch the broom and clean this place."

"Why me? It's her fault, she threw the first one."

"I don't care who it was. None of you is an angel, and you girls aren't babies anymore. When I was your age, I cooked and cleaned house; you just make messes." She shook her finger at them. "I'm telling the doctor what you've been doing." Lizzi begged her not to say they were playing with the fruit. "Did you eat your twelve, for good luck this year?"

"I tried."

"I ate mine," Didi said, "and the boxers tried to grab Luisito's."

"You didn't let those animals swallow grapes. You know that makes dogs sick."

"No," Lizzi said, "we ran them away."

"Well, I worry your fortune won't be good."

"Can't we pretend we ate them so we'll have good luck?"

"Doesn't work that way. Eating a grape means eating a grape—and you threw more around than you ate."

"Pleeese don't tell Papi we didn't eat all of them. I don't want him to catch our bad luck."

"I'll think on it. Now, run along, it's bedtime."

Lizzi tossed and turned. Something stuck in the back of her mouth. She sat up, slid out of the mosquito net, and rushed to the bathroom to gargle. The feeling lingered, so she tried coughing, but it didn't go away. She went to the hallway and bumped into Modesta.

"Lizzita, are you sick?"

She pointed to her tongue. "Grape—stuck." Modesta clasped her arm, towed her into the kitchen, and set a cup of water and saltines on the table. Lizzi crunched a cracker and swallowed it. She choked and reached out to Modesta.

"Niña, you didn't wash it down with water." Lizzi clutched her neck. Modesta grabbed a chair, draped Lizzi across her lap, and beat on her back until she coughed up crumbs. "Breathe slow now and take a sip." She cleared her throat, shook her head, and took more liquid.

She uttered a raspy sound and drank once more. "It's gone. I can talk again."

"That's good. Just you rest a minute."

The two sat at the kitchen table and held hands. "Did Papi make up the twelve grapes and good luck story?"

"Why no, folks believed that for years. Your father is following the habit. Everybody wants the best of luck."

"I love eating grapes but gulping them in a hurry wasn't fun."
"That's right, niña."
"Do you believe it's my first unlucky thing this new year?"
"Could be."

After putting Lizzi to bed, Modesta checked to make sure Dobin was in the master bedroom. No way in hell would she begin the New Year sleeping with that monster. The boxers curled on the floor in Luisito's room. The clock in the kitchen showed 12:55 a.m., and the doctor and Señora should return soon. Time to call it a night. She lay reminiscing the frightening event. A sting rippled through her spine as she fretted that the young girl could have died right before her eyes because she didn't finish her grapes. Must be a coincidence because her fortune-teller friend Elvira explained the real reason people did this stupid New Year's tradition. "They're a bunch of suckers," the palm reader said. "It started in Spain back in early 1900 when growers needed to sell a bumper crop of grapes."

She laughed that it was a clever hoax. Everyone ate a grape for each stroke of the midnight hour on New Year's Eve and got twelve months of good luck while the farmers made lots of money. As she curled on her right side, another idea ran through her mind. Only last week Elvira said the curvy palm lines showed a new direction in her life.

Changes had happened—a killing in the neighborhood— just the beginning. She twisted one way, then another. A cursed scene appeared in Elvira's crystal ball—dark clouds covered the island of Cuba, followed by the woman's haunting words: "This doesn't look good." Modesta pressed the pillow against her head to stop thoughts from racing. Dearest Buela, who helped her through childhood problems, was in heaven — could be praying time.

With eyes fixed on the ceiling, she prayed out loud. "God, you go fetch my Buela and help me with my troubles. Things will happen, and I gotta get ready for them. Buela—where are you? I'm waiting for your answer. You're the only one I ever listened to and did what you told me. I remember you saying over and over that nobody will take care of me except me. Wait—I hear you now, and that's what I'm gonna do—keep my eyes and ears open and do what's best for numero uno. Not so sure about this bad luck thing, but your grand-baby has the bases covered—I ate my twelve grapes—on time."

TWELVE

Nacional Nightmare

Hotel Nacional
December 31, 1958

Melmont squeezed his forehead. He needed strong coffee and two aspirins. Those Cuba Libres at the Tropicana did a number on him. Unlike Wichi he didn't have to make hospital rounds today. Each step magnified the pounding pain as he trudged to the bathroom and gulped the pills. He released the vise grip on his temples, separated the curtains, and unlocked the window. The balmy breeze and blinding sunlight filled the room. He fumbled for his sunglasses and wobbled to the phone on the side table.

"Good morning, room service, may I help you?"

"Yes, it's Melmont, number 203, two cups of strong black American coffee, and hurry."

He glanced at the surroundings, not caring that dirty clothes and underwear sprawled on the sofa and floor. The patriotic shirt from last night lay draped over the chair. He made it to the couch, closed his eyes, and massaged tight neck muscles. A knock promised the java; he got up, stumbled over shoes that rested where he kicked them off last evening, and fell. Another rap, "I'm coming," he said. He grabbed the doorknob, pulled himself up, and opened the door.

"Coffee you requested, sir." Melmont slumped on the chair. The man poured the steaming brew. Once he left, Melmont managed a few sips from the quivering cup. It took forever for the caffeine blood level to rise to where he could face the day.

A warm shower brought back lost vitality. He hummed "Mona Lisa" while he soothed and dried his body with the soft fluffy towel. He wished he had been tidier with his shirt but vowed to wear it, wrinkled or not. After grabbing his camera, he sauntered to the lobby. A dynamic world awaited; his stomach growled. Following lunch on the breezy deck, he spotted the Russels from the disastrous flight into Havana. He greeted them and inquired what they planned to do that day.

"Stroll along the Malecón," William said. "And you?"

"I'm just taking it easy, maybe I'll meander around Old Havana."

"Don't forget, Doctor, we meet tomorrow at one o'clock in the lobby for the ride to the airport."

Melmont grinned. "Can't afford to miss that lift."

A gust of wind blew Melmont's hat off while he mingled among the crowd of tourists and Cubans lining the streets. The Latin beat from sidewalk bands had folks dancing along the way to Old Havana. Although signs in most closed stores read: CERRADO, a peddler on the sidewalk barked, "Maní." Tourists surrounded him and held out their hands for the paper cone filled with peanuts. An elderly woman placed a small Cuban flag into his hand. The sound of music, the smell of food, smiles on peoples' faces, and others just sauntering along, made him realize why he loved this island and its people. He marveled at the towers of Havana Cathedral with their pigeon inhabitants. He clicked a picture of the magnificent Baroque church as one of the flock dropped a souvenir on him. *Damn, that bird shat on my favorite hat.* He strolled to the harbor. The blue sky behind the Morro Castle provided the perfect setting for a snapshot. The watch showed 3:30 p.m., and his feet hurt. *Time to return to the Nacional.*

Back on the avenue, he heard cracking sounds. *Fireworks started early* he supposed. As he continued the stroll, two bearded men in green fatigues snatched each of his arms and rushed him along the sidewalk. He struggled to get loose— an impossibility with their firm grip. Surely, they must have grabbed him by mistake. He attempted to speak, but they slapped his head, one side and then the other. They took him to a small alley. The shorter man punched him in the abdomen, sending him on the ground, and the other booted him in the flank; his hat rolled away. Excruciating pain ensued, and he clutched his stomach and tried to talk. A rebel yelled and spat on him. "Yankee espía."

"No spy, American doctor."

He took out his wallet and offered money to let him go. The taller man snatched the billfold, grabbed the camera, and put the end of his revolver next to Melmont's forehead. "Yankee spy die now."

"No, please, I'm no spy."

The blasts got louder. Truckloads of men with rifles held upward whizzed by the alley and yelled, "La Revolución."

Melmont feared the worst. Another rebel wearing a red bandana appeared at the corner. "Vamos, let's go," he said. The man holstered his gun, jerked Melmont, and tied his hands behind his back. They pushed him forward, and he stumbled to the avenue. Harried faces darted by as people scurried in various directions. He tripped over a couple forced to kneel on the sidewalk. The woman bawled as a renegade poked a rifle in her partner's jaw. Why didn't someone arrest these thugs? The words "La Revolución" told the story—he was trapped in a Cuban revolution. A rebel jabbed him in the back with a gun, prodded him to a nearby warehouse, and threw him against several trash cans. A frightened crowd huddled beside a wall. He supposed they were American tourists.

A woman cried, "We're Americans, someone help us!"

"Cállate, shut your mouth."

Melmont looked around and spotted the Russel family clustered in a corner. Peggy stared ahead, her face wan, while Annie held her hand. He called out William's name. The brute nearby smacked him on the head with a pistol. "You've injured him," William said. Blood flowed down Melmont's temple, but he nodded to reassure his friend. William told the man they weren't spies. They had travel papers and documents at the Hotel Nacional. The rebel walked over and pointed a gun at his skull.

Annie threw herself over her father's face. "Please don't hurt him."

The barbudo hesitated, then grabbed her neck. "Shut up, or I'll put a bullet in you." She returned an icy glare and grasped her father's hand.

A military truck appeared, and the rebels shoved the tourists on board. They untied Melmont's hands, and he faltered into the vehicle. He maneuvered to a position next to William and gave Annie a smile. A few other passengers had bloody faces, but he saw no major injuries. Many of the women wept, elbows pressed into their sides, but most people kept quiet and stared ahead. The truck rumbled through the streets. A man with a baseball bat darted along the sidewalk smashing windows. Behind, a younger kid grabbed a radio from a display. An elderly lady hobbled out of a grocery store carrying sacks of food. "What's going on?" William said. "Where are the police?"

"There are no police. We're amid a revolution."

The truck stopped at the Hotel Nacional, and the rebels prodded the tourists off with their rifles. Another vehicle arrived, and the soldiers unloaded their passengers. Melmont suspected they rounded up outsiders throughout Havana and brought them there. As he stumbled up the steps, he was blinded by a reporter's flash, likely for a propaganda picture.

Crystal chandeliers sparkled above packed tourists in the hotel lobby. Bearded rebels ordered everyone to sit on the floor. One man shouted, "You can't do this to us. We're Americans." The rebel snarled they were Yankee spies. William stood and demanded they let his wife and daughter go to their room.

"No, Americano." He pushed him downward.

"Asshole," William muttered.

"Hope he doesn't know English," Melmont said.

An older man protested. "I'm a lawyer, and we have rights. You can't hold us against our will without cause." Others demanded to leave. Chaos prevailed in the large room until one rebel fired into the ceiling, and glass from the overhead fixture fell on the crowd. A woman cried out, and the man next to her took his handkerchief and wiped blood dripping from her head. The rebels then separated Americans from others who they allowed to go to their rooms.

"Viva La Revolución," the leader said. "Viva Fidel. No more Yankee imperialism."

A young bearded punk approached a middle-aged man beside Melmont. After calling him a pig and forcing him to stand at attention, he struck the man's face and demanded he take off his gold watch. He put the timepiece on his wrist and waved it high. "Look what the Yankee imperialist has donated to the Revolution." He kicked the man and walked away.

An elderly lady fell. Melmont eased over to aid her. "How much longer can this continue?" her husband said. He assisted them to the elevator while the rebels herded Americans to their rooms.

The Russels moved by. "Peggy's unable to take this stress anymore."

The woman was in shock. "Sorry I can't help you," he said to William as he glimpsed at the surly guard behind him.

"Thanks, we'll do the best we can. Annie's my helper."

The rebel shoved Melmont off the elevator and into his room. He rifled through his belongings, stole his favorite belt, and left. Melmont locked the door and tried to call the front desk, but the phone was dead. He opened the window and saw a sea of olive-dressed militia resembling grasshoppers.

He contemplated the actions of these savages and became livid. *To think, people called Batista's men gangsters.* He rubbed his aching head and noticed blood on his fingers. The wound needed cleaning, but no water flowed from the faucet. He gaped at the bloody image in the mirror. "I'm in deep doo doo." The possibility of not seeing his family again brought back the same lump in his throat he'd experienced during the crisis on the flight. The absence of air conditioning created a sweltering atmosphere, and raising the windowpane only increased the humidity. He found a magazine, lay in the bed, and fanned himself. At first, he tossed and turned on the soaked sheet but soon didn't care. His eyes closed, and an arm fell across his chest.

Gunshots outside woke him. Men yelled, "Batista's gone. Viva Fidel." The clock showed 4:00 a.m. He hurried to the window and got a load of rebel militia celebrating and firing weapons into the air. He lay back in bed. His heart throbbed as he speculated how to get home—then his eyelids folded.

"Pan y agua," someone called from the hallway. He glimpsed at his watch, 7:00 a.m. Bread on a paper napkin and a glass of water lay by the door. He scarfed down the paltry meal and began the task of keeping cool—sitting and fanning. While daydreaming he heard a ruckus outside the room.

A pounding shook the wall. "Abre la puerta, gringo." He hesitated before opening the door. A thick black beard showed through the peephole.

"What do you want?" Melmont said. The barbudo demanded to know if he was the American doctor. "Yes," he said and turned the knob. A bloodied man lay on the floor. "What happened to him?" A spy he was told. While he stood there and wondered how this incident involved him, the brute jerked the injured fellow, shoved him into the room, and onto the bed. He barked an order to fix him. "But I don't have any medicine."

"Okay, he die." He turned and left.

Melmont didn't recognize the beaten victim grinning through bloody teeth. "You promised we'd meet again in better circumstances."

"Major Hart, I can't believe it's you."

"I've been in worse shape."

"What did they do?"

"Just roughed me up a bit."

He cleaned the wounds with a towel and dressed them with a torn pillowcase. Curiosity overcame reluctance to inquire. "How did you deserve this, Major?"

"I'm here to learn Fidel's terrorist tactics used last June when brother Raul took American hostages to the mountains."

"You're CIA, I suppose." He smiled. Melmont scratched his head. "Why take Americans captive?" Hart told him the Castro boys played a smart hand with the hostages, knowing that Batista dare not bomb the rebels for fear of harming Americans. It gave them time to regroup and rearm, plus the US had to take note of their cause. Melmont sat on the edge of the bed.

"In the meantime," the major said, "Castro received publicity around the world while he trickled the release of the prisoners over several weeks."

"I must have been too busy with my rat experiments to pay attention to the news. Looks like the Castro brothers are experts in terrorism."

Hart nodded. "You bet they are."

Melmont's eyes narrowed. "A dumb question, but why are we called Yankee imperialists?"

A deliberate look crossed the major's face. "For Fidel's Revolution to succeed, he needs a villain to target, and the US 'behemoth' who kept the corrupt Batista regime in power and 'exploited' Cuba is the perfect scapegoat."

Melmont saw that as a plausible explanation. He hated being stuck there and asked his friend the likelihood of being released. Hart believed they'd go free since Castro knew better not to be at odds with the US so soon. "Take my advice, though, don't antagonize the goons."

"Do they know you're spying?"

"I'm not sure—chances are fifty-fifty."

The third day arrived, and blackjack provided the only distraction from the heat. Fortunately, a guest left a deck of cards.

"Major, how come you always beat me at this game?"

He smirked. "Fifty-fifty plus Lady Luck."

On the fourth day, a loud knock sounded, and a deep voice yelled, "Vamos." Melmont was half-asleep and weak. Hart was in poorer shape because of his wounds. Melmont got up, staggered to the door, and opened it. A bearded green henchman stood holding a machine gun. "Get clothes and come with me."

At last they were leaving this place *but what destination?* He looked back at the major who nodded a sign of encouragement. Along the hall rebels pounded on other doors. One pulled a screaming woman from her room. "You pig, go." A barbudo prodded half-dressed guests into a single file in the hallway. A few sobbed, others carried a blank stare.

"This doesn't look good," Melmont said.

"Let's wait and see, my friend."

They were marched downstairs and handed rice and stale bread on a soiled paper plate, plus a cup of lukewarm water. Melmont hoped this wasn't his final meal. The Russels were there. Annie and William appeared in reasonable shape. Peggy looked emaciated and glassy-eyed. He leaned over to Hart. "Not a favorable sign, she needs medical help."

"Atención!" The chief rebel rose. "I have great news. Our liberator, Fidel Castro, is in control of Cuba, and Batista's evil ways are gone forever."

The rebels raised their arms and shouted, "Viva Fidel."

Melmont heard that Castro's right-hand man, Che Guevara, oversaw executions at La Cabaña prison in Morro Castle. He eyed Hart and wondered if they awaited that fate. A woman yelled she wanted to go home. "Cállete, we decide who goes and who stays," said the head rebel. A hush fell over the crowd when he announced the ones allowed to leave. He read off names on a list, and as he called each person, a cry of joy sounded.

Melmont waited and listened: "Lucas, Marshall, McConnell, Mellott."

He raised his hand. "That's me."

"No," said the lady across the room, "It's Mellott. I'm Charlotte Mellot."

He sank back, devastated. He heard wrong. Hart stroked him on the shoulder. People murmured and talked. The rumble of their voices ended with a gunshot overhead. The leader continued reading. "Melman."

"Yes, thank the Lord," an older woman cried out. Melmont's heart pounded in his chest. If they didn't call him next, he was cooked. "Mel . . ."

"Please, God, let it be me."

The head guy finished reading, "Melmont."

"I'm Richard Melmont," he shouted, and tears filled his eyes. Hart patted him. He looked at the major, then realized they had been through the Hs and his friend's name wasn't there. "You aren't on the list."

"I told you it was fifty-fifty, and the cards are still out." They read more names. Melmont was misty-eyed when they called Russel. Annie cried and William hugged his catatonic wife. After they ended with Zachary, Hart looked at him. "It's blackjack—win or lose."

The head rebel then announced there were a few more names—Barnes, Davis, Frady—Hart. "That's you," Melmont said as he grabbed his friend's arm. "You made it."

"Dealt a good hand."

The insurgents pushed and shoved the Americans out of the hotel toward two army trucks. Melmont was forced into one vehicle while they herded the major and the Russels into the other. A frightening thought crept through his mind. He remembered what the Nazis did. *Are we going to the airport—or somewhere else?* The drive lasted an eternity until the truck slowed. He shivered just before the RANCHO BOYEROS sign came into view. The place was desolate except for one Pan American DC-7 near the runway. Several military trucks with armed soldiers surrounded their ride to freedom. They pulled up and stopped. "Vamos," the rebel shouted while motioning for Melmont and others to leave the vehicle. He jumped to the pavement. The short distance to the plane seemed like a mile. He never ran so fast in his life. The engines sputtered and the props began to spin. He grabbed a window seat and peered through the glass for the other truck. They unloaded the passengers, and he saw the Russels running with Hart behind. As the major reached the first step, two rebels from the nearby truck seized his arms and pulled him away.

"No," Melmont said, "they've stopped my friend."

The soldiers shoved Hart into the back seat. He stared at the plane and gestured with his hand—five fingers and a zero—twice. The vehicle then sped off and disappeared. Melmont sniffled and lowered his head. Fifty-fifty odds—he wished this were blackjack.

"Doctor Melmont, we made it," Annie said and ran to him. He looked up and told her to wait a bit longer. William carried his listless wife and lowered her into the seat across the aisle. He smiled at his friend. Silence permeated the cabin. The engines hummed, louder and louder, and they began to taxi. Military vehicles moved alongside—he didn't understand why. The airplane stopped at the runway. A truck turned ahead of the DC-7. He couldn't see it anymore. *Is it blocking our takeoff?* A loud roar shook the craft and thrust him back in his seat. Terror gripped until he realized they were

moving along the airstrip. Faster and faster the plane acceler-
ated until he felt a bump. They were airborne. Higher and
higher the Pan American climbed, and the alligator-shaped
island disappeared behind the clouds.

"Praise God," shouted a man from the front row. Sponta-
neous outbursts of joy and cries followed throughout the
cabin.

The Captain announced, "Welcome to the United States of
America—and a belated Happy New Year."

THIRTEEN

Bearded Bogeymen

Biltmore Neighborhood
January 4, 1959

Hell broke loose, and it wasn't even noon. "American Spies Detained at the Nacional" filled the front sheet of the Havana newspaper. Wichi's coffee splattered on the table when a figure popped out of the page. "Oh, no, it's Melmont."

OP rushed into the kitchen. "What did you say?"

"Look, that's Melmont," pointing his finger. "They're holding him as a spy."

She grabbed the paper and put a hand to her mouth. Wichi rose from the table, said his friend was no spy and needed help. He was going to the Nacional. She clutched his arm and begged him not to leave; it was dangerous. He planned to wear a white coat and take his medical gear. *The rebels will allow me to visit my patient.* OP insisted it was too risky. She ran to the living room sofa and returned with an article that showed Che Guevara, a well-known Argentine communist, was in control of La Cabaña prison, and there were rumors he had begun executions. "This is what might happen to you." He tossed the paper on the table and paced back and forth. The American physician had befriended them. Since he didn't speak Spanish and couldn't communicate with the rebels, they'd crucify him. Wichi picked up a brochure from the medical meeting. He'd use his credentials to convince them Melmont was a doctor, not a spy. "Please don't go," she pleaded.

Wichi grabbed the medical items and left the house. A few blocks away a large moving van parked along the curb. Men carried boxes out of the Purcey home. Lizzi had not mentioned that Patsy was leaving. *Her father loves Cuba and the weather, so why is he going?* He guessed anti-American sentiment likely forced his company to pull their employees off the island sooner than later. The Coronet's fuel gauge sat just above empty when he reached the green dinosaur above the pumps. The gas station two miles from the house represented one of the American oil companies in Cuba. "Fill her up?" said the attendant. He nodded. The guy asked if Wichi planned to go to Fidel's celebration on January 8. He frowned and said he might watch it on TV. "Castro has fought hard in the hills for us and is on his way to Havana to free Cuba."

"What do you mean by 'free'?"

The man spat on the pavement. "Where have you been? Fidel is defending us from the Batistianos and Yankees."

"Are we at war with the US?"

"Well, my father said Batista and American companies are our enemies."

"So, if your enemy gives you a job, where does your work go if Castro decides to get rid of your oil company?"

The employee rubbed the back of his neck. After returning the nozzle to the pump, he stroked his beard and muttered, "Hadn't thought 'bout that."

Wichi cranked the engine, rounded the corner, and turned on the radio, hoping to listen to Dulce's music. Instead, a male announcer captured his attention. "Ladies and gentlemen, we bring you excerpts from a speech by Comandante Fidel Castro who has now gained control of Santiago and will soon lead a caravan to Havana." Wichi reached to turn off the radio but hesitated when he realized he'd better listen to what Fidel had to say. He had doubts about his association with Che, the communist. Since Manuel Urrutia was sworn in as president today, he was curious to learn how Castro and he might interact.

Fidel's voice came from the radio. "Personally, I can add that power doesn't interest me . . . We have all united to support the Revolution. There will be no more bloodshed . . . We won't have to employ force, nor walk around with guns, because true order is the one based on freedom, respect, and in justice, not force."

Hmm, these words don't have the tone of a dictator—he'd continue listening.

"We will re-establish our economy. We will take care of sugar cane so it doesn't burn . . . And where there is justice, we won't have revenge . . .There will be no revenge or hatred . . . Now, anyone can speak, good or bad, but anyone will speak . . . There will be absolute freedom because that's why we have made the Revolution."

Wow—freedom, justice, no more killing—words that touched his heart. At last a chance for an accountable government. He caught the last of Fidel's address before nearing the hotel.

"Manuel Urrutia, the magistrate [President], who said the

Revolution was just—I have put into his hands all legal transactions that I have exercised with maximum authority inside a liberated territory that is now our country. I will simply assume the functions that he will assign. In his hands rests all authority of the republic. We respectfully lean our arms before the civil power in the Republic of Cuba to the provisional president. I hand over my authority, and I allow him to speak to the country."

Wichi turned off the radio and felt relieved that Castro may be good for Cuba. As he drove up the winding driveway to the Hotel Nacional, he had hopes of helping his American friend and was sure the rebels would understand. In the parking lot a rifle-bearing soldier waved him to stop.

"I'm a doctor with a sick patient staying here."

"Beat it, hotel's closed."

"He's diabetic and may die if I don't treat him."

An officer in olive-green fatigues approached the car. The guard stepped aside, and his superior looked at Wichi and his medical bag on the seat. "Go ahead." He found a parking space, grabbed the bag, and started toward the entrance. A soldier stopped him and asked why he was there. He replied that a patient in the hotel was unwell.

"No one's sick here."

"You're wrong, I must attend to him or he might die."

The man asked the patient's name. Wichi stared at him and knew it was a trick question. Tall and red-headed was his answer. The soldier wiped his nose on a sleeve. "I asked you his name, not how he looks."

"Richard Melmont."

"An American, eh? You can't call on these Yankee spies."

"My patient is no spy."

"All Americans are spies and imperialists."

Wichi pushed the guard aside and hurried up the steps. Someone yelled to stop, but he kept going toward the door. Before he reached the entrance, two men grabbed him by the arms and dragged him backward. He demanded to know where they were taking him. They told him to shut his mouth. "I'm a physician," he said.

"Don't care who you are."

They threw him into the rear of a military van that smelled of urine, and roaches scurried under the rags. The barrel of a machine gun lay a few inches from his eyes. He asked if the rebel enjoyed terrorizing innocent people. "Put your tongue where the sun don't shine," he said. Wichi knew he was in trouble. These thugs were taking him somewhere, maybe to shoot him. The van stopped, the door opened, and a guard pulled him out in front of a police station. A bearded goon pushed him inside and onto the floor.

Nearby, a man cried, "I'm not with Batista."

A rebel punched him in the face. Blood gushed from his nose and mouth. "You'll pay, Batistiano."

Wichi sensed the poor guy's fate and hoped his wasn't the same. His head lowered for a moment until two black boots and green pants stood before him. The soldier grabbed his arm and pulled him to the main desk where the sergeant asked questions. "Your name and address."

"Doctor Luis Barreras, 194 . . ."

"That's enough, you assaulted our guard." He said he didn't attack anyone but was only trying to see a patient at the Hotel Nacional. "Oh, an American spy?"

"Sí, an American, but a spy, no."

"They left this morning."

"Then I'm done here." He turned to leave, but the rebel grabbed him and said no way he'd escape punishment for attacking a soldier of the Revolution. "I've told you, an ailing patient needed me." The man slapped his head, shoved him inside a small room, and locked the door. He sat in a chair against the wall and listened to wailing and groaning in the hallway. A woman cried, saying she was no Batistiana. She screeched and a thump sounded. These people were merciless.

After hours of waiting, his brain pounded. He massaged his forehead, but nothing could break the tension of worrying what lay in store. An adolescent boy in green fatigues stormed in and ordered him to stand. Wichi followed him to the front office and to a desk. The soldier seated there waved a piece of paper with his long, tobacco-stained fingernails. "I'll let you go," he said, "but if it were up to me, you'd rot in that jail cell." He breathed a sigh of relief. "Get out of here, traitor."

A rebel pushed Wichi out the door, shoved him into a waiting truck, and tossed his medical bag beside him. "You're a pig," said the driver, pulling away from the curb, "assaulting my comrade and rubbing noses with Americans."

"I don't hurt people, I treat them." As he bounced along, it astounded him how helping a friend during this Revolution generated so much violence. He stared out the window at ominous black clouds rolling in from the east.

The truck slid to a stop. "There's your American car. We'll keep an eye on you." Rain poured but it didn't matter. He jumped out and dashed for the Coronet. Safe inside, he reached for a towel on the seat to dry his trembling hands and mop a sweaty face. He wanted to get home before something else happened. The wipers were on full speed along the Malecón, but the road was barely visible. If he hit someone, he'd be taken back to rot in that station. While putting his nose against the windshield, he managed to stay right of the middle line. The rain lessened by the time he reached Quinta Avenida and had stopped when he parked in the driveway. He climbed out of the sedan, and a massive boom knocked him against the car—*they shot me*. He grabbed his chest—*no blood, maybe an explosion*. He glanced at his house and others nearby. Everything looked normal. A bolt of lightning flashed in the sky, followed by a loud rumble. *Whew, just an old-fashioned thunderstorm.* He steadied his shaky legs and faltered into the house.

OP jumped from the sofa. "Wichi, where have you been? Did you see Doctor Melmont?"

"I tried to, but they detained me at the police precinct."

"Ay, Dios mío. I told you not to go."

"I went to help my American friend, but I'm glad they let him return to the US."

"Why did they keep you?"

"Accused me of hitting a soldier—not true, then they released me."

"Gracias a Dios you're home."

"Did you catch Castro's Santiago speech earlier?" he asked. She shook her head. "Fidel promised a multitude of things that sounded good, but the rebels' brutality tells a different story. If these barbudos represent what the Revolution is all about, we're in for a more violent and repressive government than before."

OP sat back on the couch and fluffed the pillows. "Let's hope after Fidel arrives in Havana, the good things you mentioned will happen, and we can have a happy life."

Lizzi dashed into the room, crying. "I'm so sad, Patsy Purcey leaves tomorrow."

FOURTEEN

Conquering the Catholics

Biltmore Neighborhood
October 1959
Nine Months Later

"OUCH," Modesta yelped as the knife sliced her finger. She let the slippery potato flop into the sink and watched the water turn red. *Wish it were Batistiana blood, not mine.* She wrapped the cut with toilet paper before peeling the rest of the potatoes. Since Fidel marched into Havana back in January, she'd been hoping for a job other than chopping and cleaning. He promised Cubans social justice and no more tyranny. Batista's hired murderers deserved to die. Castro was her man; one who rounded them up and mowed them down. She tapped her feet, swayed to the beat of Radio Rebelde, and planned her role in the Revolution.

Soup was boiling when the announcer interrupted the music. "Comandante Fidel Castro has mandated the closure of Catholic schools; nuns and priests will be detained."

"Now they're cooking," she muttered and wiped her hand on the apron. With Catholics put away, she needed to wean Graciela from wasting time praying to that rosary and attend the Santería meeting on Saturdays. Plus, she might learn useful voodoo.

Wearing a bathing suit and balancing a dirty clothes basket on her head, Lizzi strode barefoot into the kitchen. She noticed Modesta's bloody apron. "Are you hurt?" She shrugged. Lizzi asked her to launder a school blouse for tomorrow.

"No school for you. Radio says nuns been put away."

Lizzi stared at her, point-blank. "No way, you heard wrong."

"Not deaf yet."

Lizzi said her father had the answer and knew how to fix it. Modesta shook her head and said he could do nothing. She waved a knife in the air and bragged how the Revolution was getting rid of those church-and-people-owned things. The girl glared at her. "Phooey on the stupid Revolution. Where's Papi?"

"He's taking a siesta, don't go bothering him."

A hard knock at the door awakened Wichi, and Lizzi rushed into the room. "My school's closed, and they took the nuns away."

He sat up on the bedside, held his sobbing daughter, and asked where she heard the news. Modesta, she told him. The headline in the newspaper OP left on the nightstand caught his attention: "Castro Conquers the Catholics." He read out loud, "Fidel has nationalized two Catholic schools in Havana—Maristas and Sagrado Corazón."

"That's my school," Lizzi said. "What's 'nationalized'?"

He explained the government now owned Catholic schools, and they removed God from the classroom. He didn't mention

the part referring to Catholics as social scums and having
military church-watchers sitting in pews. He pitched the paper
into the wastebasket, blew out a long deep breath, then took
Lizzi in his arms. "Esto es el colmo, the peak of craziness—
Castro hating the church." Lizzi remarked that the Pope
should help, and she wondered where he was. Wichi chuckled
and said maybe hiding under a mattress. They laughed. She
wanted to see the campus, but he shook his head—too
dangerous. The pleading gaze in her eyes melted his heart
because he knew how much the school meant to her. Since OP
had taken Didi and Luisito to a dental appointment and wasn't
around to object, he decided to take Lizzi there.

The unlocked gate provided access up the hill to Sagrado
Corazón. Lizzi suggested driving to the back of the gymna-
sium instead of the porte cochère in the main entrance. "I know
the way," she said. He glanced at his wristwatch—noon, and
no one there. After he stopped the car in the field along the
edge of the property, Lizzi grabbed the door handle and insisted to go inside the building. He caught her arm and said it
was time to leave. "Please let me walk into the gym. I had so
much fun there."

He scanned the place—no sign of soldiers. The doors and
windows were closed. Satisfied that no one was present, he
agreed to allow her to enter the school. "But I'm going with
you."

The car door shut, and an uncanny quietude prevailed, with
only the sound of tall grass rustling in the breeze. They trekked
through the field and reached a small walkway that led to the

rear entrance of the gym. The door flew open. Wichi's heart skipped a beat; he expected to have a soldier's rifle stuck in his face. Relieved that it was only the wind, he needed an excuse should the men discover them. "If we meet anyone, let's say you left your gym shorts." Lizzi squeezed his hand. They peeked into the offices and smelled smoke that lingered above ashtrays filled with smashed cigarette butts and cigars. A massive picture of Fidel Castro hung above the desk. Shadows and nail holes of former crucifixes marked the walls.

Lizzi pointed out the locker room where Sister Bernadette used to pray with the students before and after each PE class. "I miss her so much. She was a tiny nun but had such a big heart."

"Nobody's here, let's go home. This unnerving silence haunts me."

"What was that?" Lizzi said, pointing to the right. "Did you hear it?"

"Could be the men back from lunch, let's leave."

"The noise came from inside a locker," she said while thumping each green cabinet. "Anybody here?" A scratching clatter on metal grew louder as she hurried along the row. A cry originated from the end locker. Lizzi ran and placed her ear to the door. "Papi, hurry, someone's inside." A woman's voice from within asked who was there. "Lizzi Barreras," she said.

"Aleluya! It's Sister Bernadette, please help me out of here."

Wichi pulled on the rusted latch and rattled the door to no avail. Thoughts raced through his mind. The soldiers' return meant prison, but the motivation to please his daughter kept the effort going to get the nun out. Lizzi handed him a metal rod that lay nearby. "If you hit the handle from below, I know it will work." He knocked upward against the bolt—no luck. He pounded again, but it still didn't open, and time was running out. She pleaded to save Sister Bernadette, so he grabbed the rod with both hands, swung hard, and the latch moved. He yanked open the door and a petite nun dressed in a black habit fell to the floor. Lizzi hugged her.

"Praise God, you found me."

"What are you doing here?" he asked.

"Three days ago, they seized the school and took everyone away. I hid from the soldiers until I got stuck inside yesterday." Wichi inquired if she could walk. "Sí, Señor." She held out her cross. "God will give me the strength to run."

They sprinted to the car, and he reached for the keys and found nothing—and the other pocket was empty too. "OH, NO." They must have fallen out when he ran across the grassy field. The watch showed 1:00 p.m.—end of the soldiers' break. He and Lizzi rummaged through the grass, and Sister Bernadette knelt and prayed. They needed a miracle to find the keys. "No luck here," he said, "we have to search the gym again." He told the nun to stay near the automobile. She continued praying while they rushed back to the lockers and scoured the floor—nada. Drenched in sweat he glanced toward the main door. *Any minute the rebels may enter.* "We're leaving." He grabbed Lizzi and made a mad dash to the car. As they approached the nun, she lowered her outstretched arms and opened a hand containing the precious keys.

She handed them over. "God has performed a miracle today."

"Sí, please pray for one more—getting us out of here."

He clutched the wheel, with Lizzi and the sister in the rear. The tires threw rocks as they surged backward. Just as he switched gears, a man bellowed from the building, "Stop, or I'll shoot." In the doorway Wichi spotted a soldier with a pistol pointed in their direction. Lizzi's gym shorts alibi was invalid now with a nun in the car. They'd arrest him for helping a Catholic escape, and he'd die in jail or in front of a firing squad. He hit the gas and prayed the rebel had poor marksmanship. That second miracle was imperative, because they were making a run for it.

"Get down," Wichi hollered. A cloud of dust billowed behind when he pushed hard against the accelerator. A shot fired, then another as the Coronet careened around the shrubbery. *Thank God, he missed.* They raced along the curved road and back toward the front gate, and he hoped to find it open with no guards. A glimpse through the trees showed a clear entrance, but before reaching it an army truck with soldiers entered. He slammed on the brakes and stopped behind a tall row of bushes. A soft whimper sounded in the backseat. Wichi turned and put a finger to his lips. The militia moved ahead toward the porte cochère. A squint in the rearview mirror revealed the soldier from the gym sprinting towards them. "Hold on," he said as the tires spun. The man fired a final shot. Another miss and they were through the gate. The likelihood was slim that the military truck could turn around and catch them. He hoped they didn't get his license plate. One more obstacle to overcome—a soldier stationed at the neighborhood entrance. At the 192 Street intersection, the sentry stood, poised with an automatic rifle.

The man gave Wichi a penetrating gaze while he waited for the green traffic light. He grasped the steering wheel with a death grip. When the light changed, he pressed on the gas, held his breath, and looked back in the mirror. The soldier remained at his post—another miracle.

He pulled into the carport. Not a moment to rest—he must hide the nun. After opening the door, Lizzi got out first and clasped sister's hand. He followed and motioned them to hurry into the house. Inside the living room Wichi paused and took a deep breath. "Welcome to our home, Sister Bernadette."

"Muchas gracias, I owe my life to you." Tears gushed from her eyes.

"We will help you, but it will be difficult with the Catholic persecution." He grasped her hand.

Lizzi embraced her. "I'll take care of you."

OP's car rolled into the driveway. Wichi met the three at the door. "Back so soon? We have a guest," he said and faced a puzzled stare from his wife. Didi and Luisito ran past him.

Lizzi rushed to her mother. "Mami, we had a horrible day." She said her school was closed and Papi drove her there one last time. "Look who we found—Sister Bernadette."

"Señora, your husband and daughter saved my life."

"You're the PE teacher?" The nun nodded. OP smiled and threw Wichi a gesture to follow her into their bedroom. She shut the door and said, "Are you insane? Have you read the papers regarding Catholics?"

"The poor lady was trapped inside a gym locker."

"You took Lizzi to an off-limits place without my permission?"

"She cried and begged me to take her."

"I want to cry too. I'm not sleeping well since the Revolution, and now you've made more trouble for us."

"Whether you approve or not, Sister's here now."

Modesta grunted and grumbled in the kitchen. She needed extra potatoes and onions for the soup. Another mouth to feed, more dirt to clean, more clothes to wash, and more stuff to do. She picked at the scab on her finger, and fresh blood oozed. Her life shifted from nasty to horrible because they brought a sister home. Those Catholics were supposed to go away. She wondered how much importance she'd receive if the Committee for the Defense of the Revolution learned the doctor hid a nun in the house.

FIFTEEN

Hidden Habit and Heartaches

Biltmore Neighborhood
November 2, 1959

During the last several weeks, Modesta couldn't find a speck of dirt or a morsel of food on the spanking clean floor after Sister Bernadette finished mopping. By eight o'clock the nun had watered the flowers and fed the dogs. She looked good not wearing the habit, and besides, she couldn't work being covered like that. Sweet dark eyes sparkled with joy, and ebony arms— now exposed—glistened in the light as she peeled mangoes and prepared the platter for the family's breakfast.

"Sister, you're sweating too much."

"I want to help you."

"Lord knows I need it, but your pretty black hands are for praying not mopping and cutting."

"Modesta, are you Cuban?" Sister asked.

"Born in Aspiro, near Pinar del Río. Where're you from?"

"Jamaica. My mother worked for a family there, but she died. My father has a home in Key West."

"You trying to get there?"

Bernadette froze momentarily, and with a bowed head, she prayed, "Thy will be done, not mine."

"I pray that dear Buela makes my life easier, but still got to wash and iron and cook and clean cages and feed those animals."

"Work hurts no one if the peace of God is in your heart." Modesta said she'd have peace if nobody gave her orders. After the nun called her an angel for cleaning the habit and veil, she shrugged and admitted she was more of a devil. Sister made the sign of the cross. "Dios te libre, God forbid you saying that word."

"Only because you don't know me."

"I'm sure there's goodness in you." She hugged her and left to do calisthenics with the girls. This little nun puzzled Modi. She shouldn't be in the Barreras house because Catholics were bad for the Revolution. Yet here she was, helping with the chores and saying she was a good person. The sister created an unexpected problem.

Wichi made his way into the kitchen, sat at the red melamine table, and forked a juicy mango slice. "Ahh, delicioso, sweetened by the sun." He turned to Modesta. "Nice of you to serve this luscious fruit."

She chewed on her tongue. "Ripe mangoes peel easy."

"It's good to have Bernadette here."

"I suppose so."

"She doesn't have anyone now that the nuns are gone."

"Says her father lives in Key West."

"Oh?" he said while sipping coffee and mulling over the sister's safety. He was unsure how Modesta felt toward her and worried that she might tattle. Without the habit she didn't resemble a nun, but if the militia found out, grave danger awaited.

"Wichi, finish breakfast and come to your study," OP yelled from the hallway.

Amused at what burr lay under her saddle, he got up and followed. "You're on high alert, what's the problem?"

"Close the door and grab this." She puffed up a flyer, pointed to the name, Hubert Matos, and read, "Castro's former top military commander arrested." She threw the paper on the desk. "I knew him, a teacher and a fine person, who supported the Revolution because he wanted democracy for the Cuban people."

"What crime did Matos commit? And by the way, where did you get this information?"

"Margo Martin, next door, gave me a newspaper clipping. Matos committed no offense, other than he believed Castro had no intention of holding free elections. He also thought the Revolution was moving toward communism. One example was the new agrarian law—whatever that is. Matos resigned his post and gets jailed."

Wichi added, "I read an article explaining the law. The government can now take and distribute land without compensating the owner."

"Sounds like socialism."

"Exactly, and with Che Guevara advising Castro, Matos is correct. We're on the path from socialism to communism."

OP caught his arm. "Remember what these despots did to you. No telling what will happen if we're discovered hiding a nun." She told him Sister Bernadette had been there too long and needed to go.

"Give me time."

Wichi grabbed a starched lab coat, picked up his medical bag, and left the house. The drive along Quinta Avenida had a different tone; previous traffic comprised commuters heading to work. Now, military trucks hauling rifle-waving soldiers rolled past. His heart ached at the sight of graffiti on the storefronts: LA REVOLUCIÓN HASTA LA MUERTE. The last thing he fathomed—people willing to die for the Revolution and its misery. In the rearview mirror a black car kept a fixed distance and copied his every turn. It looked as if someone were following him. His jaw tightened and sweat beaded on his forehead. *They traced the nun from my license plate.* As he arrived at the office, the vehicle zoomed past. He wiped his brow. No jail time awaited him—at least for now.

Olga greeted him as he opened the door. "Buenos días."

She handed over the appointment ledger. A long red-painted nail pointed to his private office. "Rey is in there, and Sarita Fontana and her father will arrive at two o'clock."

What could be wrong—Rey here at this hour, and Pepe coming later? He hurried into the room. The mechanic wore the usual light blue, short-sleeve shirt and sat with his head lowered. "Qué Pasa, Rey? I haven't seen you in several months, are you sick?" When he didn't look up or respond, Wichi continued, hoping to lighten his spirit. "We must return to Fontana ranch again, admire the fields, and smell the manure." No comment. He shook his friend's slumped shoulder. "If you stay until two o'clock, you'll see the love of your life. Bueno, no?"

At last he raised his head. A despondent expression dominated Rey's face. He stood and averted eye contact with his boss. "Doctor, my responsibilities have changed. I've been working for Fidel Castro, and now I'm in charge of several buildings, including this one."

"No, por favor, this can't be true."

"My sergeant wants your keys. The State has confiscated the office, and you'll lease the space under our rules."

"Your rules? Damn if that's the case."

"Things are different, Doctor, the new government will control your salary, secretary, and supplies."

Wichi kicked the desk, and the lower drawer handle fell. "Open your eyes, if Batista was a canker sore, Fidel is the plague."

Rey pumped up his chest. "Fidel is good to me, and I get free things. I'm an important person, with a rifle at home and a new uniform." He held out his hand. "The keys—I must show up with them tonight."

"That's your problem, you arrogant moron. Does Sarita know you're a Fidelista?"

"Sí."

"And she still loves you?"

"No, she hates me."

"Good, she deserves someone better."

"Doctor, your keys—now."

Wichi faced Rey as a matador prepared to slay the bull. He took the ring of keys out of his pocket and threw them on the floor. "No one will ever control me or my practice. GET OUT."

Rey snatched the ring and yelled, "I'll bring my rifle next time." Every muscle in Wichi's body tensed while he watched Rey flee. He remained silent, looked at his clenched fists, and wondered what held him from punching his traitorous friend. His hands loosened, and he stumbled toward the desk. After catching himself on the arms of the chair, he sat and leaned back, both eyes fixed on the ceiling.

Olga rushed into the room. "Doctor, are you okay? I didn't think Rey had a mean bone in his body."

Wichi continued to stare overhead. "Castro has brainwashed him, and now he's a Fidelista." He pivoted. "Want to hear the latest dreadful news? The Revolution nationalized my practice." She gasped. "Rey has authority over the building, and he'll let you in, if you wish to keep working."

"I'll continue to help take care of your patients."

"Gracias. I'm not sure how much they'll pay you."

"We aren't the only ones affected," she said. "My friend works for a pediatrician, and they cut her salary."

Wichi glanced at the time—1:20 p.m., and he needed rest. He had worked hard these past fifteen years to build a medical practice, and without warning, everything now belonged to the state. He asked Olga to let him know when the next patient arrived.

At 1:45 p.m., a tap on the door, and Olga announced the Fontanas came early. "I'll see them." Pepe and Sarita lumbered into the private office, her arm around the waist of her faltering father. The robust, sun-tanned farmer had an ashen pallor and a gaunt body. "Hola, come in." Wichi helped Pepe to the chair and then embraced Sarita. A distant stare diminished her loveliness, and the once-sparkling emerald eyes now reflected sadness. "Tell me, what's the matter?"

"Papá has weakened in the last month. He won't eat and barely drinks water."

He assisted Pepe onto the examining table and found an enlarged liver. After finishing the physical, he tightened a tourniquet on the farmer's arm to get a blood sample. He looked at Pepe's sunken eyes. "You need to eat more lechón and gain weight. Your pigs are the best."

"No more pigs—militia took them." Pepe's voice quivered.

"Doctor," Sarita said, "it's not just the animals, but the government took the fertile part of our farmland with the new agrarian law and gave it to other people. Only a few meager fields are left to grow crops."

"I'm sorry to hear that, and I share your loss, for today I found out they've confiscated my office."

"From Rey, no doubt."

"Sí, and to think I considered him as a son."

"And I loved him." She wiped away a tear.

Wichi checked Pepe's lungs. "You still have the horses?"

"Gone except one."

"Camagüey?" Sarita shook her head. Wichi couldn't help but look in the other direction and clench his fist. *Those thieving bastards.* He shifted to Pepe and managed a smile. "Did you know the stallion threw me?" The old farmer nodded. "I planned to come back and ride that horse again to show him who's boss." A half-grin on Pepe's face brought a moment of joy. Sarita remained with her father while Wichi went to the lab to analyze the specimen. He pounded the counter. "Damn the Revolution and those bearded barbarians." Next, he made a blood smear and inspected it under the microscope. The centrifuge stopped spinning. Results of the tests were conclusive: Pepe had severe anemia. The fecal specimen confirmed intestinal hemorrhage. He returned to the patient. "Pepe, you have a low blood count from internal bleeding in your intestine. I need to hospitalize you this afternoon and do further tests. Did you come prepared to stay a few days?"

"Sí," Sarita said, "we won't miss what's left of the farm." Wichi accompanied them to their car and gave directions to the hospital. He'd come by later to check on them.

Back in the office, he slumped into the chair and yearned for happy memories, but pleasant thoughts were replaced with the reality that the government now owned his practice. Moments passed as he sat contemplating the future. Olga poked her head into the room. "It's been a long day. What time should I return tomorrow?"

"Let's try the usual and see how it goes."

"I'll tidy the papers on my desktop and put Señor Fontana's medical records in the filing cabinet."

Wichi heard the door close, and he walked to the laboratory to look at Pepe's blood smear once again. Considering the enlarged liver, anemia, and intestinal blood loss, it was evident Pepe suffered from advanced colon cancer. Before leaving he adjusted the window blind and spotted two military trucks parked in the street. A hard knock resonated. "Doctor Barreras, open up, NOW." *For sure they're here to arrest me—the nun, I guess.* He hesitated and considered calling OP first but had no choice other than to let them into the office. With no place to run, he must follow their orders. A siren blared outside. He opened the door, and a soldier grabbed his arm and pulled him to an ambulance stopped in front of the building. "Doctor, we arrived upon a terrible accident. The young woman insisted we escort the emergency vehicle here."

Inside, Sarita hovered over her father. "Please help him, a truck hit us." Wichi leaned over the farmer; he wasn't breathing. A finger on Pepe's neck revealed no pulse. He looked at Sarita, shook his head, and she sobbed. He held her as she wept; tears flowed in streams onto his shoulder. She caught a breath, her voice cracked. "First Mamá, the farm, and now Papá. What next?"

Wichi offered a handkerchief to wipe away the blood on her face and asked if she was okay. She nodded and said God granted a miracle that saved her life, since their little car was demolished. "I understand it's difficult to suddenly lose your father in the accident, but I can tell you he was spared days of suffering."

"What do you mean?"

"Colon cancer — Pepe had only a month to live."

She drew a long breath and exhaled. "Gracias for telling me, and I'm thankful to know he didn't endure pain at the end. Wichi said he'd help with the funeral arrangements. "No need, Doctor. Papá's brother lives in Havana, and I can get in touch with him." They walked into the office, and Sarita made a call. Within thirty minutes the relative arrived. Wichi told her to notify him if she needed anything. She dried her tears and hugged him. "Papá liked you so much; I will always remember your kindness."

"Pepe was a good man."

Sarita and the uncle went to the ambulance, and Wichi headed home. He caught a glimpse of the somber car in the mirror, gripped the steering wheel, and guessed many were being followed these days. He pulled into the driveway, and the vehicle passed. Today was a turning point in his life—for the worse. The horrible day was almost over, and two things entered his mind to end it best—his comfy chair and a shot of whiskey.

SIXTEEN

Saving Sister Bernadette

Biltmore Neighborhood
November 3, 1959

A sudden flash of light, a loud boom, and multiple thumps on the flat roof brought Wichi out of bed. He rushed to peer through the wooden slats of the jalousie window, his first thought—a counterrevolution. After seeing coconut trees sway and drop cannonball-like fruits onto the house, he realized they were in the middle of a terrible squall. Rain pounded the outside walls as if it came from a fire hose. "Get everyone into the kitchen." At six o'clock the room was dark as the children crowded under the table. Power was out, so OP lit a candle. Water seeped under the glass sliding patio door. Wichi called for Modesta to bring towels. No answer. "Where is she?" Sister Bernadette said she was hiding under the bed. Now he remembered—storms terrified her since childhood. "Leave her be," he said. "Sister, help soak up the water."

The family huddled for an hour until the wind subsided and the downpour became a steady, gentle pitter-patter. Both girls cheered as the electricity returned. Didi came from underneath the table first. Luisito remained hunkered with the dogs until Lizzi pulled him off the floor. Modesta poked out her head. "Is that awful storm over?" Wichi assured her it had ended, and she eased into the kitchen to prepare the food.

"I'll peel the mangoes," Sister said.

"Okay, that's mighty nice."

Wichi finished breakfast and motioned OP into the study. She followed, closed the door, and asked what was happening. "A shocking event occurred yesterday. You were asleep when I got home, so don't tell the children what I'm about to say." He told her the State seized his laboratory and office, and he had to surrender the keys to Rey, now a Fidelista. She slumped into the chair. "Castro has snatched doctors' practices, and Rey is in charge of my building."

"Rey, of all people, he's been like your son."

"Castro is staying true to his M-26-7 reform program—distribution of land to the peasants and nationalization of private enterprises."

"What are you going to do?"

"Rise and denounce him—just kidding—not possible without being jailed or killed."

"Do you still have a job?"

"Yes, working for Castro, who promises to provide healthcare for everyone."

"Where's he getting the cash?"

"Fidel will rob the treasury just as Batista did, taking money from everybody, even the poor, except they won't know it."

A thump hit the roof—maybe the last coconut.

Around nine o'clock, Wichi prepared to leave for work. Slivers of sunlight shone through the windows, and a boisterous backdrop of croaking toads resonated in the yard. "Papi, look at the frogs stuck on the glass," Lizzi said. "You also have them in the office. Can we go there?" When the answer was yes, she twirled twice and hugged him. The plan was for OP to drop off the children while she visited her mother. He grabbed his medical bag and left for work.

Modesta wrote a grocery list: bread and butter and potatoes and a chicken for the rice. She counted the pesos Señora had given her—just enough. Shopping provided an excuse to leave the house and attend the Committee meeting at noon. No one was at home except the nun, and after today she might not be a problem. Modi put on soft shoes that didn't hurt her corns, grabbed her Woolworth bag, and lumbered out the door. The neighborhood watch gathered at the vacant Purcey house. Glad these Americans left a building for their assembly. Her goal was to become a tattler for the Revolution. She strutted inside and found an empty chair—not a familiar face in the crowd. She had hoped to get Graciela there, but her friend's loyalty belonged to the Martin family. An officer started the meeting. "We're here to help Fidel, and your job is to uncover anti-revolutionary activities, so keep your eyes and ears open." He wanted information if any employers were Batistianos, or if they hid traitors or Catholics. "Comrades, raise your arm if you have any news to share."

A bony young woman elevated her hand high. "The people I work for helped Batista." The leader wrote the address she submitted. He asked her to stand and thanked the comrade for doing her duty. The crowd applauded.

The soldier reminded everyone they were brothers and sisters in the Revolution. "You are to spy on employers *and* keep tabs on each other, and we will reprimand traitors. Now, let's hear from another patriot." Modesta sweated, more than usual, wrung her palms, and then dried them with a handkerchief. She raised her right hand and hanky slowly in the air.

A woman nearby pointed. "This lady is lifting her arm."

The soldier looked straight at her, "Yes, comrade, what do you want to tell us?"

Modesta froze. She was close to having Bernadette jailed or executed, and then she remembered the nun's words, "I know there's goodness in you." Her fingers shifted to her forehead. "I wasn't raising my hand to tattle, just wiping my brow. Kinda warm in here."

"Gracias, comrades, anyone else? Stay vigilant and let's meet here same time next week." She stared ahead, took a deep breath, and exhaled. While gripping her bag, she stood and watched two men hanging a sign on the wall: CUBA SÍ, YANKEES NO. She waved at them as she left. She walked to the market and wrestled with the decision not to turn in the nun. The sister being so nice and helpful cost her the recognition she wanted from the Committee.

Wichi glanced out the office window and saw OP drive away. The children burst into the waiting room, and he greeted them in the hallway. Luisito wrapped both arms around his leg. "Papi," Lizzi said," I love coming here." Didi wanted to know if he was going to show them neat stuff in the microscope. He told them the frogs were waiting in the bathroom. The croaking cacophony increased when he turned on the light. A brown toad leaped two feet above the tub, and Luisito shrieked.

Didi swung around and headed toward Olga. "I'll skip the amphibian viewing."

"These are bigger than the ones at home," Lizzi said.

"They're African clawed frogs and are used to see if a lady is pregnant." She didn't understand. "I think I can explain it to you," he said. "It's called a Hogbend test. The nurse takes a urine sample from the woman in the morning and injects it under the frog's skin. By late afternoon, if the frog lays eggs, the lady will have a baby in less than a year."

"What happens to the poor frog?"

"Nothing, mi niña, she goes back in the tub with her friends until it's testing time again." Lizzi said the frogs enjoyed helping people, and that's why they croaked so much. She and Luisito amused themselves until OP arrived and announced it was time to leave.

Wichi kissed the children goodbye and retreated to his desk. He mulled over the precarious circumstances of hiding Sister Bernadette. For sure, Modesta didn't approve of her presence, and rumors abounded of domestic help snitching on private conversations within the homes. If she reported the nun, retribution awaited both the sister and him. He had to find a quick solution to get her out of the house and to safety. Olga tapped the door. "It's lunchtime and no patients on the schedule." He told her to enjoy the afternoon, and he'd see her tomorrow.

Wichi leaned back in his chair to ponder solutions and

recalled that Modesta said Sister Bernadette's father lived in Key West. Getting the nun there required passage across the water, so he perused the filing cabinet and hoped to locate a patient with a boat. After thumbing halfway through the list, he came up empty-handed. While flipping through the Ks, he saw the Kim family from Guanabo on the coast. Lottie Kim was a leukemia patient before she died. Her husband, Peng, and son, Wong, had relatives in Key West, and they had fished often in the Florida Straits. Time to take them up on an offer to eat fresh fish. He opened the Kim chart and looked for the phone number. Several years had transpired since he saw the family, and he hoped the information remained current.

He dialed the number. Three rings and a soft voice answered, "Peng Kim here."

"Señor Kim—Doctor Barreras, do you remember me?"

"Aah, sí."

"Are you fishing these days?"

"We try."

"You promised me fresh fish a long time ago."

"Come to Guanabo, you eat red snapper today."

"I'll be there." He wrote the directions on his prescription pad, called OP, and said to expect him late.

The town of Guanabo had the backdrop of a glistening turquoise ocean. The American gas station on the outskirts of the village was a landmark, located across the street from Peng's place. Wichi came to a stop in front of his small cinderblock house. Peng stood on the steps and waved. He stepped out of the car. They bowed to each other. "How are you and Wong?"

"Fine, Doctor, fine."

"My daughter had a swim meet here several years ago. Nice town."

"Come inside house. Wong cook red snapper."

The tantalizing aroma of fresh fish in the skillet had Wichi licking his chops. He parted the beaded curtain that led into the kitchen. "Wong, good to see you."

"Nín hǎo, Doctor."

"Please have seat," Peng said.

They sat at a rickety table; Wong served Wichi a whole red snapper. "Fish swim in ocean this morning."

"Delicioso." He asked if they still had their boat and took people fishing.

"You want to catch fish?" Wong said.

"Not me, maybe a friend."

Wong scratched his bald head. "No problem."

"I remember you telling me angling is great in the Florida Straits."

"Sí, can't fish there now," Peng said. "Rebel boats shoot."

"Have you ever been to Key West?"

"Many times, older sister live there," Wong said.

Peng rose to his feet. "Come to pier, see boat."

The three walked the short distance to where the Kims' boat bobbed in the water.

Across the stern were the words "LA ESTRELLITA, little star." Wichi liked the name.

"Nice boat," Peng said. "Thirty-foot, cabin covered — keep dry. Have 1955 outboard engine — run good."

"It should take you a long way."

Peng stepped inside the cabin and brought out a brass mariner's compass. He said it belonged to his grandfather. "Use compass, can reach China." They cracked a rowdy laugh.

"How about making it to the Keys?" Wichi said.

"Not subject talk outside. "He sensed a sudden seriousness in the older man's tone. They moseyed back into the house and sat on a worn sofa. "Very unhappy since rebels steal laundry business."

"Me too, Castro took over my practice."

"So sorry."

"Big secret—Peng and Wong leave Cuba for Key West soon in boat."

Wichi flinched. He hadn't expected this opportunity. "Your secret—my secret. Will you carry my friend with you?"

"Hard to take more person, need gasoline and supplies."

"I'll pay."

"Man—how old—how big?"

"Not old—very little."

"Man young—small. Maybe no problem."

"Uh, how about a little young nun?"

"Nun—no, no, no, no. Too dangerous, Castro hate nuns."

"Por favor, Señor Kim, if she stays, they may kill her."

"Trip too hard for woman nun—not possible."

Wong grabbed his father's arm and pulled him aside. They talked and argued in Chinese. Wichi thought Wong wanted his father to take the sister, but the older man looked reluctant. After hearing Wong mention Ma-ma, Peng changed his demeanor. He now hoped these men included the nun. This was the one chance to get her from his house to safety. They returned. Peng spoke first. "Wong remind father how doctor help Lottie when she was sick. Peng owe you favor. We bring nun to Key West."

He grabbed Peng's hand, shook it again and again. He circled both arms around Wong's chest and lifted him off the ground. Wichi left, hopeful the cards fell exactly right to solve the nun problem, but that still meant a tricky hand to play.

SEVENTEEN

No Rest for the Weary

Guanabo, Cuba
November 3, 1959

Wichi departed Guanabo late in the evening after planning Sister Bernadette's secret escape with his friends. At the outskirts of the town, gunshots sounded; people yelled and ran along the road. Flashing red lights lit the darkness as he pulled up behind an automobile stopped by a roadblock.

"Turn off the motor and get out," roared a male voice outside the car.

"Un momento, por favor, I'm Doctor Barreras, just going home to my family."

The bearded rebel jerked open the door, shoved a flashlight in Wichi's face, and yanked him out of the Coronet. The light blinded his eyes. "Don't give a damn who you are, raise your hands and lean against the car." The young barbudo did a pat-down and pocketed Wichi's favorite pen. Gunfire erupted from inside the auto ahead as it crashed through the blockade. Instinctively, he hit the ground at the same time as the man who frisked him. The soldiers fired machine guns at the getaway vehicle. A hundred feet away, it exploded in a ball of fire.

"We got those traitors," a guard hollered. "Viva La Revolución."

Wichi noticed the guy who stopped him didn't move. A rebel rushed to the barbudo and shouted, "Rico's hit." Blood seeped on the pavement around the body of the bearded man. The rebel grabbed Wichi by the shirt. "They say you're a doctor. Get your ass over here; you got work to do." He shoved him to the soldier lying in the crimson pool. Blood gushed from the left side of his thorax. He gurgled as more liquid poured from the mouth, his thick dark beard now red. Wichi tore off Rico's shirt to evaluate the injury while the rebel yelled at him, "You better fix him, or else."

He placed his hand on the man's chest. "He won't make it; the bullet pierced his heart. There's nothing I can do. I'm sorry."

The victim took one last gasp and lay motionless. The rebel shrieked, put his pistol to Wichi's head, and cocked the hammer. Wichi squeezed his eyelids together—a lifetime flashed across his mind—he hoped for a swift death. An eternity lapsed before the pressure of the barrel released from his brow. He opened his eyes; another trooper had grabbed the rebel's arm, pulled him back, and said, "Let the doctor go, he tried."

"Somebody's got to pay for Rico." The rebel growled and marched over to a half-dozen people huddled on the grass—four men and two women. Saliva foamed from the corners of his mouth. "Who wants to volunteer?"

His eyes focused on a dark-headed woman. "Not me," she screamed, "I'm innocent." She tried to crawl away, but he grabbed a leg and dragged her beside his fallen brother.

An older man seated by the pavement rose to his feet and pleaded. "Please don't shoot her," he said. A militiaman pushed him back to the ground with the rifle stock and told him to keep quiet, or he'd be next. The sobbing woman lay beside Rico's body. The rebel snatched her by the hair and held a gun to her head. She begged him to release her.

"No," Wichi yelled, "enough killing."

The guy pointed the weapon at him with eyes so penetrating they alone could have pulled the trigger. "Shut up," he said, "unless you want to take her place."

He pressed the pistol to the woman's temple and fired the bullet. Blood splattered and hit Wichi's face as she fell limp beside the dead soldier. The rebel cackled and discharged another shot into the air. Wichi turned his head and retched. He had observed death many times, but never the wanton murder of a blameless person in this manner. "You killed her in cold blood." His voice trembled.

The goon's lips drew back in a snarl. "Saved the firing squad the trouble. Anyone against the Revolution deserves to die."

Wichi's heartbeat pounded in his ears. "Let me go," he said. "I haven't committed a crime."

The rebel pointed to the five clustered on the ground. "Get out of my sight, or you'll join them."

He staggered back to the car. Once inside, he locked the door, his hands quivered as he wiped blood off his face. Several miles from the gory scene, he pulled off to the side of the road and burst into tears. It wasn't manlike to cry, but witnessing these atrocities exceeded the ability to control his emotions. After regaining composure and taking a few deep breaths, he focused on the goal ahead—hurry and get home.

A sweaty shirt clung to his chest. He longed to dispose of the filthy, bloody clothes. Something in the rearview mirror caught his attention. That sinister car was on his tail. *What should I do, outrun it?* He took a quick right turn at the next intersection and glanced back. The black sedan turned. His heart throbbed, he drove faster, and it followed. Wichi stopped the wheels—no getting away—the vehicle halted about two hundred feet behind. After the earlier experience, didn't matter what happened now. He killed the lights, stopped the engine, and prepared for the worst. A good ten minutes passed, the black car doors remained shut. The headlights burned, so he didn't know who was inside. He looked in the mirror again. *Damn the torpedoes,* he was going home. He started the Coronet and raced along the narrow street. The vehicle mirrored his movements. He turned onto 194 Street; it passed out of sight. *What's going on?* At this point, who cared, he needed a warm shower.

Not a soul stirred in Biltmore. The house was dark as he pulled into the carport and turned off the headlights. A shadowy figure emerged around OP's car. He gasped—must be the guy who chased him. He got out and stood tall, fists gripped. The man came closer, and a faint beam of light caught his face. "Rey, what are you doing here?"

"Didn't mean to startle you, Doctor."

"You come to arrest me?"

"No, sir. That's blood—are you hurt?"

"Why should you care?"

Rey hung his head and said he couldn't bear the thought of losing his second father. He began sobbing. Wichi walked over and laid a palm on him. Rey continued to weep and admitted his behavior was that of an ungrateful son. "So why did you do it?"

"I felt the Revolution made me an important man."

He grabbed Rey's shoulders and peered into his eyes. "You've always been important to me." Wichi asked why he came tonight.

"My sergeant ordered me to arrest and beat up a tenant they called a Batista informer. It sickened me when they executed the innocent man the next day." He tried to overlook it but was haunted by such brutality. "I joined Castro's rebels to advance my position and be somebody, not help send people to the firing squad."

"Fidel preys on you and others who sense they're victims." Wichi embraced him. "What are you going to do?"

"Don't know since I agreed to the terms of the Revolution." Wichi said they'd kill him if he broke the rules. Rey admitted he'd have to play the game but promised never to hurt him or his family. He hoped it was the truth. "It is," Rey said. "In fact, working for Castro may provide opportunities to help you."

"I believe you." He hesitated, and a thought flashed in his head. "Since you offered, I can use a favor."

"Whatever, Doctor, I'll do it."

EIGHTEEN

New Moon, Little Star

Guanabo, Cuba
November 15, 1959

Wong awakened early and examined the lengthy things-to-do list. He questioned the merit of undertaking the dangerous journey to Key West, and the nun made it worse, but so much had changed in Guanabo under Castro's regime. Life for him and his father wasn't promising. After Peng fixed breakfast, he rummaged through an old chest and found rolled-up papers. "Here are navigational charts we need to study. It's been a while since the last trip, and we need to travel in darkness of new moon."

"How many days for the trip?" Wong said.

"Good weather—one day. Bad weather—two days."

"I better get busy, boat needs repairing." After he finished breakfast, Wong gathered tools and headed for the pier. The fuel lines showed cracks and he had to replace them. He loosened the clamp to the carburetor.

A twenty-foot skiff docked beside the *Little Star*. The man turned off the engine. "What are you doing with that wreck?"

Wong looked over at the bearded, weather-beaten face of the neighbor. His bloodshot eyes with drooping bags stared at him. "Hola, José—fixing boat."

"You're wasting time, fish aren't biting."

"Next time."

"How can you afford that boat since the laundry business went away?"

"My business, not yours."

"Everything is my business. I work for the Revolution."

"So, you snooper now."

"Yeah, we fish for anti-Castro activities."

"What happens when person get caught?"

"The Committee decides, most get prison."

Wong watched as the neighbor staggered off the boat, carrying a knapsack and a bottle of rum. He wondered how the man, stoned most of the time, could pilot the craft, much less fish. Castro chose the scum of the earth to do his dirty work of tattling. He and Peng must be careful around him. A woman called out from José's shack. "You bum, take out the trash, rats crawling everywhere."

"That bitch thinks I'm her slave. Soon I'll be somebody important and ditch her."

Wong continued to repair the boat. He glanced at the drunk stumbling toward the house—another good reason to leave Guanabo.

Late afternoon Peng approached the pier. "Something wrong, son looks troubled?"

"José snoops for Fidel. Watch your words; he's a snake."

"We go sooner than expected. New moon comes on November 30, so we leave in darkness after midnight."

Wong stared at his father; wrinkles formed on his forehead. "Rebel patrol boats are a big problem at night."

Peng pulled at his graying goatee. "Since they pass by

every hour, we must go at one-thirty." He put his hands on Wong's shoulders. "We need the courage of our ancestors." Both placed their palms together and bowed.

The following day, Wichi received a call from Peng. "Doctor, we leave last day this month, one-thirty in morning, sharp."

"Perfect."

"Who bring nun?"

"Rey, my mechanic."

"Man also bring twenty gallons gas, smoked fish, rain gear." Wichi said not to worry. He took a deep breath and hoped Rey was sincere at his word to undertake this dangerous mission.

Wichi gathered the family and the nun into the living room. Modesta was off for the weekend. He cleared his throat. "Sister, we love having you here, but it's temporary until we can get you out of the country." He explained the getaway plan. Bernadette dropped to her knees and thanked God for answered prayers.

"Who's taking Sister to the coast?" OP asked and gave him a not-you stare.

"I'm arranging it."

Bernadette turned to the family. "You've shown love and kindness. Bless you for letting me stay here."

"I'll miss you." Lizzi sobbed and reached into a pocket. "Take this pack of gum." Didi hugged Sister and placed a Hershey bar in her hand. Luisito put his favorite rock inside her bag.

"You need strength," Wichi said. He held her arm and they strode along the hall. "This trip may be dangerous."

"Sí, and I don't worry. God will provide. Gracias, Doctor."

He hurried to the study and dialed Rey. "Can you talk now?"

"Sí, Doctor."

"You said you will help me."

"For sure."

"A friend of the family needs a ride to Guanabo." Wichi gave him the date, and said he needed to bring supplies. "She must be at the pier before one o'clock in the morning."

"She?"

"A nun."

"A nun? Sounds dangerous."

"Getting cold feet?"

"No, I'll do it."

"Come to my neighborhood at midnight, park your truck on 192 Street, and Bernadette will be there. Peng and Wong––father and son, will wait on a boat named *La Estrellita* docked on the harbor pier. They have to leave at one-thirty in the morning."

"That's it?"

"One more thing—bring twenty gallons of gas, a sack of smoked fish, and rain gear."

"That's three things, Doctor."

Wichi snickered, 'twas the old Rey he knew. "Promise me you won't leave until you see their boat disappear."

"You have my word."

℘

Rey hung up the receiver and realized he'd gotten himself in a mess. If it turned sour and they discovered the nun—end of game for him. While he pondered if saving Sister Bernadette warranted risking his neck, the innocent man he arrested—and they killed—came to mind. He didn't even know this woman, but a helpless Catholic sister shouldn't rot in jail or die on the firing squad. He lost Sarita, the love of his life, because he followed Castro. That wrong decision taught him a hard lesson. Now he must do his part to ensure the nun left the shores of Cuba.

Late afternoon on November 30, Rey finished mechanic duties and drove to the gas station. They sold him the last twenty gallons because he wore his green fatigues. He returned to the shop to pick up the homemade wooden crate to conceal the nun. It resembled a mechanic's storage box, with tools in the top and a space below where she'd squeeze into the bottom compartment. Around eleven-thirty he headed toward Biltmore. It was midnight when he stopped and shut off the ignition on 192 Street. Unwavering stars in the cloudless sky glittered on the hood of his truck. Crickets chirped while he waited, a peaceful scene until a knock on the door. "Meet your passenger, Sister Bernadette," Wichi said. Rey got out and shook her tiny, clammy hand. Tears gushed from her bloodshot eyes. Wichi embraced her, patted the mechanic's shoulder, and disappeared into the inky night.

Rey helped her into the truck and they left. Beyond the city limits sign, he turned onto a desolate road, stopped, and said, "Hurry, get in the back, and I'll fit you inside the box." He opened the secret door, and Sister Bernadette scrunched into the small space. "Sorry, it's only a short ride from here and I made air holes." He started the engine and headed to Guanabo. While he drove along the dark road with the nun behind, thoughts turned to Sarita. He wondered if he had any chance of getting her back. It might help if he saved Bernadette. Lights shone ahead. As he came closer, his worst nightmare materialized — a check point. Soon he'd know if the contraption worked to hide the sister. If not, they'd shoot him and imprison her. The guard held up an arm, and Rey stopped. One bearded rebel shined a flashlight into the cab while another looked in the rear. His heart raced, and he prayed Bernadette made no sound, then showed the man his papers.

"A little mechanic work to do, comrade?" He nodded. The guardsman shouted from the back, "Nice tools you got in the box."

His stomach drew up in knots, and his voice cracked. "Army truck outside Guanabo needs fixing."

"Better let him go quick, don't want Sarge on our backs." Rey thanked them; his knee shook so much he barely kept his foot on the accelerator.

He arrived after midnight and found the place dark—the gas station sign turned off and no streetlights. The silhouette of the distant pier was difficult to see. He parked the truck in the shadows, opened the crate door, and the tiny woman popped out, her arms wringing wet. Must have been a gut-wrenching experience with the soldier standing by the box. For sure God looked out for her. He smiled and grabbed two tanks of fuel; she took the supplies, and they crept to the dock. The rickety boards squeaked, and he stumbled on a nail. It was a tough hike without the moon to guide them. Stars reflected on the ocean and provided just enough illumination to make out two forms waving them ahead. "Get in," Wong said. Peng helped the nun into the boat. Rey hurried back to the truck and soon returned breathless with the remaining gas. Wong placed the containers in the rear and told Rey the 1:00 a.m. patrol had not passed by. That explained the concerned expression on the men's faces. Twenty minutes later—nothing. No choice but to wait. The silence on the dock broke by discordant singing not far away. "José, neighbor, nasty bum," Wong murmured. Sister Bernadette prayed aloud; Rey covered her mouth. They watched as the man waved a pistol and stumbled toward them, closer and closer. "He gets on dock, no can leave"

"José on pier with gun—one bad luck. Patrol boat no pass by—two bad luck," Peng said.

A light showed on the neighbor's porch, and a woman howled, "José, get your fat ass back in my bed." The drunk stopped, turned around, and cursed. He staggered toward the house and fell on the ground.

"Man leave," Wong said. "One good luck."

"Patrol boat just go by," Peng said, pointing to the moving light on the water. "Two good luck—we go now." Rey hugged the nun, shook the men's hands, and left *The Little Star*. The engine cranked, and the small vessel backed out of the slip. He watched as it moved over the black water and disappeared. He then raced along the pier, stepped on a rotten plank, and it broke with a heavy cracking sound.

The drunk's voice shouted, "Who's there? Stop, or I'll shoot." He fired one shot; Rey kept running. Another crack, and a sharp pain pricked his outer right thigh. He touched his leg and felt blood. The man fired a third round and missed. *Good thing he's drunk.* Rey leaped into his truck and peeled out. By morning Guanabo would crawl with militia looking for them.

His fear heightened as he approached a barricade outside the town. *Oh, no, God, don't let them see this blood.* After grabbing a towel, he wiped his hands and threw it under the seat. He pulled the truck to a stop. The guard poked a flashlight in his face, asked for identification, and Rey handed it over.

"You're one of our comrades."

"Sí, Viva La Revolución."

The man inspected the back. "So, you're a mechanic. Been doing emergency work in Guanabo?"

"Army truck threw a rod, tough job."

"Get going." Sharp pains shot through his thigh, but he drove onward. Headlights from a passing car showed blood oozing through his pants. He should be able to make it home. By four o'clock in the morning, he reached his apartment and faltered up the steps. He fumbled for the keys, staggered inside, and collapsed on the floor by the bed. He grabbed a bedsheet and tied it around his leg. Weariness overtook him. His eyes folded; he smiled and envisioned the nun on *La Estrellita* to Key West.

NINETEEN

Sun, Sand, and Soldiers

Biltmore Neighborhood
December 1, 1959

By mid-morning, Wichi sat at his study desk and sipped espresso. Since Castro took over his practice, patients had dropped off, so today he'd go in later. Eager to know if Rey managed the nun's escape, he dialed the number. A groggy voice answered. "Have to sleep, can't talk."

Whew, Rey made it home. "What happened?"

"Tired."

"Hmm, I'll check on you later."

The folded neighborhood paper on the desktop caught his attention. On opening the front page, he stared at the headline: "Havana Biltmore Club Closed." As he finger-combed his hair, he swiveled the chair around and pondered—another private takeover by Fidel's new government. The family had many pleasant memories there, especially Lizzi's swim meets. A squeak from the door, and she poked in her head. "Papi, can Didi and I invite Margie and Rosie to go swimming today?"

"Come here for a minute," he said.

She sprawled on the comfy chair and looked at him. "What's the matter, Papi, you look sad?"

"I have terrible news, mi niña. Castro has closed Biltmore Club."

"No, Papi, this can't be true. I love that place." He shook his head and told her it was real. Lizzi groaned and said Castro was a mean man, but she didn't understand why he wanted to close the club. Wichi explained that Fidel's government controlled it and wouldn't allow them to go there. His answer wasn't convincing. "I've worked hard to be a good swimmer; don't I deserve a place to practice?"

"Sí, but life's not always fair." She asked him to call Tutu because he was an important man at Biltmore. The sadness in his daughter's face prompted him to hold her and gaze into the tearing brown eyes. "There's no need for a swim coach anymore."

"Papi, I can't live without swimming." She said how much she looked forward to competing in Miami with the team next year. "I hate Castro with his nasty beard."

"I don't want you to say the word 'hate.'"

"Castro doesn't own the pool."

"At this moment he does, and we have to accept his command." She dashed to the bedroom and slammed the door. Following close behind, he asked her to open it. She said she'd stay in her room until they allowed her into the club. "You're not to go there. It's dangerous. Do you understand?" No answer, just howling and weeping.

He returned to the study, rested in his chair, and watched a fly light on the edge of the desk. He rolled the newspaper and smashed the bug. "Bingo—I'd like to handle Castro this way."

Modesta walked by carrying a load of laundry and

stopped at the door. "Sister Bernadette wasn't in her room this morning. You know where she might be?"

Expecting this question, he was ready with an answer. "A priest wearing street clothes came by last night while you were asleep and assured safe passage out of Cuba for the nun. Bernadette went with him."

"All for the best, I suppose."

"Please make sure the children don't go to Biltmore Club. It's closed."

"Sí, Señor. Too bad about the club."

Wichi left home and drove to Rey's apartment before going to work. He climbed the stairs and knocked. Photos of Che Guevara stuck along the walls, and bright red banners with hammers and sickles hung overhead. A harder strike this time. "It's Doctor Barreras."

After a brief pause, Rey opened the door and peered both directions in the hallway. He pulled him inside. "A bullet got me last night."

"How serious?"

He hobbled across the room and plummeted onto the worn sofa. "My leg."

Wichi rushed to him. "Let me examine it."

Blood had dried on the wound and stuck the scab and hairs to the trouser. Rey muffled groans as Wichi cut the pants and separated the fabric from his body. The bullet had entered the outer part of his right thigh. Men chatted outside the door. A thump on the wall and a man yelled, "Rey, you there?" Wichi froze and motioned for him to say something.

"Yeah, let me sleep."

"Catch us later, we're going for a beer."

Wichi waited until they disappeared and ran to fetch his medical bag from the car. He cleansed the wound, applied antibiotic ointment to the skin, and wrapped it with gauze. "Lucky the bullet hit near the surface and spared major blood vessels."

"Thank God," Rey said.

"Please tell me Bernadette and the Kims left the pier."

"Sí, Doctor."

He clapped. "That's wonderful news, but how did you get shot?"

He said a Fidelista neighbor nailed him. Wichi asked how he made it home. Rey explained the checkpoint and how his uniform and ID card got him past the guards. "Told you my membership in Fidel's army might be useful."

Wichi grasped his hand. "I knew you'd come through for me." The young man's eyes watered. Wichi asked him how he'd explain the injury at work, then breathed a sigh of relief when Rey said he had overtime to take off three days. "Good excuse, I'll see you later." He stood and looked at his friend. "You're a brave man."

"No, Doctor, I want to make up for my horrible mistakes." Wichi leaned over and hugged him. "Will Sarita ever love me again?"

"Women always love heroes."

Lizzi paced the floor, eager to visit the club. She peeked out of her room and strolled into the kitchen to see who was there. Modesta just left for the fruit stand. Dobin slept on cool tiles, and boxers romped in the backyard. With Mami teaching kindergarten until Christmas, Luisito at a friend's party, and Didi next door at Margie's, the house was quiet, and Papi wouldn't return until later. The Biltmore closing worried her, and she needed more information. After slipping on a bathing suit and T-shirt, she grabbed goggles and tennis shoes, determined to go to Biltmore even though Papi's warning flashed in her mind.

Dark clouds gathered, so she'd better hurry. She biked hard the entire mile and gasped at the CERRADO sign at the club entrance. Papi was right; Castro closed it. Didn't matter, the crystalline water called her. Seagulls squawked and accompanied her to a favorite spot on the beach. She took off her shoes, wiggled toes in the warm sand, and sat cross-legged on the shore. The hypnotic lapping of the gentle waves soothed her mind. This crystal sea meant home. A perfect-shaped starfish lay four feet away. She got up, eased over, and caressed it. As she waded waist-deep, the dreamlike surroundings reminded her of the many times hundreds of multi-colored angelfish swam alongside. Yellow angels appeared within reach. A hand through the water and a swish separated them into glittering schools. The sea took on an iridescent color as sun rays appeared among the clouds. She dove among a group of blue tangs and followed a smiling parrotfish. She surfaced and returned to the shore. Lizzi lay on the wet sand and gazed at the aquamarine ocean that splashed softly against her legs. A tiny hermit crab crawled up her arm and liked staying there. This was the life she relished. These were the creatures she loved, and Fidel dare not take them away from her.

"Get up, beach is closed," yelled a man's voice.

Her heart skipped a beat, and she turned and glared at a soldier in olive-green uniform. "Julito, you scared me. Why are you wearing those clothes?"

"I belong to Castro's militia," he said.

"Why do you have that gun pointed at me?"

"You're trespassing on government property. This club is cerrado."

"But my family has a membership."

"Not anymore, so leave now."

"I have to practice for future meets."

"You can't swim here. It's not for rich people."

"We're not wealthy. Pilar's the rich girl with a huge house, and we have a small one." She jumped up and shook her finger in his face. "Your family belongs to the club too. Are you rich?"

"You're confusing me with those questions. Go away."

"You kissed Didi at the beach last year, and she'll hate you for kicking me out of my favorite place."

"She thinks I'm stupid."

"You are." The words slipped out before she caught them.

She turned, put on her shoes, and sprinted to the front entrance. A thunderclap struck nearby—time to leave. Before she reached the bicycle, a guard grabbed her shoulder and snarled. "What are you doing here?" She told him she had to get home, but he insisted she intruded on government property and wasn't going anywhere. "Can't you read español? The sign outside—what did it say?"

"Cerrado."

"So, you're not stupid."

She squirmed. "Por favor, let me go."

The rain began, first small drops, and soon a downpour. The man motioned her with his rifle to the canopy next to the building. Another guard grabbed her chin, shook it, and stared at her face. "What's your age, eight—maybe ten?"

"Get your dirty hand off me."

"You'll go to jail." She wailed as the man tugged at her arm.

Julito ran toward them. "I confronted this suspect earlier during my patrol and interrogated the girl. She left her bike here and returned for it. Release her now."

"What do you mean? I'm putting her behind bars."

"She's my prisoner. I found the girl and took care of the problem." Julito led her to the bicycle. "Go home and don't return."

Lizzi peddled until her thighs burned. Droplets pelted her cheeks as she squinted to keep water out of her eyes. Halfway home Papi's warning rang in her brain. She might have stayed in jail forever. The rain pounded and blinded the way. The bike hit the curb, and she flew over the handlebars and landed in a palmetto hedge. She wiped her face and rubbed a few scratches on her arms. With a flat front tire, she couldn't ride anymore. The downpour washed away the streaming tears on her cheeks.

On arriving home she dreaded facing her father and the deserved punishment. She opened the front door and stood drenched in the foyer. Didi came around the corner and eyeballed her. "Where have you been? You're wet—and a mess."

"I'll tell you in a minute. Is Papi here?"

"No, only Modesta and me, but she's in the kitchen."

"You won't believe what I saw today. Can you keep a secret?" Didi nodded. She informed her Julito enlisted with Castro's army, patrolled the Biltmore Club, and had a real rifle. Didi snickered and said the idiot couldn't shoot straight. "He ordered me to leave the beach. Another soldier arrested me, but Julito lied and said I was there to get my bike."

"He's still a punk, and you shouldn't have been there."

"Por favor, don't tell Papi, promise?"

"Okay." Didi paused a moment. "Forget Julito. We broke up a long time ago."

Lizzi chewed a nail. "I'm getting sick at my stomach with Castro closing our school and now our favorite place. What can we do?"

Didi frowned and put her hand over Lizzi's lips. "You must keep your mouth shut with government stuff. If we aren't careful, Papi will get in big trouble when someone hears us talk against the bearded one."

"I miss Sister Bernadette and hope Papi's secret plan worked, and she made it to Key West."

"Don't breathe a word to anybody, Modesta for sure." Lizzi nodded and lowered her head—a happy life ended that day.

Modesta licked her lips and eased from the hallway to the kitchen, glad that she listened to those stories. She knew there was something fishy with the nun's leaving. How she wished

the doctor hadn't lied—a big strike against him. He'd pay for
that. She needed to keep tabs on any suspicious things against
the Revolution. At the next Committee meeting, she might find
a reason to raise her hand and get recognition. Besides, Modi
was the sharpest spy in the neighborhood and deserved to be
famous.

TWENTY

Woolworth Woes

Havana, Cuba
December 10, 1959

María Teresa paced the floor of the small dwelling on the third level of Apartamentos Celestiales, a far cry from the heavenly apartment as advertised. The window casements cracked and peeled, and the wooden floors sagged. Horns blared as she looked below at San Rafael Street where Ofelia Perfecta's car had just arrived. The doors opened, and her granddaughters darted toward the building. Content to see them and happy that Luisito didn't come, she bemoaned that her only grandson rode around on his stick horse and pointed a toy pistol at her when she visited. The boy inherited the lack of respect from the father. Wichi had many imperfections, and the one that irritated her most—he shortened her daughter's beautiful name to OP. She knew he did it to aggravate her. She recalled the day the priest baptized her only child—Ofelia Perfecta, the perfect appellation—and Wichi had to ruin it. Placing the café con leche on the table, she wiped her lips with a napkin. A metal knocker rapped against the massive wooden door. "Abuela, Abuela, we're here."

She lumbered across the room, her legs heavy and ankles

swollen. A friend said she needed compression stockings. She opened the door. "Look at you two wearing shorts. Niñas, I told your mother to dress you in lacy blouses and felt skirts, but she never listens."

Lizzi flared her pants. "We wear fancy clothes to church."

"How will you girls learn to be ladies surrounded by animals and birds in the outskirts of Havana?"

"Why don't you have any birds?"

"Nasty creatures, I'm not spending my days cleaning cages."

"Mami adores her three canaries."

"Your mother can take care of the ingrates, not me."

Didi pulled on María Teresa's arm and complained of boredom since Castro closed Biltmore Club and their school. The girls made faces when Abuela asked if they enjoyed their mother having them recite poetry and read books on Spanish literature. "Can we do something exciting today?" Didi said.

She released her granddaughter's hand. "I'm too old for fun."

Didi rubbed her tummy. "You enjoy going to Woolworth's soda fountain for lunch."

"I do, but it may not be open since the government took over businesses."

"Castro better not close it. That's where I buy Hershey bars and Bazooka bubble gum and costume jewelry."

She had them wait while she coiled her hair into a bun. "Where is the nun?"

"She escaped on a boat last week, but we're not supposed to say a word."

María Teresa shook her head and considered it another one of Wichi's crazy ideas. After reaching for an umbrella and patent leather purse hanging on the hall tree, she dialed for a cab. They descended twenty marble steps, climbed over a high wooden threshold, and waited for the Cubataxi. She entered first and told the driver to go to Galiano and San Rafael. The three exited near El Encanto store. She ordered them to stay by her side. Even at Christmastime, she didn't want to spend money, so they stood in front of the "Enchanted Store" and looked at the window displays. The absence of Christmas decorations surprised her. She turned to the girls. "Qué feo. Everything is so ugly without the trees and lights. Have they forgotten it's almost Christmas?"

"Last year the store had a Santi Clos," said Lizzi. "I loved the way he waved Feliz Navidad."

A lady standing nearby whispered in María Teresa's ear. "Fidel will ban Christmas in Cuba."

She grimaced, thumped the tip of her umbrella on the sidewalk, and noticed disappointment in the girls' faces. "The nerve of that atheist, thinking of ending Christmas in a Catholic country."

"Feliz Navidad." The woman smiled and walked away.

As they ambled along Galiano Street, Didi pointed ahead. "That man wearing a black coat is handing roses to the ladies."

"Keep walking straight and ignore him. He's called the Caballero de Paris."

Lizzi tugged at Abuela's shirtsleeve. "We live in Havana, not Paris."

"He claims to be a French gentleman, but his real name is José María Lopez." He came closer, and Abuela saw Lizzi

staring at his curvy, brown fingernails and black top hat.
"Don't pay attention to him, a homeless bum who roams
Havana and talks to strangers."

Didi smiled. "I think he's neat."

"Vamos before he blabs nonsense."

No sooner had she spoken when the man stepped onto a
bench. He raised his hands in the air and sang of his love who
never made it to Havana but died in France, and he would
always be her Caballero de Paris. Bystanders gathered
around, and soon an army truck appeared at the scene. Two
soldiers rushed out, grabbed, and handcuffed the caballero.
The crowd booed and raised their fists. One soldier said he
was crazy, and they were taking him away for mental
treatment. They loaded him into the vehicle while he howled
for his lost love. People continued to protest until a trooper
took out his pistol and fired a shot over their heads. Everyone
scattered. María Teresa clutched the girls and tugged them
away to the next block.

"That poor man," Didi said, "the soldiers arrested him."

"He's crazy, but they lock up anyone these days." Abuela
tightened her grip on the girls' hands.

"I'm hungry," Didi said.

Lizzi smacked her lips. "Me too."

"I'm exhausted. Good thing we're here at Woolworth, and
the soda fountain is open." Waitresses in red shirts and black
skirts jingled coins inside their short, white aprons. María
Teresa sat on a swivel bar stool away from the ceiling fans,
because she hated for a breeze to touch her face and ruffle her
hair. She ordered three medianoches.

"Sorry," said the server, "our midnight sandwiches have

changed. We have ham and pickles and sweet bread, but no pork or Swiss cheese." Abuela's stomach growled, so she had no choice but to take the abbreviated bocaditos. Lizzi asked if the lady would press it flat. She smiled. "Sure can, honey."

"Do you have Coca-Colas?" Didi asked.

"Sí, but they're room temperature."

"My granddaughters want ice cream."

"Sorry, Señora, no helado in two months."

Half-eaten sandwiches and warm drinks sat abandoned at the bar when a dozen or more government troops swarmed into the store. They shouted, "Viva Fidel," as they destroyed Woolworth signs. María Teresa grasped the girls and asked the waitress why the soldiers appeared. She said her boss warned that Castro planned to take over Woolworth and get rid of the American name. A loud commotion from the main aisle terrified Abuela. Military men dragged a struggling, well-dressed man out of the building.

"That's our manager," cried the waitress. "Señora, you and las niñas need to go as soon as possible." María Teresa took each granddaughter's hand and headed toward the door. As they hastened past the jewelry counter, two of the militia stuffed watches and rings into their pockets. Others yelled obscenities at customers.

One man shoved her and the girls aside. "Leave, old woman, you're not eating or shopping here anymore."

Lizzi and Didi towed her to the front entrance. "Easy, my heart can't take this stress." Didi waved a taxi. Abuela shuddered, and they scrambled into the car.

"What's going on inside Woolworth, Señora?" asked the driver.

"It's terrible, just get us home." They passed military trucks with soldiers shouting, "Viva La Revolución."

María Teresa inhaled short, erratic breaths. The cabbie stopped at the apartment and she paid the fare. *How will I climb the steps?* She began but wavered after the second level. The girls put their palms on her buttocks and pushed her. She wanted no one to help her, but this time she needed the boost. She sneered, realizing her own daughter had never assisted her up the stairs. Lizzi counted each step until they reached the top. Once inside, Abuela collapsed into a small, flowered chair. She reached for a white linen handkerchief from her purse, wiped her forehead, and took off the black pumps. She yawned. "I didn't digest my food because of the commotion," she said and closed her eyes.

"She's asleep and snoring," Lizzi said. "Poor Abuela, this hasn't been an enjoyable day for her."

"I don't think she has any good days," Didi replied.

"We had fun pushing her up the steps, even though she didn't like it." Lizzi poked her sister, and they laughed when their grandmother snorted. Didi stated that she didn't like many things—or people—mainly Papi and Luisito. Lizzi understood her not liking their little brother since he always pestered her but didn't know what she had against Papi. She glanced at Abuela's desk and saw a photograph. "Come look at this," she said. "It's a picture when Luisito was baptized. Abuela didn't look happy then."

On the oak dresser Lizzi spotted old newspaper clippings tied with a black string. She unfastened them and separated the papers. "Here's an article from Camagüey on January 20, 1940." She motioned for Didi to join her on the twin bed covered with a blanket that smelled of moth balls. The story read: "Blanca Ronquillo, wife of Filiberto Sala, wealthy cattle farmer, was found murdered in the bedroom after he returned from a poker game late at night."

Didi scooted closer. "Oh no, she was Abuela's sister!"

"There's more," Lizzi said. "The rancher had made an enormous profit from a sale and kept the money in his nightstand. Blanca apparently awakened and recognized the thief, who used a pillow to suffocate her. The police have the butler in custody and charged for the murder."

"How horrible," Didi said. "Now I know why our grand-mother's grumpy and doesn't smile."

"Well, she still has a brother, Tío Nicolás.

"Uncle Nicolás is strange."

"But he gave us Dobin."

"Yes," Didi said, "but he doesn't come to see Abuela often, and Mami told me how much she loved Blanca." Lizzi asked about Papi's mother. Didi told her Abuela Mercedes died at the age of thirty-six while delivering her ninth child. "And the poor baby died too."

"I'm sorry we never knew her," Lizzi said, "but I love Papi's family—Charo and Tío Cuco and Tía Nena and Tía Yoya."

Pfffft! sounded across the room. They both giggled.

María Teresa squirmed, her eyes flew open, and she grimaced at the foul odor that lingered. "Ay," she groaned as she struggled to sit up straight. "I think I ate spoiled food." She couldn't get out of the chair alone, so she called for her granddaughters. "Hurry, I need to change my underwear." They held their noses while helping put on her slippers. Each one took a hand, and they lifted her out of the seat. She shuffled to the bathroom and the girls stood by. Although their faces disclosed nothing, they must have suspected. *How embarrassing.*

She returned to the living room and said it was best to ignore the Woolworth incident. "Let's not tell your mother, because she won't let you visit me after today." She clasped her hands together. "Plus, I'm not up to her reprimand."

"Count on us," Didi said.

Lizzi nodded. "Not a word."

"Now, for the greatest part of the day. Come into my bedroom."

Lizzi ran in front, her eyes widened. "Is it a surprise?"

"Be patient, and you'll see."

She flipped on a lamp, sidled to a large wooden armoire, unlocked it, and opened the heavy doors. The shelves lined in black velvet had a mirror in the back. Rows of necklaces and brooches and rings glimmered inside. Lizzi wanted to know if it was a treasure chest. Didi reached for an earring. "NO, I will choose what you're allowed to touch." The girls cowered. She placed a few favorite things on a purple cloth while they sat on the bed and gazed. Lizzi stretched her arm toward a pearl choker, and María Teresa slapped her hand. "That one is for Didi when she turns fifteen." Lizzi squinted at her sibling. Abuela removed a ring, her lips quivered at the side. "See this two-carat diamond solitaire, it belonged to my sister, Blanca." They gasped. "This is for your mother."

"When does she get it?" Lizzi said.

"Oh, one day."

"I have a tenth birthday next week. Is something here for me?"

"No, these precious gemstones are only for special occasions." Lizzi lowered her head. "I have your gift. Open this box." She took the present—bonbons from Woolworth.

Didi smirked and gave a smile. "Lucky girl, at least you don't have to wait till you're fifteen."

María Teresa plucked a chocolate. "I bought them last month. Mmm, still good." A strong thwack rattled the front door. She flinched and hoped the soldiers hadn't followed her home. She grabbed her precious jewels and locked them inside the armoire. "Stay here, girls."

A second clatter, and a woman's voice shouted, "Open up, it's me." Another thump. What an impatient daughter she had raised. Didn't she know how much her knees hurt? She unfastened the door. "Took you a long time," Ofelia Perfecta said as she stood there with hands on her hips. "Did you take las niñas to Woolworth?"

TWENTY-ONE

Do Not Pass GO

Biltmore Neighborhood
January 1960

Modesta knew children were nosey creatures and understood what grownups said. She wasn't privy to gossip at the Martins' since Graciela didn't spy, but with Margie and Rosie here in the doctor's house, she had a golden opportunity to get information. She waited until the four friends settled in the bedroom, eased into the hallway, and took a position outside the door where she listened to their conversations.

"In case Mami comes, both of you hide under the bed and keep quiet," Didi said. "She wants us to take naps."

Rosie asked, "Lizzi, can I have a bonbon?" She told her to pick one. "Mmm, yummy, where did you get them?"

"Abuela bought them at Woolworth for my birthday."

"Papá told us Castro took over the place and changed the name."

"Sí, we were there when the soldiers destroyed the Woolworth signs." Modesta gave a thumbs up—Castro got rid of another American store.

"Anybody hurt?" Margie said.

"They dragged the poor manager out of the building and pushed Abuela."

"The government has our parents worried."

"Ours too," Didi said, "since they took over Biltmore." Modesta's eyes widened. She kept listening.

"Have you seen Julito?"

"The half-wit has joined Fidel's army."

"He ordered me out of the club," Lizzi said.

"What were you doing there? It's closed."

"I know. I got caught by the rebels, but Julito lied and saved me."

"Shh," Didi said. "You're talking too loud."

"Did you hear something in the hall?"

"Let's check and see." Modesta darted around the nearby corner, leaned against the wall, and waited. The door opened. "No one's here." After it closed she slinked back into position. Margie told them her father worried because they were Catholic, and Castro hated religion. Before their priest left, she said soldiers with guns stood inside the church, and one man made a mean face and scared her. Didi said, "Look, Margie, I found an old copy of a teenage magazine."

"Lizzi and I need to get to work on our secret project," Rosie said. Modesta's ears perked—more juicy news on the way.

"Forget your stupid project," Didi replied. "Mami will wake up soon, and you and Margie must leave now."

"I'll make our treasure map later, Rosie, and give it to you then," Lizzi said.

"Come over to our house and let's play Monopoly," Margie announced.

Monopoly—that was the American game they discussed

at the last Committee meeting. Castro ordered it destroyed so Yankee imperialist ideas didn't corrupt children's minds. The Revolution wanted everybody equal, but that board game had winners and losers. To report it was her chance to get recognized. She slipped into the kitchen as Margie and Rosie dashed home. A few moments later, in came Señora. "Had a nice siesta?" Modi asked.

"Sí, since I stopped teaching, I love my relaxation time. It's always good when the girls rest too."

"I'm not so sure 'bout . . ."

"Hi Mami," Lizzi said as she and Didi burst into the room.

"Were you going to say something, Modesta?" The two glared at her.

"No, Señora, nothing important."

Lizzi asked permission to play Monopoly. "It's such a fun game; we can buy property, charge rent, and build houses and hotels."

"You even get $200 when you pass GO," Didi said.

"Okay, since you rested."

The girls hurried to the Martin house. Modesta's fist tightened. She needed to talk to Graciela. Castro banned Monopoly, and her duty was to enforce the law. An excuse came to mind. "Señora, sugar's almost gone, can I borrow a cup from Graciela?" She nodded. Modesta finished drying the dishes and ambled next door.

Graciela invited her inside. "Why Modi, what are you doing, girl? You haven't been over in a month of Sundays."

"Is Señora Martin here?" she said and glanced around the kitchen.

"No, she left to the store. Be back in a while."

"Good, we need to talk."

Graciela pulled up a chair for her. "What's the matter, Modi, something troubling you?" She said that Fidel didn't allow anyone to play those Monopoly games. Graciela leaned back in the seat and said it was news to her.

"That's because Señor Martin didn't tell you; he knows it's wrong."

"Señor is a good man."

"Not so sure about that."

"Modi, he may not favor the government, but he's no anti-revolutionary." She told Graci if soldiers found the game there, they'd put her in jail. "I'm not worried about a soldier getting this old lady." Modesta glowered at the girls outside in the carport engaging in that evil pastime. She picked up the phone. Graciela held her arm. "Don't do it."

"I have to—gotta keep you out of trouble." After shaking off the old woman's hand, she dialed the Committee's number and reported the children playing Monopoly. "They're coming over," she said and clapped.

"Modi, Lord knows what you've done. It's not right, and I'm gonna pray nobody gets hurt." Modesta assured there'd be no harm done if they stood by Fidel. She grasped the door handle and paused. "Almost forgot, I need a cup of sugar."

Lizzi rolled the dice and landed on Illinois Avenue. "I just went past GO," Rosie said. "Please give me $200."

"You don't get to keep it because you hit the Income Tax space," Didi said.

"That's not fair."

Didi landed on Rosie's Park Place. "What makes you say, 'not fair'? With your two houses, I have to pay you $500."

"I like this game."

Lizzi saw a military truck pull into the driveway, and two armed soldiers got out. A tall man approached them. "What do you think you're doing?"

"Playing Monopoly," Didi said.

"It's against the Revolution to play this Yankee capitalist game."

"What's a Yankee capitalist?" Rosie said.

"Shut up," said the other militiaman as he leaned over and swept everything to the ground. The Monopoly pieces bounced everywhere, and a gust of wind sent the money flying. "Pick 'em up and pile 'em on the concrete." Lizzi sobbed, and they struggled to do what he ordered. The tall guy took out a lighter and lit the paper. The other threw gasoline on the pile. Flames exploded and Lizzi fell backward. Her face burned and her hair smelled stinky. Rosie screamed when the bottom of her dress caught on fire. Graciela rushed out the door, snatched her, and smothered the flame.

The Martins' car pulled up in front of the house. Señora Margo jumped out and shouted, "Children—what's going on here?"

The tall man stood in front and grabbed her arm. "They were playing Monopoly."

"You're crazy. Let go of me."

He pushed her forward. "You and your husband know this game is illegal."

She hurried over to Rosie, hugged her, and turned to him. "What are you saying?"

"Monopoly—it's forbidden." She said they weren't aware playing Monopoly was against the law. He threatened to take her to jail after she called him an animal. "You're lucky that my orders were only to destroy this game."

Didi left and said she was going to get her mother. They returned and Mami hurried toward Lizzi. "My cheeks are hot," she said.

"Look at my daughter's burned face," she cried out, "and you singed her eyebrows." She shook her fist at the soldiers. Lizzi had never seen Mami this angry and thought she would punch the tall guy. He grabbed the gas can, scrambled, and the two left. The men looked like dogs running away with tails tucked between their legs.

Lizzi heard Señora Martin tell her mother, "I can't wait to get out of here." She didn't understand what it meant, and Mami looked puzzled. The Señora said she'd visit later and explain. She turned to Graciela. "How did this happen?"

"I don't know. It wasn't supposed to turn out this way."

"What did you say?"

"Nothing, I'm just upset and confused."

The moment OP opened the front door, Margo burst into tears. She helped the neighbor to the sofa and fetched a hanky. "OP, I am so sorry what happened with those awful soldiers," she said, dabbing her cheeks. "I hate to think what they could have done to our girls." OP gave assurance it wasn't her fault, just something they had to live with. "Not us," she said. OP flinched and asked what she meant. Margo informed her Mani had just gotten home and was so angry he couldn't come over to talk. They had considered leaving Cuba ever since his firm offered a transfer to Venezuela several months ago. After today's incident they made up their mind to go. Margo's eyes swelled with tears as she lamented abandoning everything behind—home, church, school, and friends.

"Wichi and I will miss you and Mani." She glanced toward the bedrooms. "This is devastating news for the girls; they treat each other as sisters." OP volunteered to help with the move and see them off to the airport. They hugged, and she walked Margo out the door. The daughters had to be told. She called them into the living room and asked Modesta to make lemonade.

"You won't punish us for playing Monopoly, will you?" Lizzi said. She told her no, but there was sad news—the Martins were moving to Venezuela.

"Why, because of that game?" Didi said. OP mentioned there were other reasons.

"Such as the mean things Fidel's doing?" Lizzi said as Modesta entered with a tray of drinks. OP squeezed her hand, and Didi shushed her with a finger over the lips. They waited in silence while the busybody walked back to the kitchen. "Can we go with them?" Lizzi said.

OP shook her head, "It's not that easy."

"I'm losing my best friend, and I'll never pass GO again."

TWENTY-TWO

Agonizing Adioses

Havana, Cuba
March 1960

"I don't want Rosie to leave." Lizzi bawled on the way to Rancho Boyeros Airport. Her neighbor waved from the Cubataxi ahead. Lizzi stuck her head out the window and yelled, "Rosie, Rosie." Her eyes, flooded with tears, made it hard to see the car filled with the Martin family. "She's my best amiga in the whole wide world. What will I do without her?"

"Please, mi niña," Papi said, "don't be sad, you'll find another friend."

"No, I won't. Nobody else has pigtails and cute dimples like Rosie."

Mami looked at her. "Be happy for Rosie, the family's going to Venezuela, and who knows, maybe they'll return soon."

Lizzi put her face in her hands and cried. Then she looked up and saw a VIVA FIDEL sign. "Because of that awful man, I'm losing my best friend." Papi told her to be careful what she said, it could get them in trouble. She asked why they had to leave, and he told her Señor Martin's company offered another job. Lizzi knew Papi wasn't happy living in Cuba. "Why don't we move too?" He didn't utter a word.

Mami turned around with watery eyes, and Lizzi noticed sadness in her face. "Your father is a doctor," she said, "and his work differs from Señor Martin. We can't go anywhere now."

"Are you crying too?"

"We're heartbroken that Rosie's family is leaving. Margo and I are good friends."

The Coronet stopped behind the taxi. The cabbie lifted the trunk and distributed the suitcases. When Rosie grabbed her bag, Lizzi jumped out of the car. She ran to the cab and they embraced. "Please don't go." Both wept until the mothers came and separated them. The two families walked into the terminal. Lizzi and Rosie held hands. Didi and Margie sauntered ahead. On reaching the departure section, Señor Martin had them stop. He pointed to the sign: FLIGHTS TO SOUTH AMERICA.

Rosie rummaged through her carry-on bag, took out a First Communion rosary, and gave it to Lizzi. "I'll hide it just like we planned," she said. "Here's the secret map I made last week so you can find it when you return." Rosie rolled-up the brown paper and stuffed it among her things. A guard approached them, stopped, and snatched the bag. Rosie screamed. Lizzi gripped her hand and said to him, "What do you want?"

"You're hiding something." He pulled out the paper. "Aha, a map, what does it show?"

Papi stepped up. "Señor, the girls buried packs of chewing gum in the backyard and marked it as a treasure." The guard asked his name. "I'm Doctor Barreras, neighbor to the Martins."

"You mean these worms leaving the glorious Revolution."

He grabbed Señor Martin's arm. "Is this your daughter with the map?" He nodded. The man barked that she didn't need it anymore and flipped on his lighter. Lizzi snatched the paper from his hand and said he couldn't do that; it was her friend's map. He took it away and pushed her backward. The soldier snarled as he set fire to the paper and snickered at the clump of ashes on the floor. He walked ahead, lit a cigarette, and laughed.

Lizzi ran after him and tugged on his sleeve. "Why are you so mean?" He stopped and blew a puff of smoke into her nose. It made her cough. Papi rushed over to them, his face was red. She knew he was angry, and she covered his fist and looked him in the eye. He relaxed the grip and gave her a smile. The guard sneered and tromped through the corridor.

A paunchy militiaman approached the Martins. "Gusanos, get in line against the wall."

Lizzi wondered why they called people worms. Papi explained gusano was a nasty name for those who leave Cuba. She watched the soldiers searching the passengers. "Why are they doing that?" He told her they wanted money and jewels—things to keep or sell later.

An announcement blared. "Cuban gusanos going to South America, move it. Don't take all day."

"Well, Mani this is it. I wish you the best."

"Thanks." The men shook hands. Señor Martin motioned for the family to follow him.

Lizzi grabbed Rosie, hugged her, and bawled. "I thought I lost you that day at the beach, but now I will lose you." She wiped Lizzi's cheeks and said to think of her every night before she fell asleep. Margie pulled Rosie away as the soldiers scooted the Martins toward La Pecera. Lizzi knew why they call it the fishbowl. Once inside you became a goldfish. She waved at her best friend in the glass room and hoped to see her again.

"No more goodbyes to the worms," yelled a guard.

Papi said it was time to leave. Outside in the parking lot, a crowd gathered around a guy who stood on the hood of a car and shouted, "Fidel is a socialist. There'll be no elections. He and Che Guevara will soon make Cuba communist." Didi inquired what the man said. Papi was about to answer when a military truck screeched and stopped. Armed militia jumped out and yelled for the protestor to shut his mouth. "What did I tell you, there's no free speech here," he said. One soldier grabbed his legs and pulled him off the car and onto the pavement. "Cuba is no longer free." Another punched his face; he fell limp, and blood gushed alongside the nose. Lizzi gagged. The soldiers dragged him to the vehicle and left a red trail smeared on the road. She grasped her father's arm. They hustled to the Coronet and headed toward Biltmore. The sky darkened as the afternoon sun disappeared behind a cloud. Lizzi heard her father mutter that a black car followed them. When they turned into the neighborhood, she noticed it went straight ahead. *Happy to be home, but hard to say goodbye to someone I love.*

Modesta made sure Luisito napped when the family returned from the airport. Off for the weekend, she couldn't wait to inspect the neighbor's place before catching the bus. The

Martins owned nice stuff, and Fidel said that things in gusanos' houses belonged to everyone. She knocked on the back door. "Bet that's you, Modi," said the sweet voice. Graciela held a mop in her left hand, pulled open the door, and let her into the kitchen.

"Why are you still laboring? You're not getting paid anymore."

"Girl, can't leave a house dirty. You know I work that way."

"You don't owe them." Graci patted her arm and said the Martins were good folks, even gave her something extra. She held an envelope stuffed with twenty pesos. Modesta lowered her eyebrows and growled it should have been more.

"Honey, you shouldn't say that, because they were nice people and treated me right."

"Well, they're gone now, and a deserving family gets this house."

"I suppose so. They won't be needing me."

"Gotta leave before we miss the last bus." She opened a drawer in the dining room, pulled out a small silver box, and stuck it into her purse.

"Modi, you shouldn't."

"It's mine as much as anybody's. Let's go." She took her friend's hand and they walked out the front door. Graciela sighed and stared at the house, then put a palm to her chest.

"You okay?"

"Sweetie, I worked here a long time. Just felt sadness in my heart."

"Better hurry, don't want to miss the ride."

They reached the bus stop. Graciela slouched on the

wooden bench and got out her prayer book. "Modi, I've been praying for your soul because you did something awful, calling those mean soldiers to come for that Monopoly game. Lordy knows I forgive you, but it's not good what you did."

Modesta placed her hands on her lap and took a deep breath, "Graci, things are changing. The Committee will recognize me as the best snooper in the neighborhood."

"Lord a mercy, muchacha, is that what you want?"

"You bet; I aim to be important."

"Tattling is no way to be somebody."

"I'm working to help the Revolution arrest people against Fidel."

Graciela pulled up her stockings. "Revolution's paying you nothing, and no poor man's gonna give you a job."

"I understand, but I'll soon be giving orders."

"They're making you lots of promises, and how do you know if . . ."

"Bus is coming, we got to go."

The driver stopped the clunker at the curb. The motor sputtered and a breeze blew the fumes aside. He opened the door. "Last bus to Regla. Vamos."

Graciela lugged her bag and panted up the metal steps. Modi took her heavy tote and asked if she brought a sample of the Martin's stuff. "You know me better than that. Señora gave me pots and pans, and even wanted me to have her own necklace." Black diesel smoke spewed forth as the coach lunged forward. The old woman stumbled. Modi caught her and questioned if she was okay. "Honey, I'm just tired."

Modesta helped Graciela with her belongings, and they sat together. She flapped her hanky in the air. "I'm happy we're away from that fat, stinky sergeant a few rows ahead." Graciela asked what happened to Concepción. She said she quit the job with the Batistianos a long time ago. Graci was glad they didn't discover her uncle killed the lieutenant colonel, otherwise she'd be dead. "He hid long enough until Batista left," said Modesta. "Now he's a corporal in the Revolution and has a chance to get even."

"Getting even's not gonna bring back his son."

"Sí, but the devil knows sweet revenge."

"No, he doesn't." Graciela made the sign of the cross.

The brakes squealed as the old bus jerked to a halt—not the Regla stop. The smelly sergeant stood up, waddled to the front, and shouted a roadblock was ahead. After he got off and joined other militiamen gathered along the road, two young troopers came aboard and searched the passengers' belongings. One man opened Graciela's bag, took Señora's necklace, and reached for his pocket. Modesta grabbed his arm. "What do you think you're doing? This belongs to her." He pushed her back and barked that it was government property. Modi stood in his face and said she was a member for the Defense of the Revolution, and the jewelry was the old lady's. He ordered her to shut up and grabbed the handle of his pistol.

Graciela held her arm. "Modi, let him be. Don't need a necklace."

"That necklace in his pocket won't go to the Revolution," she muttered.

Graciela smiled at the man. "Don't mind her. She's just talking to herself." He sneered and walked to the front of the bus. "Sweetie, I know you're trying to help me, but you got to hold back."

The sergeant banged his pistol on the metal rail. "An army truck ahead crashed with lots of injuries, and we're using this bus as an ambulance. Everyone to the rear." They brought the wounded inside and placed stretchers across the seats and on the floor.

"Lord, we'll never get home tonight." Graciela prayed as sweat dripped from her brow. An injured soldier lay nearby and stared and moaned. His body shook; he coughed up blood. She leaned over, took his hand, and said, "Don't you be afraid; God is with you." She kissed his forehead. His eyes became fixed—he stopped breathing. Graciela folded her hands and prayed. "He's in heaven now." Modesta held her palm while they watched soldiers writhe in pain. The bus pulled into the emergency platform. Medics unloaded the victims. "Modi, I feel dizzy," Graciela said and grabbed her chest.

"Don't you get sick on me, sweet lady."

"Not sick. It's my heart."

"You're just tired."

"Gonna be with the Lord soon."

"No, Graci, you stay here with me." She squeezed her hands.

"You're a good girl. Watch out for those Committee people making you do bad things."

"Nobody's making me do anything."

"But they're lying to you about what's right and what's wrong." She struggled to catch her breath.

Modesta held her hand and wept. "Please don't leave me, Graci."

The old lady murmured, "Promise me, Modi, you'll do the

right thing." Modesta hesitated, looked at her friend, then nodded. Graciela smiled and began making the sign of the cross. Her hand stalled and dropped before she finished. She sighed, her eyes closed.

Modesta patted her cheeks. "Speak to me, Graci." She turned and called for help. A medic came, checked Graciela's neck pulse, and listened for breathing. He looked at Modesta and shook his head. "No, no." She wailed; the man put his hand on her shoulder, but she brushed it aside. Didn't want to lose Graciela; she needed her, and it wasn't fair that the Lord called. She had only a few precious moments left with her old friend. Modesta kissed her forehead, stood, and held her hand until it slipped onto the stretcher as they took her away. "Adiós, Mama Graci. It pains me deep saying goodbye to you."

TWENTY-THREE

New Neighbors

Playa (Biltmore) Neighborhood
May 1960

Bored beyond belief since her best friend Rosie left, Lizzi became a snooper. Military trucks brought new people into the
neighborhood. Noises came from the Martin house. *Someone's
there.* She hopped on Didi's bike and rode across the street to
a palmetto bush, a perfect place to spy. A large woman
dressed in a flowered muumuu climbed off the back of an
army truck parked in front of Rosie's old house. She carried
a big bucket in one arm and a mop in the other. She blurted
at the man behind. "Pick up that kettle and wash pan, I'm not
doing all the work." A little girl followed, holding something,
maybe a doll. Behind her a young boy ran out of the truck
and chased a ball. While biking along the street, Lizzi saw
children playing tag in the yard two doors from the Purcey
house. Three boys played baseball in the vacant lot. Farther
away, a naked youngster rode a tricycle in the driveway and
made her blush.

At the end of the block, she stopped under a big sign with a
red ATENCIÓN at the top. The Defense for the Revolution had
changed Biltmore's name to PLAYA. She pondered for a

moment—her school, the club, and now Biltmore neighborhood.
Castro continued to do bad things to make life miserable. She
raced home and told her father the news. His brow wrinkled.
"Sorry, Papi. I didn't mean to upset you."

"That's okay, mi niña, I'm not surprised."

"New neighbors are in Rosie's house, and I want to meet
them."

"You can be the neighborhood spy but stay away from
those soldiers."

The midday sun beat on the patio by the kitchen. The
mamoncillo hedge provided the perfect shady spot to pry on
the neighbor's backyard. Lizzi grabbed the gardening clippers
and cut enough branches for a peephole and a place to sit. Soon
the back door opened, and the woman she saw earlier tossed
out a bucket of garbage. *Hmm, trash doesn't go in the yard.* She
slurped on a mamoncillo ball while waiting and wiped the
sweet juice that dripped from the corners of her mouth. The
little girl came out carrying a doll. She lifted her tattered dress,
squatted, and peed in the grass. It flabbergasted Lizzi to see
someone go to the bathroom in the yard. The girl pulled up her
pants and ran to the swing set nearby. Her stringy black hair
shifted over her shoulders and half-covered a dirty face as she
swung back and forth. Lizzi noticed scratches on her skinny
arms and legs, and no smile showed on her face. She climbed
the monkey bars, fell, and hit the ground. Lizzi burst through
the hedge and ran to help. The girl saw her, squealed, and hid
her face. "Are you hurt?" The child peeked through her
fingers. Lizzi touched her shoulder and said, "Don't be afraid,

I'm Lizzi, and I live next door." She removed her hands and revealed two big brown eyes. "What's your name?"

"P . . . Pita."

"How old are you?" Eight fingers showed. Lizzi said she was ten and they could be friends. She extended her arm. Pita hesitated, then smiled and took her hand. Modesta shouted that lunch was ready. "I'm coming," Lizzi said and turned to Pita. "Are you hungry?" She nodded. "Come with me." She led her to the kitchen.

Modesta stood by the stove and stirred a pot. "Who's that young'n?"

Lizzi informed her that she lived in the Martin's house. Modesta acted surprised that a family moved in so soon. Lizzi said she invited her for lunch. "First get her clean." The two girls skipped to the bathroom. She turned on the faucet. Pita cupped her hands and took a swig. Lizzi told her they drink water from a glass. She washed her hands, picked up a cloth, and cleaned her face and arms. They dashed back to the kitchen. "Where were you, niña? I thought you two had left."

"I want to teach Pita manners because she uses the bathroom in the yard."

"Campesino folks from the country use the toilet in outhouses; others make a hole and squat in the fields." Lizzi learned something new. Modesta served the girls chicken soup. Pita took a slice of garlic bread and dunked it before stuffing it into her mouth. She reached, grabbed another piece, and did the same. Lizzi couldn't help but stare at her new friend. Never had she seen anyone eat that way. Pita picked up the bowl, tipped it, and slurped the last bit of soup. Noodles covered her face. Then she gobbled a helping of rice pudding. Modesta shook her head. "That child sure was hungry and still is dirty." Lizzi took her to the bathroom, removed her clothes, and Pita jumped into the tub. After filling the bathtub with water and bubble bath, the little girl giggled as she splashed the suds on her body.

The door opened and Mami stood there. "Qué pasa? Who is she?"

"Pita, our new neighbor."

She motioned Lizzi into the hallway and closed the door. "You didn't ask my permission to bring her into this house."

"Pita's my new friend, and we had lunch."

"She's not your responsibility. Take her home." Lizzi returned to the tub and laughed. Pita had bubbles on top of her head.

A woman's shrill voice came through the open window. "Pita, where are you?" She flinched and jumped to the floor. She grabbed her clothes and sprinted naked. Lizzi followed.

"Don't chase that child," Modesta said. "She's wild, leave her be."

Lizzi returned, flopped into a kitchen chair, and whimpered. Modesta handed her a glass of lemonade. She wiped her eyes and sat for a time, thinking. "Why did Pita's family move here?"

Modesta cleared her throat. "Fidel is helping the poor."

"Fiddlesticks," she said. "I'm the one trying to help her."

"Don't you fret. Our comandante knows what's best for us."

"I'm not sure. He changed the name of our neighborhood."

A horn blared from the street. Lizzi dashed to the living room window and saw Pita in the road; a large truck headed for her. The driver swerved and slammed into a palm tree. She started out the front door to see if Pita was okay, but Mami stopped her. "Don't go out there." Lizzi trembled at the thought the truck may have hit her. "Your father needs to handle this, but he's taking a siesta after a hard night at the hospital. Don't bother him."

Lizzi ignored Mami, ran to the bedroom, and shook him. "Papi, Papi, wake up. A truck ran into a tree, and my friend may be hurt."

"A wreck, who's injured?"

"Pita, the little girl who moved next door."

Wichi splashed water on his face, dressed, and snatched his medical bag. He told everyone to remain in the house. Screams sounded from the truck bent around the tree. Steam spewed from the radiator. He hurried to the scene, and in the back, at least a dozen people appeared dazed from the crash. Chickens squawked and scurried in several directions. A hen's wing slapped his arm as she flew to the ground. One woman clutched a crying baby. He had a man take off his shirt and apply pressure to stop the bleeding on a boy's knee. A girl grabbed a goat by the horns. No one looked critical, simply scared folks with cuts and bruises. "The driver is bleeding," shouted a man's voice. Wichi hustled and encountered an unconscious soldier slumped over the steering wheel. He noticed a laceration on the forehead, and blood covered his face. By the looks of the cracked windshield, the victim took a hard hit to the skull. Wichi checked his neck and found a normal pulse. As he placed his stethoscope on the victim's chest, a hand jerked his shoulder backward.

"Who are you, and what're you doing?"

"Doctor Barreras, and I'm attending to this injured man."

"I'm Sergeant Paco, and you have no jurisdiction here."

"He has a head injury and may die without immediate medical attention."

"We take care of our own. Get out or I'll arrest you."

He put his stethoscope back in the bag and glanced again at the driver. The nerve of these idiots—they didn't know what's best for anyone, even themselves. He brushed the sergeant aside and walked away from the truck. The man hollered at him. "I'm told a girl ran in front of the vehicle and caused this wreck. Are you her father?"

He stopped and turned. "No, is she injured?"

"That's none of your business."

"This is my house and my neighborhood."

"Everything here belongs to the government."

Wichi realized he'd better keep his mouth shut—no reasoning with these thugs. He rounded the back of the truck, bent over, and pretended to check his shoe while looking under the vehicle for a body. No girl—he breathed a sigh of relief. The campesino he aided before stopped him. "Gracias, Doctor, you helped my boy's leg."

"How's he doing?"

"Okay, his knee quit bleeding."

"You have a nasty cut above your eye; I didn't notice that earlier." The man said he tried to break up a fight between two hombres over a house. A large home with five bedrooms went to an older fellow with two kids, while the younger guy with six children got a three-bedroom house. "I thought the Revolution treated everyone the same."

"Supposed to, except I saw the first dude slip a few pesos to Sargent Paco."

"Money still talks, eh?" The man smiled and nodded. Wichi asked if he lived in the neighborhood. He pointed to a cream-colored house. "Did you come here by choice?" He said the military herded everybody into a truck and told them to occupy houses left by gusanos, but his father stayed in Pinar del Río. He refused to live in someone else's home.

The sergeant moved toward Wichi and threatened to arrest him if he didn't leave, so he trod back to the house as a military truck pulled behind his car. He tapped on the door and asked the driver, "How do you expect me to get to the hospital in an emergency with that vehicle blocking my driveway?"

"If you have to go somewhere, you'll need permission from Sergeant Paco."

Wichi knew better not to argue with these gun-bearing bullies, or he'd end up back in the police precinct. He slammed the front door, entered the study, and plunged into a chair. He gritted his teeth. *Does this house—this property— belong to me?* Not anymore. A bottle of rare scotch lay stashed inside a cabinet. He poured a hefty drink, swirled the glass a few times, and took a swig. He reclined and lowered his eyelids; the day's events weighed heavily on his mind. His neighborhood had become a hellhole.

TWENTY-FOUR

Two Lost Birds

Playa Neighborhood
June 1960

CLEAN CAGE

DO NOT LET CANARY OUT.

Modesta glared at the sign above the kitchen sink. After turning the faucet, she threw water on her face and frowned at more reminders on the counter:

Today is Coquita's turn for a good cage wash. Don't forget the vitamins and change the dirty newspaper.

The high-and-mighty Señora thought she couldn't remember things. Serve her right if that precious bird weren't around anymore. She stomped to the wall, unhooked the canary's coop, and swung it as she returned to the kitchen. Coquita squawked. "Shut your beak, I'm not through with you." She shoved dirty dishes aside, set the cage by the sink, and opened the wire door. The stench of the gray water in the glass bowl disgusted her. Coquita screeched and pecked her wrist. "Stop, or I'll dunk you in your own slime." She fumbled the dish, and it dropped on the floor and shattered. She picked up a sponge and cleaned up the pieces. "Ouch." Blood dripped from her index digit, and a glass splinter stuck in the skin. "Bird, look what you did to me." She pointed a finger at Coquita, and the fowl flew to the back and spread her yellow wings against the bars. "Afraid of Modi, huh? You'd better be." The canary tilted her head and blinked its tiny black eyes.

Modesta needed mambo to liven up the place and help finish the icky job. She wrapped her finger, turned on the radio, and dialed up Radio Rebelde. "Just you, me, and the music, bird." She pointed at her. "Look at this muck," she said as she threw away the shitty paper. Coquita flew to the swing and pooped on the paperless bottom. "You nasty, inconsiderate feather-head, couldn't wait for a new liner." She cleaned the mess and grabbed a fresh newspaper that showed a photo of Fidel shaking hands with the leader of her neighborhood Committee. Below the image read: "Committees prepare to celebrate the anniversary of Fidel's 26 of July Movement." Her eyes brightened as she continued reading. Hard to believe it started on that glorious day in 1953, and Comandante Castro had now been in power for a year and a half. Here was his picture with her Committee boss, but next time she'd be standing there. She placed the paper aside. *No way is that bird gonna crap on Fidel.* Her finger again aimed at the canary at the top of the cage, hanging upside down. "Idiot bird."

A stack of newspapers lay in the living room. She sorted through them to make sure no revolutionary material was used to catch poop. Thoughts of becoming a famous patriot flashed through her mind; important folks never clean cages. After opening the fridge, she poured mango juice and imagined a photograph of Castro shaking her hand. She took a long swallow, glanced at the empty cage, and gasped—the bird flew the coop. Coquita screeched from the light overhead and fluttered its wings. Modesta cupped her hands and shouted, "You fly back inside this cage, you wretched fowl."

A net hung by the broom closet; she seized it, dragged a chair, and swatted the stick as the bird flew to another fixture. Modesta swung again and missed. She mopped her forehead with her apron. The canary lit on the cabinet above the sink. "You stay still." While gripping the net, she aimed with precision. "Gotcha, bird." Had to move fast so she didn't fly out again. Reaching into the mesh with her right hand, she grabbed Coquita—no movement. She poked its head with her long fingernail. Still no motion—she covered her mouth——*Modi's in trouble.*

Lizzi came into the kitchen. "I'm thirsty."

Modesta jerked an arm behind her back. "Mango juice in the fridge."

Lizzi gaped at the cage in the sink. "It's open. Where's Coquita?"

"I turn away one minute . . ."

"Where is she?"

Modesta brought her hand in front and opened it. Lizzi took the bird, cradled it, and coaxed it to move, and when nothing happened, she squealed, "Coquita's dead." Tears cascaded on her cheeks. She took a napkin to wrap the canary.

"Sorry, niña, it was an accident."

"Mami will be mad."

"Still has Sashita and Rosita."

"But Coquita was her favorite."

"I know." A car door slammed. "Here she comes."

Señora dropped the groceries on the counter, then looked at Lizzi. "Mi niña, why the long face?"

"Co . . . Coquita." She burst into tears.

"Qué pasó?"

"Uh, Uh, well, I—" Modesta's lip quivered. "Something bad happened."

"Where's Coquita?" she said and stared at the vacant cage. Modesta swallowed hard. "She flew out."

"My precious Coqui—gone. NO, NO."

"Modesta tried to net her."

"What's in the napkin?"

"Coquita."

"You killed my birdie!" Shaking her finger at Modesta, she screamed, "You didn't read my signs."

"Wasn't my fault."

"You're fired. Get out of my sight."

"Not leaving until the doctor pays me."

"Clean up this mess now."

"I'll finish it, but I'm done here."

Señora turned off the radio, sobbed, and caressed the lifeless yellow feathers. "My beloved bird, what will I do without you?"

Modesta tramped to her bedroom. "Hateful woman— stupid bird. She may be 'OP' to the doctor, but to me, she's 'Old Pig.'" She pulled her bag from underneath the bed and packed her clothes. While the wailing continued in the kitchen, she folded her blouse, paused, and imagined OP shedding less tears when her husband passed.

Wichi finished his last patient around noon, and his stomach grumbled. He asked Olga if there were afternoon patients. She checked the schedule and shook her head but said there was a letter from Doctor da Silva. *Hmm,* he thought it was interesting. They hadn't spoken since the Revolution began. She handed him the note and said adiós. While sitting at his desk, he tore open the envelope.

> *Wichi, hope this letter finds you well. Sorry, for not keeping in touch. Following Dec '58, my practice has been on the decline, and my family is unhappy, so we're leaving for Mexico tomorrow. A gift will arrive from us, and I believe you will enjoy him.*
>
> *So long,*
> *Tony*

He sighed and hoped it wasn't another dog. After folding the letter, he placed it inside his front pocket and gave it a pat. He closed the office door, walked toward the car, and stared at bins overflowing with trash. The stench necessitated a handkerchief to cover his nose. An old man chased away lanky, stray dogs from the pile of rubbish he had collected. Wichi kicked away a crumpled newspaper blown against his leg.

Driving home he turned on the radio and yearned for good music. A man's voice said, "Next month we honor the anniversary of our glorious leader's 26 . . ." He pushed the OFF button. That scumbag and his 26 of July Movement have taken us from prosperous businesses and clean streets to boarded shops and stinking garbage. As he passed by a magnificent mansion, now with broken windows and covered with graffiti, he shook his head—more of Fidel's July disaster.

He reached the house and turned into the carport.

Modesta stood by the front door holding her suitcase and a Woolworth bag. "Are you going somewhere?"

"It was the bird, it went and died."

"That's no reason to leave."

"Señora got mad and let me go, need my money for June." She wiped her nose with her hand. "I'm so sorry, loved that bird. Tell me I'm not fired?"

"You're not," he said. "Go prepare dinner."

OP came running out. "Why's she returning to the house?"

"To cook for us."

"But I fired her, she killed my bird."

"And I rehired her, we have to eat."

Wichi heard Modesta shouting from the kitchen, "Somebody is hollering for help." *What now?* He darted outside and followed the aroma of beans cooking in the neighbor's front yard. A large kettle hung over a shallow pit in the ground, and a young boy stood crying as he held out an extended arm. A tall, skinny man stared at the boy's hand.

Wichi approached them. "Can I help you?"

The man looked at him. "Who are you?"

"I'm Doctor Barreras, your neighbor."

"Please do something for my son, Pablito."

Wichi took the niño's hand, turned it, and saw seared flesh. The child cried but didn't move. "Bring a bucket of cool water and towels." He comforted the lad while the father dashed inside and soon returned. Wichi sat in the grass beside the youngster and dipped his palm into the water while Pablito squirmed. After questioning the man how the son burned his hand, the answer was that he grabbed the hot kettle handle.

"I was hungry," the niño said.

Wichi finished wrapping a towel around the boy's hand when sunlight behind disappeared, and a large shadow engulfed the three. Startled, he turned and gawked. A massive flowered muumuu covering two basketball protuberances towered overhead. She snorted. "Chicho, qué pasa? Who is this hombre?"

"Vaquita, mi amor, he's a doctor who lives next door, and he's fixing Pablito's burned hand."

"Ay, mi niño, your hand's hurt and my Pita's missing. Chicho, if you don't find her soon, I'll hang you by the balls."

Wichi gulped and remained seated on the ground, eclipsed and intimidated by this amazon. He wiped the sweat off his brow and exhaled. "My daughter, Lizzi, saw Pita yesterday."

"Are you hiding her?"

"No, Señora."

"You better not. I want my baby girl now."

"I'll ask Lizzi if she knows Pita's whereabouts." He eased his way into the upright position.

Vaquita huffed and puffed. "I cut people's throats who lie to me."

Chicho squeezed between the two, "Vaqui, he's just trying to help us."

Wichi hurried home. OP waited by the window when he entered the house. "What were those campesinos doing?"

"Cooking beans in the yard, and the little boy burned his

hand." Country bumpkins was her reply. "Sí, but I got to meet a 'little cow.'"

"Be serious, Wichi."

"I met Pita's parents, Vaquita and Chicho. Her brother, Pablito, was the one with the injury."

"Vaquita—she's the 'little cow'?"

"Sí, and don't plan any parties with her." OP looked puzzled and didn't get the joke. He'd let her find out later.

Time for a snack, so he headed to the kitchen to join Lizzi. "Mi niña, you have work to do."

"What?"

"Pita is missing, and you need to find her. Be careful, though, her mother is big and mean."

Lizzi thought for a while before Pita's location hit her—the hedge hideout—a safe place for the little girl. She prowled to the post and discovered Pita, sleeping soundly and clutching her doll. She knocked on the back door of the Martin house. An enormous leg appeared. Next thing she knew, the biggest person she had ever seen lifted her off her feet.

"Who are you; what do you want?"

"I'mm . . . Lizzi, your neighbor. I'll show you where Pita is."

"Take me to my baby." The huge woman lowered her to the ground and hollered, "Chicho, put your pants on, a girl found Pita."

"Follow me," Lizzi said. She jumped over a row of prickly bushes. The branches cracked and snapped under Vaquita's feet as she stomped behind. "We're here," Lizzi said as she moved aside mamoncillo limbs covering the opening of the hideout. Pita remained asleep. Vaquita lifted her daughter and slobbered her with wet kisses.

She awakened. "Vasilo took me, but I ran from him. Look what he did." She pointed to a scratch on her arm.

"Your no-good father, I told him to stay away from you."

Lizzi's eyes opened wide, for she couldn't help but stare at this huge woman holding her little friend.

"Chicho, he hurt my baby's arm, you find him."

"He's grande."

"I'll handle him," she said. Vaquita held Pita to her chest and thundered toward the house.

Lizzi watched until they closed the door. She hurried back through the hedge and ran home to deliver the news, but Luisito burst into the room and spoke first. "We've got a horse in the carport."

TWENTY-FIVE

Choo-Choo Chicken

Playa Neighborhood
July 1, 1960

Modesta stripped the linens off Didi's bed. She heard the dogs barking through the open window and spotted Lizzi and Luisito trying to ride the new nag around the backyard. Just what this family needed—another huge animal to feed and leave manure to dirty her shoes. The doctor was to blame for this latest addition. He was a sucker to have the creature pawned off on him by a friend who didn't have the balls to send the beast to the glue factory. She gathered up the pile of sheets and bathroom towels and carried everything to the Norge washer in the kitchen. She tossed in a cup of coconut soap flakes and let the lid bang shut, then she shuffled to the sink to clean dishes. "I'm still hungry," Lizzi said as she charged through the back door. "Modesta, will you please serve more mangoes?"

"I'll slice one, but we got to save a few for the familia coming to visit."

"I can't wait for cousin Charo to get here and spend three days teaching us to ride our horse."

"He arrived with no name," the doctor said. "Let's give him one." He scratched his chin. "How does Botín sound?"

"I like the name," Lizzi said. "When will Charo, Tío Cuco, and Tía Nena get here?"

"Cuco's letter said five-fifteen, but the Camagüey train is always late. Hope they arrive in time for Nena to cook something for dinner."

Modi was tired of hearing how good that relative from Camagüey prepared food. She'd wait and see if it were just talk. Didn't matter, though, might be less work for her.

"Modesta, look at those clouds," Señora said. "Hurry and get the laundry on the line before it rains and put clean sheets on the beds."

"Can't stop the washer till it's done."

"She's right," the doctor said. "Be patient."

"Okay, then while you're waiting, go wipe the cobwebs and dried lizards from underneath the beds. I don't want Nena to think I'm a poor housekeeper."

Modesta was eager to remind OP, the "Old Pig" who tried to get rid of her, that she didn't know how to keep a house, but figured it best to stay mum. The doctor peered out the window and said the sky was clearing. He asked for scrambled eggs. "You want it done before I do the cleaning the Señora told me to do?" He told her his stomach came first. She smiled as she sauntered toward the stove. The Old Pig glared back. Modesta fired up the skillet, scrambled eight eggs, and placed them on the table.

"Tasty," he said, "but you needn't have cooked so many."

"I want you to have plenty to eat." Truth was, she needed a good excuse to get out of the house to attend the noon Committee meeting. Shopping for more eggs and milk provided the perfect alibi. The washer finished the cycle, which meant she didn't have to clean under the beds—

another great way to irritate OP. She whistled and carried the laundry basket to the backyard. Sunshine returned and the wash should dry soon. Modi grabbed a sheet and laid it across the clothesline. A gust of wind made it flutter. She took a clothespin out of her mouth, and while fastening the cloth to the line, something behind snorted. She turned and faced the nose of the horse, spat out another clothespin, screamed, and ran toward the house. The doctor opened the door as she clutched the handle. He asked her what was wrong. "You know what's wrong—that horse-of-a-creature out there."

"He won't hurt you, we'll keep him inside the rickety shed."

"I can't stand horses."

He asked her why. She explained when she was young, a horse kicked her brother in the head and made him crazy. "Can't work around those animals."

"You needn't go near him if he scares you."

"What about the clothes on the line? I'm not hanging no more."

"The Señora will do it."

"Whaat?" OP said.

Modesta snickered.

Wichi reached the office mid-afternoon. His practice had dwindled, and only two patients remained on the schedule. Between appointments he sat at the desk and pondered the new horse. To add this animal to the menagerie created another problem for Modesta. He couldn't have her quit with company on the way. A total disaster loomed if OP took over housekeeping chores and meal preparation. After the last patient left, he came from the private office and stood in amazement as Olga handed him two burlap sacks. "Doctor," she said, "the man didn't have any money to pay you, but he said these two fine hens will make a good meal." He chuckled and took the bags, a proper payment with Nena coming. Now he'd have the best pollo asado, roasted chicken, in Havana. Olga locked the door behind him. Gripping the clucking birds, he sauntered toward the Coronet.

His watch showed 4:30 p.m., plenty of time to get to the train station, and with light traffic he crossed the railroad tracks in less than thirty minutes. A shady spot awaited to park the car and keep the chickens cool. He strolled to the depot and glanced at the familiar HAVANA CENTRAL RAILWAY STATION sign. The loudspeaker blared. "The 5:15 p.m. train from Camagüey will arrive on platform number four at 6:00 p.m." Late again, nothing different from his days in medical school when he traveled the same train home to visit his father. Around six-thirty, black smoke in the distance signaled the old locomotive chugging toward the station. The clickety-clack slowed to a screech. The wheels locked, and the cars came to a halt. A horn blew. When the doors opened, a railway attendant descended the metal stairs and had everyone move back to allow passengers off the car.

Wichi scanned the small, dingy windows as people walked to the doorway. No sign of the relatives, so he found entertainment watching travelers disembark. An older woman pushed and shoved others waiting their turns. "Get out of my way," she said. "I need fresh air." The steward helped her as she stumbled to the platform.

Soon most passengers had exited, and Wichi wondered if his family made the trip. He sat on a wooden bench, then spotted his brother detrain. "Cuco," he said, "I thought you weren't aboard."

They embraced. "Had to freshen up. A few rodents joined us for the trip."

Wichi laughed. "Descendants of the ones that rode with me years ago." He backed up and inspected his younger brother. "Hermano, you look mighty dapper in that white guayabera." Cuco slapped him on the back and said how much he missed seeing him. Wichi glanced at the crowd and watched for Nena and Charo. Cuco said they were still in the lavatory since it was a long and dirty ride. They hugged again. "You're looking healthy, must be the fresh air in Camagüey."

"I take my vitamins, and Nena keeps me busy."

Wichi nodded and smiled. He felt a bump as someone grabbed him from behind. He spun around, laughed, and hugged his niece, her ponytail bounced while he tickled her. "Charo, look how you've grown. I like those blue jeans and cowboy boots." She strutted a few steps away, turned, lifted her head, and told him she was soon going to high school. He squeezed her ear and said Didi wanted to know if she wore makeup. Charo questioned why her cousins weren't there. "No room in the car," he said, "but Lizzi and Luisito are waiting for you to teach them how to ride their horse."

"You have a horse?" He said Botín wasn't a stallion, but a pet for the children.

"What's Didi doing?"

"Not riding horses, but she wants you to paint her fingernails." Wichi glanced at the station as Nena stepped off the train. He swept her up in a hug. "You haven't grown an inch."

"And you look ten years older," she said and pinched his cheek. "You and OP been squabbling lately?"

"Just the usual, although she tried to fire the cook."

Nena gave him a mischievous smile. "You'd starve without someone to prepare a meal." He admitted the problem was solved and Modesta remained, but she might be a tattler. "I'll check her out," Nena said. Wichi marveled at her ability to understand people. She read OP like a book and could handle her and anyone else.

They reached the car, and once the suitcases were in the trunk, Cuco climbed in the front while Nena and Charo got in the back. A clucking sound came from the sacks on the seat. "Wichi Barreras, don't tell me you're in the chicken business now. Last time I heard, you were a doctor, not a guajiro hick."

"A patient paid me today with two hens. These ladies will provide dinner tonight."

"Who will wring their necks and prepare them?"

"You, of course, the best cook in Camagüey."

"Aah, Wichi, so you invited me to be the chef?"

"Maybe not, but if Modesta leaves, you have the job."

"Ha, I can't imagine anyone working for 'La Señora.'"

"Now, now—you can manage OP."

"I'll soften up Modesta first and teach her how to make roasted chicken."

Wichi patted his stomach. "Thinking of those hens simmering in olive oil, onions, garlic, and tomatoes makes me hungry."

"You've memorized my recipe. What do you think of besides food?"

"Keeping a cook, the only person between me and starvation." They burst out in roaring laughter. Charo said she couldn't wait to see Biltmore. "Sorry, mi niña, it's now called Playa. Fidel can't stand American names."

"Life's also tough in Camagüey," Nena said. "The Revolution has taken most of our property under the agrarian law. My brothers basically work the land as government employees." Sadness showed in her eyes.

"What a shame, I've always loved your family farm." Charo begged Wichi to take her along the Malecón. "Better roll up your window or you'll get a salty shower." He drove through a wave as it swept across the promenade. Charo stuck her head out and squealed when the brine sprayed her hair. Soon he pulled into the carport.

Charo darted to the door. "Didi, Lizzi, where are you?" She bumped into OP, gave her a half-hug, and continued into the house.

OP strolled toward the car. "Nena, Cuco, you made it."

Nena opened her arms wide, moved toward her, holding a chicken in each hand. "Here, I brought your dinner."

OP backed away. "Ay, Nena, you never change."

"You're the same, too."

"Cuco needs a shot of whiskey after that exhausting train ride," Wichi said to OP.

He led the way to the kitchen with Nena swinging the hens. Modesta peeled onions over the sink. She turned when they entered. "Are you that good cook from Camagüey?"

"Sí, so you've heard of me." Nena laughed. "Bring a bucket and follow me to the backyard." Modesta reached in the cabinet, picked up a container, and accompanied her.

Wichi heard fluttering, and Nena appeared with two lifeless hens. He gave a thumbs-up. Modesta's eyes widened. "My goodness, this woman sure knows how to wring a chicken's neck." Nena smiled and said home economics taught her many things.

"Modesta will help you prepare dinner," Wichi said as he opened the cabinet and grabbed several glasses. "While she gets the hens ready, Nena, come have a drink." They joined OP and Cuco in the living room. Wichi put his finger to his lips and spoke in a low tone. "We have to be cautious talking politics." He pointed to the kitchen and turned to Nena. "Remember what I told you, she's dubious, so be careful." She nodded and winked. After pouring four drinks of whiskey, he handed them out and raised his glass. "Here's to Cuco and Nena and Charo. Good to have you here with us."

Modesta had the water boiling in the pots ready for the hens. She grabbed the chickens by the feet, then dipped and scalded them before plucking. While pulling the feathers she recalled the earlier Committee meeting. A stroke of luck those two whippersnappers appeared. She convinced them they were the right ones to help get rid of that awful horse by stealing him under the doctor's nose. The animal belonged to the Revolution, and she wanted revenge for the Old Pig trying to fire her. Nobody messed with Modi and got away with it.

TWENTY-SIX

Nena, the Countess, and the Dragon

Playa Neighborhood
July 2, 1960

Nena watched Modesta scrape the remaining bit of grease off the roasting pan from last night's dinner. "Señora Nena, you can make tough hens taste like young capons. What's your secret?" She told her salt, pepper, minced garlic, and olive oil—and don't overcook the chicken. "It looks so easy. That bird came out golden brown." Nena said how much she loved to cook.

Modesta wiped her hands on the apron. "Me too but can't stand the cleaning bit—birds and dogs and toilets and floors." Nena explained that she studied hard and became a home economics teacher, but it took time and effort to succeed. Modi placed both hands on her hips and said she wanted respect.

"You'll get it by doing a good job with a positive outlook." Modesta cocked an eye and said she'd be somebody important in Fidel's new government. "What position do you want?" Nena asked as she hurried to lower the burner on the boiling pot.

"Not sure yet, but first I gotta get them to recognize me."

"Who's 'them'?" she said, stirring the black beans.

"The Committee." She took a breath and covered her mouth. "Not saying any more."

Nena held the stool while Modesta removed a bag of rice off the top shelf and placed it on the counter. She told the cook it was right to better herself, but to watch out for liars. "Damn right," she said. "Nobody lies to me and gets by with it." She noticed anger in Modesta's eyes, threw an arm on her shoulder, and said it was no lie—their lunch was *the* best in Havana. Modesta returned a smile and removed four eggs from the refrigerator.

OP came into the kitchen and asked what was for lunch. Nena told her black beans and rice, fried plantains, and a delicious flan for dessert. "Mother just called; she and a friend are dining with us." Modesta snarled and left after OP asked her to mop the bathroom floors. "As soon as Wichi found out Mother's coming, he made plans to take Cuco and the children to the city." Nena asked if he and María Teresa were getting along. OP said, "They shoot daggers at each other whenever they're together." She picked up a towel, dried her hands, and agreed nothing had changed. OP admitted after twenty years, she continued to hear that Wichi was the wrong man for her. Nena mentioned the last time she saw María Teresa was at Luisito's baptism, and she appeared sad. OP had seen no smiles since Blanca's tragic death, and the pain lingered.

"Murder is a terrible way to lose a sister," Nena replied. OP wiped an eye and said she'd like to have her mother more often, but she couldn't drive." Nena asked how she'd get there, and OP answered by Candelaria, the Countess of Luganillo, her only friend and driver. Nena placed her palms together. "I'm to meet a countess?"

"Of sorts, she's a socialite without credentials."

"I can't wait." A balmy breeze wafted the scent of lilies into the house. She inhaled a whiff and knew the perfect dining room table centerpiece suitable for royalty.

María Teresa and Candelaria descended the marble steps of Apartamentos Celestiales and crossed the street to her friend's 1955 black sedan. The countess helped her into the car and settled into the driver's seat. She squinted and lowered the visor. "Ready to go?"

"No, give me my walking stick. I need it to keep those animals from under my feet." She grumbled, took the cane, and placed it against the seat between them. "Do you know the way to Playa?"

"I thought they lived in Biltmore."

"Castro changed the name."

"Sí, just as he did with Woolworth," the countess said. "Now it's called Variedades." María Teresa told her she experienced that awful rebel takeover while in the store with her granddaughters. Candelaria looked ahead, pressed her black leather pump on the pedal, and the vehicle lunged forward. She hit the brakes at the next block. "Ahh, my Caddy has a new engine sound."

"Your automobile may hum, but you can't handle it."

"I beg your pardon, madam."

"I've been watching you drive, one foot on the accelerator and the other on the brake. Often you press both at the same time."

"Well, you're the first passenger to offer instructions how to operate my car."

"Maybe someone should have since I'm getting sick." She covered her lips with a handkerchief and gagged. "I may vomit." Candelaria patted her Virgen de la Caridad medallion, stepped on the brakes, and stopped the sedan. She said to lower the window and throw up outside. The maid quit, so there was no one to clean the mess. María Teresa dug into her purse. "I'll spare you the untidiness, I found a peppermint." She chewed and sighed. "That's better." The countess sped up again, looked in the mirror, and adjusted her feathered hat. María Teresa punched her shoulder. "You can't see the road with that big bonnet."

"I have perfect eyesight."

"And why are you wearing black gloves in this heat?"

She stared straight ahead, raised her chin, and declared that she was a countess and needed protection for her hands from Ofelia Perfecta's beasts. María Teresa fanned herself with a hankie and said her son-in-law added another member to the zoo. "What is it?" the countess said. After hearing the animal was a horse, Candelaria swerved the car to the right, then wheeled it back to the lane. María Teresa grumbled she was going to get them killed, just because her delusional son-in-law got a nag instead of providing books for the children. "Are your granddaughters attending classes these days?" She gave a negative answer. Since Castro closed Catholic schools, Ofelia Perfecta tried teaching them poetry but only bored them with the lessons. The countess advised that young ladies needed refinement. María Teresa lamented that the family lived like savages; the girls pranced around in bathing suits. She bought dresses last week, but they didn't wear them. A horn blared and

Candelaria gripped the steering wheel. "Did you see that man? He made an indecent gesture."

"Are you blind? You pulled in front of him; I told you the hat was too big. Keep your eyes on the road." María Teresa then remembered to tell her friend that relatives from the Barreras clan in Camagüey were visiting.

The countess replied, "Hope there's enough food."

"Don't miss the 194 Street marker." She turned, parked the car in Wichi's driveway, and helped her passenger to the front entrance. María Teresa leaned on her cane and groaned as they waited. Candelaria pulled up her gloves and rang the buzzer. No sound. María Teresa pounded on the door and the dogs barked. "Ofelia Perfecta where are you?"

"Coming, Mother."

Nena watched as OP let them inside; one boxer jumped on María Teresa, and another sniffed the countess's derriere. "Ofelia Perfecta, fix the doorbell so I don't have to wait. I need to use the bathroom." She rushed past her daughter.

Candelaria stepped into the living room. "Countess, your hat is stunning," OP said. "Black becomes you."

"Yes, it always has."

"Por favor, meet my sister-in-law, Nena Barreras."

Candelaria raised her nose. "Encantada, a pleasure, and from where do you originate?"

Nena extended a hand, smiled, and elevated her chin. "I'm from the exceptional province of Camagüey."

"I hear the region has never progressed."

"Beg your pardon, Countess, our privies surpass the ones in Havana."

"I prefer to live in a city with panache."

"But of course, and I believe your houses of ill repute greatly outnumber ours."

OP cleared her throat. "Señora, Mother informs us you have Spanish aristocracy."

"Indeed, I bear the title of Countess of Luganillo, handed to me in Madrid by the queen of Spain."

Nena offered a curtsy. María Teresa reappeared and extended Nena a half-hearted embrace. "We were just discussing Camagüey," she said as she turned to the countess and swept an arm towards OP. "María Teresa's daughter was born there and given a name fit for royalty."

"It's not important," OP said.

María Teresa hissed. "Yes, it is, and to this day, I don't know why your guajiro husband calls you OP. It diminishes your status." She returned a frown.

The countess placed her hands together and nodded at María Teresa. "Do tell me the name."

"With pleasure." María Teresa took a deep breath. "Ofelia Perfecta María del Corazón de Jesús Álvarez-Baragaña y Ronquillo," and she quietly added, "Barreras."

Nena beamed. "A royal appellation, I must say."

"An overstatement," Candelaria replied.

"Countess, I am likewise compelled to disclose my regal name—Ana Magdalena—derived from a princess in the court of Queen Isabella." She gave OP a wink.

Candelaria worked on a smile. She placed both hands on her hips. "Lunchtime awaits and I eat punctually."

Nena snapped a finger. "Modesta, we'll partake of the meal in the dining room."

"Sí, Señora."

The four ladies sat at the table. The countess removed her gloves and placed a palm under one lily. "Lovely flowers, no doubt from your garden. The fragrance resembles my delicate French perfume." Nena told her they weren't local— the Parisian ambassador delivered them that morning.

Modesta served black beans, rice, and fried plantains. The countess requested a hefty helping of the beans. Nena smirked as the royal guest dug into the legumes. Soon she'd have her own propulsion for the return trip. Modesta poured the espresso coffee. Candelaria lifted the cup with her pinkie in the air and brought the demitasse to her lips. A loud thump rattled the front door and the countess jumped. "An intruder," she said, "and we haven't had dessert."

OP sent Modesta to peek through the side jalousies. She glanced and yelled it was Vaquita, the neighbor. "What's she doing here?" OP said, then opened the door. Vaquita stood there, holding a squawking chicken by the leg in one hand and a machete in the other.

She snorted. "Where's that damn boxer dog? I'm gonna teach the killer how to walk on three legs."

"No, you can't do that to my pet."

"Then, I'll cut off yer leg." She moved toward her.

OP stumbled backward. "Don't hurt me."

"Which leg don't you need?" Nena rushed between the hulk and OP, her head at the level of Vaquita's watermelon breasts. "Git out of my way, sister, or I'll trample over you."

"Vaquita, do you want to rot in a prison cell the rest of your life?"

She peered downward. "Me go to jail? This here woman's dog broke my chicken's leg."

"I'll help you," Nena said as she touched the massive arm. She caught Vaquita's eyes, and her sweet smile caused the angry woman to lower the big knife—the dragon's fire was extinguished.

"Dios mío," OP shouted from across the room. "The countess fell to the floor."

Nena glanced at María Teresa and OP standing over the snobby lady. "Get a cool compress for her head—I'm busy." Nena continued gazing at the battle-ax. She removed the machete from her hand. "Vaqui, tell me what happened." She explained that the boxers came through the hedge and chased her hen. One animal grabbed its leg, broke it, and left it dangling by the skin. Then she ran the dogs back home. Somebody had to pay for ruining her chicken. "La Señora is to blame," said Nena, "but you don't get even this way."

Vaquita told her the hen was their meal for tomorrow, but now the one-legged bird needed butchering today. "I can't fix dinner for tonight, 'cause I gotta be at the police station to make sure Vasilo does time for stealin' my Pita."

"Give me the chicken and I'll cook you the best arroz con pollo you ever tasted."

"Little lady, does you know how to wring a hen's neck and cook it with rice?" Modesta stepped forward and said she was the finest cook in Camagüey. "Well, I'll be damned. Bird's yers, honey."

"Supper will be waiting." Nena smiled, took the fowl, and gave it to Modesta. The amazon picked her up, hugged and kissed her. Nena held her breath and hoped her ribs didn't break. Vaquita lowered her, pivoted, and trudged out the door.

"She's gone," OP said. "What did you do?"

She grinned. "Just offered to fix her supper." OP stared, eyes widened, at her sister-in-law. Nena looked around the room. "I prefer your neighbor over the phony socialite. Where is she?"

"In my bed, recovering." They scampered to the bedroom.

María Teresa grabbed OP's arm and said Candelaria's irregular breathing concerned her. Nena propped up the countess. She swallowed a sip of water, gurgled, and spat. "I dreamt of a giant woman and a three-legged dog. Must have been those beans I ate." Nena bent over laughing. OP turned to her mother and asked if Candelaria was in shape to drive home. She swung her legs over the side of the bed. "I certainly am. Let's go."

Nena helped María Teresa into the car. She shut the door and leaned through the window to say goodbye to the countess. "Next time you're in Spain, tell the queen that Ana Magdalena said hola."

The following morning, Wichi knocked on Cuco's bedroom door. "Get up, hermano, let's have breakfast." He replied it'd be a minute. Wichi waited at the kitchen table and sipped coffee. Cuco lumbered into the room, shoulders slumped, holding three train tickets. Wichi stared at his brother. "Qué pasa, why the sad face?" He said the printed dates were wrong. "What do you mean?" Wichi noticed the return was noon today instead of tomorrow. "Caramba, they made a terrible mistake—typical incompetence since Fidel took control." He called the station, but they refused to change the tickets. Cuco rushed to tell the family to get ready.

Lizzi came in crying. "Does Charo have to leave now? She hasn't given me enough riding lessons."

"I'm afraid she has to go, mi niña. The train leaves soon, so help her pack." She ran whimpering along the hall.

Cuco carried two suitcases and dropped them by the front door. He disappeared out the back. Nena dragged her bags from the bedroom, and Wichi loaded them into the trunk. Cuco returned around the corner of the house with a large box. "Can't leave without mangoes," he said and shoved them into the seat.

Lizzi and Didi were teary-eyed and hugged Charo goodbye. Luisito told her he learned how to ride Botín like a cowboy, and OP thanked Nena for preparing the meals. Wichi looked at his watch. "We have to go—train doesn't wait." They climbed into the Coronet, and the family waved as the car rolled out of the driveway. Morning traffic was heavier than usual. He hoped there weren't any roadblocks to cause them to miss the ride.

Nena tapped him on the shoulder. "Short stay, but a good time."

"Sí, and thanks to you—delicious food."

He reached the station and stopped. Passengers were boarding the train. He turned to Nena. "One more thing—any information on Modesta?"

"None, other than she mentioned a committee. She's a sly fox and not trustworthy."

"And how was lunchtime with the countess and María Teresa?"

"Okay, since I saved OP's leg from Vaquita's machete."

"Wha . . . What did you say?"

The train's horn blared.

TWENTY-SEVEN

Borrowing Botín

December 18, 1960
Playa Neighborhood

Moonbeams glared between the jalousie slats and awakened Wichi out of a deep slumber. Not bothered by the cacophony of snoring between Dobin on the floor and OP beside him, he couldn't handle the celestial light. He lifted the mosquito net aside, got out of bed, and adjusted the window. As he cranked the knob, a vague figure moved in the far backyard. He blinked, and another followed. Both headed toward Botín's lean-to shed in the overgrown field behind the house. The clock displayed 2:00 a.m.—*the girls traipsing in the yard at this hour? No way.* He'd check to make sure. He peeked into Luisito's bedroom; the boy slept in good company with the boxers. Modesta was away, so he tiptoed along the hallway and checked on the girls. Enough moonlight showed Didi asleep. Lizzi sat up, pulled back the mesh, and said she dreamed of her birthday and going to Hershey Central.

He told her to go to sleep and rushed to grab a pair of tennis shoes. Whoever trespassed on his property had no business there. With no gun to defend himself, he grabbed a flashlight and picked up Luisito's baseball bat off the hallway floor. He opened the glass sliding door, and with long strides, eased around the margin of the yard, and crouched behind the scattered bushes. The night air aroma, composed of rain-soaked grass, augmented the croaking of frogs as he sneaked closer to Botín. *What are these guys doing?* He'd investigate and scare them away, so he crawled between bales of hay stacked beside the shed. He knew to be careful in case they had weapons. A knothole in the old wallboard provided the perfect peephole. The moonlight gave enough illumination to show silhouettes of two young men.

"Where's the rope?" said the taller one.

"I forgot it," said his short, paunchy companion.

"You bumbling idiota, how are we going to take this horse without a rope?"

Take the horse? Wichi jerked his head. Time to yell and scare these thieves away, but something restrained him. These pranksters didn't resemble dangerous burglars. He put his eye back to the board.

"Can they shoot us for doing this?" said the short one.

"You're a wimp. We're not robbers; he's property of the Revolution."

"Are you sure?"

"The woman told us it was okay."

Wichi scratched his head. Take Botín for the Revolution? *Did the guy say, "the woman"?* He needed answers, so he scurried to the front of the shed with the baseball bat positioned over his shoulder.

The boys scrambled on the ground and found a bridle. "Do something useful and put it around his neck," said the tall one.

The two tried to harness Botín when Wichi switched on the flashlight. "What the hell are you doing?" The pair shrieked and dropped the halter.

"Just borrowing the horse."

"Borrowing?" Wichi said, tightening his grip on the bat. "Ha, that's a good one."

"Please don't hurt us," pleaded the fat robber.

"Who put you up to this?"

"Nobody," the tall boy said as he scampered aside and darted away. The short thief tried to run, but Wichi blocked the path. He headed for a narrow side opening. Botín snorted and kicked him in the thigh. He groaned and fell. Wichi scrambled to where he lay and pressed the bat against his chest.

"Tell me who sent you to steal my horse."

The bandit gasped. "It wuz the woman, Señor."

"What's her name?" He pressed the bat harder against the young man's sternum.

"I don't know, she said this horse belongs to the Revolution."

"I ought to take this bat to you. This horse belongs to me."

"Don't hit me, Señor, I wuz just obeying orders."

Wichi grabbed his neck and pushed him toward the door. The thief ran, limping like a mutt after a dogfight. He turned to Botín and patted his neck. "You're smarter than I imagined." The horse whinnied and nodded his head. Wichi returned to the house. Everyone was asleep, even the dogs— useless animals for guarding the property. A warm glass of milk tasted good before getting back to bed for a much-needed rest; a long day awaited. He put on his pajamas and slipped into the mosquito net. OP and Dobin continued snoring, and as he lay there, thoughts raced through his mind. *Who was "the woman" behind this mischief?* No answer tonight—time to sleep.

Wichi had just opened his eyes when the three children scrambled onto the bed. He gave them a group hug, kissed Lizzi, and wished her a happy eleventh birthday. "Can we buy chocolate kisses in Hershey?" she said. He told her they'd have to wait and see.

OP clapped. "Let your father get dressed. We leave in an hour."

Once the children dragged their feet out of the bedroom, Wichi stretched and sucked in a yawn. "Last night two morons awakened me and tried to steal Botín."

"No, who wants that nag?"

He explained the story. "They were stealing him for some-one else—'the woman'—and she gave them permission."

OP brushed her hair back and frowned. "It must be Vaquita. I haven't forgotten she had the nerve to burst into our house."

"Nor have I forgotten that Nena told me she threatened to cut off your leg with her machete." He muffled a chuckle.

"Don't you dare laugh. That hulk and the campesinos are capable of many kinds of trouble."

"Stop it, Vaquita's not 'the woman' they mentioned." He lay back in bed and pondered the strange things that tran-spired since Fidel's takeover—the mysterious black car and now "borrowing" Botín.

TWENTY-EIGHT

Hershey, Cuba

December 18, 1960
Playa Neighborhood

"Forget horse stealing," Wichi said. "Today is Lizzi's birthday, and we're going on a trip." OP admitted having little knowledge of the town named Hershey they planned to visit and wanted to learn more. She laughed that the children said the streets were lined with chocolate kisses. Wichi mentioned a patient whose friend knew Milton Hershey, who came to Cuba in 1918 to build a sugar refinery.

"Is he the chocolate man?"

"Sí, and he built a Cuban town, modeled after Hershey, Pennsylvania."

OP pulled out a history book and read a paragraph on Mister Hershey. "They awarded him Cuba's highest honor, the Grand Cross of the National Order of Carlos Manuel de Céspedes, the 'Father of the Fatherland.'" Wichi commented it was a distinctive tribute to an American. OP agreed and closed the pages. "I'm ready to go to Hershey, Cuba."

"Let's lower our expectations. I've heard Castro renamed the town Camilo Cienfuegos to honor one of his top commanders."

"I hope he hasn't destroyed it as he did the other American businesses."

"Me too, keep your fingers crossed." The children were in the car when he opened the front door. He glanced at his watch and told everyone it was time to leave.

They cruised beside the coast, and he pointed to the crystal, aquamarine sea on the left. "Aah, the air is so refreshing. Everyone, take a deep breath." He planned to have lunch in Tarará, a beach on the way, but when they arrived, his chin dropped. No one walked the deserted sand. Businesses along the main drag were boarded, and the big green dino on top of the gas station had only two legs and half a body.

"I'm hungry," said Lizzi. "I thought we came to eat."

A restaurant nearby had a charred sign advertising fresh red snapper. The blackened building had broken windows. A yellow board nailed to the wall read: CAFÉ with an arrow pointing next door. After parking the car, he got out and told the children and OP to wait. A scruffy, gray-bearded old man sat in a dilapidated, wooden chair in front of the little café, his leathery hand trembled as he lifted a rolled cigarette to his mouth. A half-empty rum bottle lay a foot away. Wichi rubbed his stomach. "Señor, is red snapper served here?"

The man stood and staggered toward him. "Mister," he said, his speech slurred, "revolutionary bastards burned my business, and I got no reason to live."

The ripped screen door swung open, and a young, dark-headed woman, wearing a hair net and apron, motioned for

Wichi and the family to come indoors. "Who's that person?" he said, pointing to the man.

"My father—he owned the restaurant. People came from everywhere to eat here. What's left is this shabby place." Wichi wanted to know what changed. "Papá wasn't able to get enough fresh fish for the customers because the new government made him serve the best seafood to Fidel's henchmen." He asked why they burned the building. She said her father bought black-market fish to keep the diner open, but a jealous snooper set fire to the premises.

"How unfortunate," OP said.

"Depression and alcohol have conquered him." The waitress wiped tearing eyes with her apron.

"Is this your café?"

"Café and our home, Papá and I live upstairs."

Wichi noticed the children squirming. Lizzi wanted a drink. The lady offered mango juice and gave them the menu—black beans and rice. She apologized for not having chicken or pork. "Do you have any fish?" he said.

"A few came in, but they go to Castro's militia."

Wichi's heart poured out for her. "We'll have the beans and rice."

The children were more interested in chocolate than eating lunch. Wichi finished the meal and paid for the food. Outside in the parking lot, rowdy men chanted, "Viva Fidel." He looked through the window. A military convoy had arrived. "Trouble is brewing," he said to the waitress.

"Sí, your family must go."

Before they left, two armed soldiers entered. The one with two stripes on his sleeve grabbed the waitress' arm, pulled her to his chest and kissed her. "Stop it," she said and pushed him away, "we've got customers here."

"We're the only customers you need, pretty woman. Grill us red snapper with lots of lemons."

The soldier with three stripes motioned for her. "Word has it you do other things good besides cooking." He tossed his holster on the table, lifted the young woman, and carried her up the stairs. She kicked and screamed to let her go.

Wichi gasped, then stepped forward, but OP held him back. Quarters could fit in the girls' eyes. Luisito clung to his mother. The door slammed shut. They listened to muffled noises and thumps on the ceiling. He looked at OP and she blinked. He drew his daughters toward the entrance, and OP followed with Luisito. Two soldiers stood there. "Going somewhere, mister?" said one.

"He don't want our company," said the other.

"My family needs to leave."

"Since we nationalized this property, you need our permission to come and go."

Wichi knew he remained in dangerous territory with these hoodlums. Two things moved the goons—force and greed. The first was out of the question. After one soldier ambled to the table and sat with the two-striped comrade, Wichi pulled out ten pesos, and eased the money into the hand of the soldier standing beside him. The guy slipped it in his pocket and shoved them outdoors. The girls touched the car first and rushed inside. OP pushed Luisito next to them and slammed the door. Wichi inhaled a heavy breath before he cranked the engine and left, pondering what to say to the children. He peered at OP and she shook her head. It troubled him to have the girls exposed to Castro's ruffians and their repulsive behavior. To shield them from these evils had become impossible. Visiting Hershey town promised a brighter side of life. Didi broke the silence. "That soldier mistreated our waitress."

"Yes, he did, now let's talk fun things. We're on the road to Hershey."

Didi liked to watch the map. "We turn here, Papi," she said. But as they approached the road marker, she told him to stop. "I'm mistaken, the sign reads: CAMILO CIENFUEGOS, not Hershey."

"That's it, Castro changed the name." They went several miles, stopped, and parked the car near the train station. He glanced in several directions—another disappointment—tall weeds grew everywhere. A sign still showed: HERSHEY. Everyone got out and strolled toward the town. Goats frolicked ahead, stray dogs roamed, and a scrawny cow mooed and grazed in an empty lot. A little boy on a rusty bicycle bumped over grass growing through cracks in the concrete. An old woman struggled to push a three-wheeled grocery cart carrying mangoes and coconuts.

"Papi, where are the chocolates?" Didi asked.

No quick answer came to mind, so they ambled along and avoided horse manure and cow pies. Luisito kicked stones into the potholes. How naïve of him to expect a vibrant town after two years of Castro's Revolution. OP sat on the curb to empty rocks from her shoe. Luisito chased a chicken, and Lizzi whined that she didn't want to stay there anymore.

"Soon we'll go," he said.

Across the street the wind flapped sheets airing on a clothesline. An elderly Black woman with snow-white hair lumbered out of a shabby, concrete house, its light blue paint peeled away, and its color faded. A frayed tarp failed to cover the sagged, wooden roof. She removed her wash from the line and placed it in a straw basket. A strong gust blew a pillowcase his way, and he reached up and caught it in midair. When he handed it to her, she smiled, and they exchanged greetings.

"What brings you to Hershey?" she asked. He told her the family wanted to see a chocolate town. "Not what you expected, is it?"

"No, but can you tell me its history?"

She said her husband came to work for Mr. Hershey right after he built the town in 1918. She was in her early thirties, and her man had a good job working at the sugar mill. The company paid well, and the children attended school. A medical clinic was right there when folks got sick. Since they were Blacks, they couldn't go to every place where the Whites went, and she resented it. Wichi asked if she still felt that way.

"I look at things different now." Mr. Hershey provided for his employees, no matter their race, even built a school for orphans. Her nephew lost both parents in a train wreck and lived in the orphanage. She lowered her head and told him how Castro's rebels destroyed the golf course and anything else that looked American and left them with a horrible-looking place. "Today, Blacks live in bigger houses and can go anywhere they please, but the town's in shambles, and people have no money to buy goods or fix up their places. Folks—whatever their color—now all got the same misery." Tears welled up in her eyes as she reflected on a life alone since her husband passed and the children left home. "If you want to know the truth—I'm worse off since the Revolution." Wichi looked at her and shook his head. She pointed across the road. "Is that your family over there?"

"Sí, today's my daughter's eleventh birthday."

"She looks disappointed."

"The children expected to see chocolate hanging on the trees."

She suppressed a laugh. "Wait here," she said while she hobbled into the house and soon returned carrying a small box. "Give this to your birthday girl."

"You needn't do that."

"Yes, I do. Have her open it later."

"Gracias." Wichi gave her a hug, told her to take care, and began walking.

"One more thing I didn't tell you," she said. He stopped and pivoted. "I named my oldest boy Milton."

They smiled at each other, and he waved and moseyed across the pavement. "Well, I guess it's time to go," he said to the family. Lizzi wept and ran toward the car. When they reached the Coronet, she sat wiping her eyes while staring out the window. Wichi got in, glanced over his shoulder, and saw the sadness in her face. It gripped his soul and broke his heart. Her birthday had been a complete disaster. He started the motor and headed home, regretting his family had to experience the repugnance of the Revolution.

"We didn't get any chocolate," Didi said.

"I'm sorry." He told OP to give the box to Lizzi and said it was from the nice lady across the road. "It's for your birthday, open it." Her squeal made him swerve the car. "What did she give you?" he said.

"Three Hershey bars!"

TWENTY-NINE

Movie Madness

Playa Neighborhood
January 4, 1961

"I'm gonna wash that guy . . . hmm, hmm." Didi bounced into the kitchen as she dried her long black hair.

"What's that humming?" Wichi looked at her and crunched on a piece of dry toast.

"I want to be an actress just like Mitzi Gaynor." Modesta handed over a glass of papaya juice and toasted more bread in the oven.

"Papi, can we go to a matinee today?"

"I'm afraid not." He smiled and said to practice more acting since he had no desire to take the family anywhere after the chocolate fiasco. He strode outside, picked up the paper, and walked to the study to check the news. The headline smacked him in the face: "The United States Severs Diplomatic Ties with Cuba." He read that President Eisenhower closed the American Embassy in Havana. Clutching the paper in his fist, he yelled, "We're doomed."

OP rushed into the room. "Wichi, why did you raise your voice?" He shouted that the Americans obviously consider Castro a communist because of his close ties with the Soviet

Union, his Marxist agrarian reform, and seizure of US companies. He slammed his fist on the desk. "Without American trade our country will suffer economically, and my practice will go to hell if I can't get US supplies and drugs. I had a gut feeling this Cuban snake would be our downfall."

"He fooled us," OP said as she plopped into a chair. "Remember they showed the white dove that landed on Castro's shoulder during the January 1959 speech. Even the nuns thought God blessed him, until he kicked them out."

"The bird lit for the purpose of crapping on the ruthless son of a bitch who came to destroy its island." She remarked that it was ironic a Catholic archbishop saved Fidel's life after the 1953 Moncada attack. Wichi smirked. "Maybe now they're praying to get rid of him."

"Shush." She pointed to the kitchen.

He covered his mouth and realized the anger inside boiled so much he forgot Modesta was there and heard every word. He closed the door. "I was mad and didn't consider her. She may tell on us."

"What do you suggest?" OP asked. He told her she had to go. "Remember," she said, "I warned you and I fired her."

"Okay, but you're the reason she's still here." OP placed both hands on her hips and said she didn't plan to mop floors or cook. "Plans alter," he said as she walked to the door. He knew the break with the US represented a game-changer. Disaster loomed since Castro crawled into bed with the Soviets.

Lizzi wandered into the office and asked to see *20,000 Leagues Under the Sea* playing at the Teatro Blanquita. He thought for a moment and realized earlier he'd told Didi they couldn't go, but after reconsideration a movie may be a good distraction. "Okay, tell your sister I changed my mind. Get ready." She raced to her room. Wichi took a quick shave, grabbed the keys, and followed OP out the front. The girls and Luisito were waiting in the car. He opened the door. "What's with the ironed blouses and poodle felt skirts?"

"We dressed up for the movie," Didi said.

Lizzi placed her legs on top of the seat and showed her penny-loafers and white socks. He said he didn't remember the last time she wore shoes. Near the theater he spotted two army trucks at the entrance. OP wanted to leave, but he shook his head, parked the car, and remarked that Fidel had taken enough from them, and today they'd see a show. The children cheered. He told them to wait while he bought tickets. Following a short hike to the box office, he got behind a dozen people waiting in line. A sign on a glass enclosure made his eyes bulge. COMANDANTE CASTRO HAS RENAMED THIS THEATER TO EL TEATRO KARL MARX. The woman in the booth announced they canceled *20,000 Leagues Under the Sea* and instead were showing a documentary on the life of Karl Marx. As folks moved ahead, Wichi stood dumbfounded. A man behind tapped on his shoulder and asked if he was in line. He stepped sideways and turned. "No, movie's not my choosing." He trudged back to the family and dreaded disappointing them once again. Anger burned in his gut—*the nerve of these communist asses*. The car was easily spotted with Lizzi's shoes dangling out the window. Didi waved and asked if he had the tickets. He shook his head, cranked the engine, and announced Castro's people scrapped the movie.

"Let's find another theater." Lizzi said. Luisito wanted to see Porky Pig.

"Impossible."

Didi sobbed. "How can I become an actress if I can't attend movies?"

Heartbroken, he turned onto the avenue while the three sniveled in the back seat. Several blocks away they stopped crying, but the silence was even more distressing. After a deep breath, he apologized and admitted being discouraged and frustrated as they were.

"We used to have fun, but now everything's gloomy," Lizzi said. Didi wanted to go live with Margie and Rosie in Venezuela.

"No connections there," he answered and glanced in the rearview mirror. A black car followed. He turned onto 194 Street, looked back, and the vehicle kept going. One day he'd solve this enigma, but for now, time to face the family and their movie madness. He pulled into the carport, browsed across the road, and spotted Mister Crawley trimming hibiscus shrubs. He and Carina were away for a year, and he was glad to see him back at home. OP and the children stomped into the house while he ambled to greet his neighbor. "Mister Crawley, we've missed you. How are things?"

"Tickety-boo, did a long film shoot in England."

"Cuba's different now, afraid you weren't returning."

"Been keeping abreast of the news, old chap," Crawley said as he whacked on a bush. "We'll stick around a bit longer, Carina's mother in Matanzas has been unwell."

"One day at a time for me, just forget today."

"I say, old man, you look knackered."

"I'm in hot water with my kids; promised them a movie and Fidel nixed it."

"By jove, I've got the solution. Brought back a new projector and reels from London. Let's have dinner tonight and a film."

Wichi leaned backward. "You've saved me."

"Jolly well mosey over at six for drinks and dinner before the show. Carina will have popcorn later for the young ones."

"I can't wait to inform the family. Modesta can feed the children, and we'll call them when it's movie time."

Crawley hailed him as he crossed the street. "Tell them it's *The African Queen*."

He waved at the Brit, said they'd love it, then sprinted to the living room. OP read a magazine while Didi combed her hair. Lizzi and Luisito lay on the floor with the dogs. "We're going to a movie tonight," he shouted. OP folded the paper and the rest jumped to their feet.

"Por favor, say it's true," Lizzi said.

OP warned him. "Don't let it be a joke." Luisito said he wanted to see Bugs Bunny.

"It's not a cartoon, but you'll enjoy it."

"Tell us, tell us, Papi," Didi begged.

"The movie is—*The African Queen*." She cheered, and then announced the stars were Humphrey Bogart and Katharine Hepburn. "Sí, that's the one. Mister Crawley invited us to watch it at his house. Your mother and I are going over first for dinner, and we'll call when the movie begins."

"Well, I guess I'd better get ready," OP said as the children ran to the rooms. Didi hollered something about a movie magazine she wanted Lizzi to see. OP showered and put on white pants and a flowered, sleeveless shirt. Wichi splashed on cologne, careful not to spill any on the white guayabera.

Minutes before six o'clock, Wichi closed the front door. A passing cloud captured part of the orange sunset. The familiar, dark vehicle whizzed by before they reached the sidewalk, but tonight he'd see a movie and forget unpleasant thoughts. Mister Crawley greeted with a bienvenido. He kissed OP and shook Wichi's hand. "Say, old chap, we are guayabera twins." Crawley smoothed a hand over his shirt.

"Your linen beats my cotton," Wichi said. Crawley patted him on the shoulder.

Carina rushed from the kitchen. "Sorry I didn't make it to the door," she said while untying her apron. "The arroz con pollo required more attention."

"Give the bird plenty of time," Wichi said. "Whatever you cook is always delectable."

OP hugged Carina. "Welcome back. Your sleek white dress is stunning."

"We're often told we make a bloody handsome couple," Crawley said, "me, the pale-skin Brit and Carina, the ebony islander."

"A well-deserved compliment," OP said.

Crawley made drinks, and they sat on the patio. "What a splendid evening with good friends," Wichi said. "It's unfortunate this paradise is ending."

"Cuba's all to pot," Crawley said.

Wichi took a sip of whiskey. "I've seen horrible brutality and killing by Fidel's thugs."

"Sounds a bloody bit akin to Batista."

"We traded the devil for his twin brother."

Crawley looked at his watch. "I'll be gobsmacked, we'd better roll the cinema. Ring the children."

Wichi dialed the phone and Modesta answered. Voices shouted in the distance—it was movie time.

THIRTY

An Unhappy Ending

Playa Neighborhood
January 4, 1961

Modesta watched the children cross the street and made sure they entered the Crawley's house. For sure the doctor was using the movie to plot something anti-revolutionary. Now was her chance to be honored by the Committee for exposing traitors. She missed an earlier opportunity to receive a medal because the idiots botched stealing the horse. Too bad dear Graciela wasn't with her, though the old lady didn't like the spying and killing necessary to keep the Revolution alive. It was getting-even time for the doctor lying about the nun's escape and the Old Pig firing her for killing that stupid canary.

She dialed the Committee headquarters. "Hola, comrade Modesta speaking. I want to report a counterrevolutionary meeting happening across the street. The ringleader is Doctor Luis Barreras, and he doesn't favor Fidel." She gave the address and details.

"Comandante Castro thanks you," said the male voice on the line. She put the receiver back in the cradle and smiled. Modi made the necessary move for fame and power.

Wichi nestled in the sofa with the children while the Brit drew the curtains and turned on the projector. Midway through the film, Lizzi yelped when the *African Queen* hit a wave sending Bogart and Hepburn into the water. "Will the actors drown?" Didi asked. Wichi prepared to answer when a bang resonated on the front door.

A loud voice outside yelled, "Abre la puerta." Mister Crawley reached for the projector cord, stumbled, and hit his knee. He asked Wichi to turn on the lights. Harder knocks sounded. "Open now or we'll shoot the lock." Wichi flipped the switch and rushed the women and children into the back room. After returning to the foyer, he unfastened the bolt and stood beside Crawley. A tall, bearded soldier in green fatigues lunged inside, flanked by two rifle-carrying troops. The yard swarmed with commandos. The leader made them raise their arms while he sent men to search the rooms.

"Why are you doing this? We have nothing to hide, just watching a movie," Wichi said. Muffled cries echoed from the bedroom, and a guard headed that way. "Por favor, leave my family alone."

"Shut your mouth, I give orders." More troopers stormed inside and trampled throughout the house. Drawers thumped as they hit the floor. The leader shouted to keep looking. Glassware broke in the kitchen, and feathers fluttered in the living room while they watched soldiers rip cushions and upholstery with knife blades.

"No guns, Sarge."

"Take the whiskey. We'll celebrate later." They emptied Crawley's liquor cabinet. The sergeant turned to Wichi and asked his name.

"Doctor Luis Barreras."

"I have orders to arrest you." Wichi replied they had broken no rules. The soldier pointed to Crawley. "He hasn't. It's you we want."

Wichi gasped. "I'm innocent too." The guy handcuffed his wrists, pushed him outside and into a military van. He wondered where they were taking him—to a police station or an isolated place to shoot him. It was agonizing to leave without saying goodbye to his family, who he prayed they didn't harm. Sweat bubbled from his temples as the truck bounced along until it stopped. The door opened in front of the nasty headquarters where he was detained at several years ago. Militiamen prodded him out of the vehicle and into the building and forced him to stand at attention in front of a counter. His legs ached while the man stationed there ignored his presence and continued to shuffle papers.

About fifteen minutes later, the soldier closed the folders. With elbows on the desktop and chin in his palms, he glared at Wichi. "You're Barreras, the anti-revolutionary." He gulped; they knew his name. The deputy shouted to the other soldiers nearby, "Rounded up another traitor, thanks to comrade Modesta." Wichi's heart skipped a beat. He recalled the horse thief had mentioned "the woman." Nena had it right, and he'd been so gullible. He told the man the housekeeper got it wrong. The neighbor invited them to see a movie at his home. He wasn't plotting against the Revolution.

The soldier smirked. "We have here a rich Batistiano exploiting domestic help instead of using his pretty hands to clean shit off the toilet, huh?"

"Not rich, never been a Batistiano, and I pay my help."

The man stroked his beard. "The report said you're against Fidel, our glorious leader, and you conducted a meeting against the Revolution, using a movie as an excuse." Wichi said it wasn't true. The officer ordered him placed on a bench between two rows of jail cells. The area bulged with prisoners; roaches scurried along the walls, and the stench of urine made him gag. The guard pointed to the cell on his left. "At La Cabaña tomorrow, those men die. Maybe you can join them." His heart pounded. A prisoner with a bloody forehead two cells away caught his attention. The man looked familiar. *Where have I seen him?* Then, he remembered—Pilar's father, Captain Joaquin Lopez, the soldier with many medals. *No more swim meets for him.* Wichi contemplated his own destiny. A crime against the government meant severe punishment, and he faced the identical fate as Lopez. Perspiration streamed from his brow and dripped onto his face. Cuffed hands behind made it impossible to scratch an itchy nose. The lieutenant approached, and Wichi suspected the worst.

The officer gave him a penetrating and bone-chilling stare. "Wish I could send you to the firing squad, but I'll release you this time."

Sweat soaked the guayabera he and Crawley laughed about earlier in the evening. A soldier jerked him from the seat and removed the handcuffs. He pushed him to the front and toward a telephone. "Call a friend or spend the night with us."

The phone quavered as he dialed Crawley's number. His voice cracked. "Can you drive me home? I'm at the central police station."

"Be there in a flash, old chap."

Wichi hung up and staggered outside to wait. Sitting on the curb, he glanced to the right. The black car he'd seen before waited across the street. The engine started; the vehicle flew by and disappeared around the corner. *Damn*, it happened so fast he didn't recognize the driver. While pondering, head in hands, a familiar "aooga" cut through the early-morning stillness. Mister Crawley's 1956 horn was a heavenly sound.

"Hurry, old man, we need to tear arse." Wichi jumped in, and they sped away. "You look gutted. What did the blokes do to you?" When he heard the atrocities of the Revolution, Crawley trembled. The car pulled into Wichi's driveway; he stumbled out of the auto and thanked the Brit. He entered the house and went straight to the kitchen to ease his parched throat. He turned on the light and gulped a glass of lukewarm tap water. A noise startled him. Modesta peeked her head from behind the door—her eyes wide open.

"Surprised to see me?"

THIRTY-ONE

The Red Scarf

Playa Neighborhood
January 5, 1961

The door flew open, and Wichi staggered into the bedroom; he slumped onto the side of the mattress—face drooped and shoulders stooped. "I'm beat," he said.

OP jumped out of the bed. "You're home, gracias a Dios. It's two o'clock in the morning and you had me petrified." She closed the door.

"You don't know the half. I endured an eternity of grueling doubt and thought I was on the way to La Cabaña for execution."

"What, for watching a movie?" Pointing toward the kitchen, he informed her that Modesta turned him in for plotting against the government. "That bird slayer is the one who deserves La Cabaña," she said. "What are we going to do?"

"I saw Modesta a few moments ago, and it was the perfect time to fire her, but my exhaustion prevented it." Wichi leaned over and questioned if the soldiers had harmed them. She shook her head and said they left after taking him away. He sighed and his body went limp. "I need to sleep." She kissed his cheek. With eyes transfixed on the ceiling, a brain fog encircled his mind, his eyelids drooped, then folded.

At dawn, Wichi pushed aside the sheet and mosquito netting. Better face Modesta before the children and OP awakened. He stepped to the bathroom, showered, and dressed. A quiet house afforded the opportunity to complete an unpleasant job. The kitchen was dark; he flipped on the light and knocked on her bedroom door but got no response. He tapped again. "It's Doctor Barreras, need to talk." Still no answer, so he turned the knob. She wasn't there—clothes and suitcase, everything—gone. On top of the disheveled bed lay a photograph. He picked it up and glared at it. Modesta spared the chore of firing her but left with a parting shot—a picture of the person he hated the most—Castro. VIVA FIDEL in red lipstick appeared across the tyrant's image.

OP bustled into the kitchen as he came from Modesta's quarters. He rushed the photo into his back pocket. "Well, tell me she's fired." He bit his lip and nodded. "What are you hiding?" He shrugged as OP circled, reached behind, and pulled out the photograph. "That woman did mean things and didn't belong here."

"Now you're the housekeeper."

She gave him a wicked glare. "Funny, I can tattle too." A rumpled apron lay on the counter; she wrapped it around her waist, opened the refrigerator, and removed an egg carton.

While eating runny yolks and burned toast, Wichi perused the morning paper that featured the men Castro considered traitors. Captain Lopez was on the list; his beaten face haunted him, and by now the Batistiano had met his Maker. What a horrible way to die. Fate could have dealt him the same blow, but they spared him, and he didn't know why.

A squeal from the children got his attention as they dashed into the room. Wichi held out his arms and hugged them. They wanted to know what happened to him, and he reassured them that all was well. Didi wanted to finish the movie at their house. He pinched her nose. "No, mi niña, it's too dangerous."

Lizzi stuck her head into Modesta's room. "Where is she?" He explained she didn't work there anymore. Luisito said that Dobin can sleep by the kitchen again.

Didi stared at the burned toast. "We'll starve without her." OP scowled. "Don't be theatrical."

Wichi opened the fridge for a bottle of juice, caught sight of a squashed egg on the tile, and spotted a cucaracha dart under the counter. "This kitchen floor needs mopping; I won't live in a pig sty." Today was a turning point for the Barreras family. Without domestic help the daughters must cook and clean. "Niñas, your mother requires a hand with cages and dogs and dirty dishes."

"When?" Lizzi said.

"Later, now go feed the dogs and play." The youngsters filled four bowls of dog food and raced out the door. OP flopped a slice of ham in the skillet. "Keep the food warm," Wichi said. "First, we have to discuss the children's education." He turned on the radio to drown their conversation. "Caray, the only station on the air is Radio Rebelde."

A newscaster interrupted the music to read an important message from Fidel Castro, who proclaimed that 1961 was the year of education, and the government had proposed the ambitious goal of eradicating illiteracy in only one year. OP laughed and wondered if Castro was a magician as well as a dictator. "We shall set up an army of educators and send them to every corner of the country," Fidel said. The announcer added that these literacy squads included Che and others.

Wichi clicked off the radio, and OP stood bewildered. He sniggered. "Che, the butcher of La Cabaña, pretending to be an educator—ha." OP sniffed and admitted Castro was correct in only one thing—children needed to be in school. She said she was qualified to teach the girls history at home, but math was out of the question. He thought the plan might work if they found a mathematics instructor. The big problem was Luisito starting first grade in a government classroom. He'd heard the primer was *We Shall Conquer*, and it sounded communist. He smacked his fist on the table, furious that Castro decided how to educate his children. "Now we know what's behind the Revolution—the indoctrination of Cuba's youth."

The door opened, and Luisito ran into the room. "Let's go horseback riding, Papi," he said. *Not a bad idea—and a great diversion from Castro's illiteracy crap.* Good thing his patient-friend down the street allowed him to take his horse around the neighborhood. They'd saddle up Botín, and he and Luisito would have an hour to ride before he left for the office.

OP sipped mango juice and extended her legs over the end of the rattan sofa. The girls finished a long list of chores and now studied a reading assignment. A strong tap at the front door brought OP peering through the window. *How odd*—Ester Ramirez, a colleague from university days, *but why in military uniform*? She opened the door. "Ester, come in, what a surprise."

"Sorry for not calling, but since it's my week to recruit children in Playa, I came for a visit." OP invited her to sit in the living room. Ester grazed the canary cages as she passed by and questioned if she still liked birds. She nodded, and the query persisted. The inquisitive woman asked her marital status and even mentioned her poetry recitation in years past. She settled in a wicker chair and fanned her face. OP apologized for the heat, saying they were conserving energy. "That's nice for the Revolution."

"It's not for Castro's benefit, just reducing our electricity bill."

Ester handed OP a brochure and bragged on the Revolution's campaign to eradicate illiteracy. Her jaw dropped as she inspected the folder. "This is Soviet curriculum," she said.

"The Revolution mandates that schools instruct Marxist doctrines." OP thought it was peculiar to promote Russian over Cuban history. "Fidel believes in the ideas developed by Karl Marx to achieve an exceptional society," Ester said. "The state provides free education and healthcare and food."

"Nothing's free," OP said. "Everything costs money, and someone has to pay for the handouts." Ester raised an eyebrow, and OP decided it was time to get to the point. "May I ask why the visit today?"

"Luisito is ready for first grade, and you need to enroll him into the Communist Youth Groups and train him to recite the matutino, the morning chant."

"What are you saying?"

"Before the school day begins, students form a circle, grip hands, and repeat after the teacher, 'We are pioneers for communism, and we shall all be like Che.'"

"That's preposterous. I don't want my son to imitate Che Guevara."

"Oh, you have to, the chant's mandatory." It bedazzled OP

that this woman fell for such nonsense. OP informed Ester she taught an exceptional public kindergarten class, even under Batista. The colleague shivered and said, "Don't mention that corrupt man."

"Yes, he was a mobster, but I didn't indoctrinate my students to mimic him." She begged OP to consider enrolling Luisito since pupils received a crimson scarf following the chant and wore it with pride every day. The little neighbor Pita had one. OP swallowed hard, her face reddened. "I'm not sure this characterizes a proper education."

"If you want to see the school, here's my card. Other families wait for me. Buen día."

OP walked her to the door, stared at the material, and watched her former classmate march toward another house as Wichi and Luisito returned. He told his son to walk Botín to the shed and he'd be there in a minute. While standing in the doorway, he asked OP who was the lady in the green uniform. "Ester Ramirez, an associate from my university days." He scratched his head and wanted to know the purpose of the social call. "Not a social call, she wants to register Luisito for first grade at Lenin Elementary."

Wichi slammed the door shut. "The hell she does." He mentioned the likelihood of their being forced to send the child to a communist elementary and wanted OP to get more information.

The next afternoon OP drove toward the school. She slowed for a goat that crossed the street to feast on lilies once grown by gardening friends. The destination was a palatial estate and

Pilar's former home. Lizzi had been there for swim parties, and OP thought of the young girl, now fatherless after the captain's brutal execution. A sign at the gated entrance read: THE LENIN ELEMENTARY SCHOOL. A military guard stopped the car and demanded her credentials.

"I'm Ofelia Perfecta Barreras, a kindergarten teacher." The man wiped his nose and told her to go home; they weren't a day care center. She showed him Ester's card and he motioned her ahead. She drove along the winding driveway and parked near the house. As she stepped out of the car, another sign hung over the entryway: WE SHALL OVERCOME. A tightness gripped her stomach. She squared her shoulders and strode to the door.

"What do you want?" said the soldier pointing a machine gun in her direction. She told him she was invited to observe a classroom. "Go wait inside."

OP dodged an overhead crystalline chandelier hanging by an electrical cord. She slumped onto a chair with a torn, velvet cushion. Soon a mature, uniformed woman approached. "Who are you, and what's your business?"

"Ofelia Perfecta Barreras. Comrade Ester Ramirez suggested that I view the first-grade class."

"There's not much time. The young pioneers for Che have nearly finished lessons for the day." She pointed to the left and gave strict instructions not to enter classes or talk with any pupil or teacher. OP reached the classroom, peeked through a small windowpane, and gawked at the many pictures of Lenin and Karl Marx. Crisp collars with the infamous crimson kerchiefs adorned the youngsters. They sat attentively at wooden desks while the instructor directed their attention to the blackboard dwarfed by a massive overhead red star. OP noticed a boy in the back of the class not wearing a scarf. The teacher made the child stand and then motioned him into the hallway. He sat on the floor, crossed his arms, and sobbed. OP handed him a tissue, and between sniffles, he said he didn't want to do the chant or wear the red scarf. The sound of clonking boots on the tile floor echoed in the hall. The matron marched toward her. "Señora, you disobeyed my rules."

"I only gave the child a tissue."

"We have laws." She waved her hand. "Guard." A female soldier grabbed the child and led him away.

A soldier approached OP and prodded her to a chair inside a dingy office. Behind a desk sat a bald barbudo blowing smoke rings. He laid a cigar on an inverted jar lid. "Señora, weren't you told not to speak with anyone?"

"Sí, Señor, I didn't speak, only listened."

"Because you disobeyed us, you're under arrest."

"What? I broke no rules."

The man propped his legs on the desktop. "We'll take you to the precinct for questioning." A soldier yanked her out of the chair and escorted her to the hallway toward the entrance. OP protested and said she wished to contact her husband. The guard said no calls and shoved her into the passenger seat of a truck parked outside the door.

"This is insane, you can't detain me."

"You're mistaken, Señora, you *are* in detention." The man turned the ignition and hurried along the driveway. When they reached the entrance, a trooper motioned for the vehicle to stop and ordered her release. The turn of events shocked her. *No questions asked—just leave.* She sprinted by a parked black automobile on the way to her car. Breathing was difficult and her heart throbbed as she cranked the ignition and sped toward the gate. In the meantime the vehicle had disappeared.

On the road back to Playa, OP glimpsed at the rearview mirror—the dark car followed. After making the turn onto 194 Street, the mystery sedan continued straight. She pulled into the carport and loosened her grip on the steering wheel. She turned off the ignition, took a deep breath, and blew out a sigh before feeling strong enough to stand. Wichi paused cleaning the Coronet's windshield. "Why are you home so late?"

"They wouldn't let me go." He kept scrubbing the glass. "Wichi, no joke," her voice rose. "They arrested me."

He dropped the rag. "What happened at the school?"

She was in the middle of the story when Luisito and Pita came running. "Pita got a red scarf at school. Watch me Mami, I can get one too."

The two children held hands and chanted, "We're pioneers for *cominism.* Yay."

Wichi glowered in OP's direction. He clenched his jaw, made a fist, and kicked a tire. "Over my dead body."

"Mine too."

THIRTY-TWO

Outré Office Visits

February 1961
Vedado Office

Wichi surveyed the medicine cabinet. Only two bottles of iron pills and no aspirins remained. No supplies had arrived since the US cut ties with Cuba. Olga threw her arms in the air. "Doctor, I'm ready to cut and run. We can't maintain a medical practice with an empty pharmacy." The weary expression of his loyal employee of eleven years pained him, and he sensed plans were brewing for her to exit Cuba. The office must stay open if possible. He asked her to stick around and said they were in the boat together. "If it's traveling to Key West, you'd see my husband aboard." She told him after Castro confiscated the American oil companies, he lost his job.

"An abomination across the board," he said. "Good thing you don't have youngsters, Fidel is brainwashing first graders." She couldn't believe it. "OP teaches the girls poetry and history at home. We will not let Fidel indoctrinate our children to become Che Guevara clones."

Olga tapped her finger on the desk. "Doctor, what's the US's opinion of this monster, Castro?" He told her they can't be happy having a communist-leaning dictator ninety miles from Florida. "Speaking of communists—Colonel García comes with Albertito at four," she said. Wichi paused, placed a thumb under his chin, and rubbed an itchy nose. He said that illness didn't respect politics, so they treated patients and ignored their political views. "You're correct, and I'm sorry, Doctor. I've grown to love that little boy and admire how his father cares for him."

He patted her shoulder. "Life sometimes throws twists when we least expect them."

The phone rang. "Doctor Barreras's office, may I help you? But he has another patient scheduled . . . Okay . . ." She hung up the receiver. "That was Yoya—your sister insists to come now."

"For her, everything is crucial. Once, she'll surprise me with an urgent matter."

Olga promised a signal when she arrived. With a few moments to spare, Wichi gravitated to the microscope. This was his escape from mundane problems as he explored the world of red blood cells carrying their precious cargo of oxygen throughout the body. Odd-shaped cells with blisters caught his eye. He raised his head from the lenses and wrinkled his forehead. This phenomenon represented an unusual finding. A rap sounded, and he peeked at the clock— fifteen minutes had passed. Yoya arrived and ended the moment of exhilaration. The instant he opened the door, she rushed toward him, huffing and puffing. The impeccable stylist now had a bouffant hairdo, with eggshells stuck among hair shafts as if a bird had nested on top. Half-dried eggs splotched her face and wet yolks soiled the "Yoya Salon" black smock. She stopped and waved a finger, her long, red nail quivered in the air. "Look at what these disgusting bearded idiots have done to me."

"Been in an egg fight?"

Her hands trembled. "First, I need to wash my face." Olga handed a towel, led her into the restroom, then helped her onto the exam table. She was still shaking when Wichi queried what happened. "Two soldiers burst in, pointing guns at my customers and me." She panted again. "They asked if I owned the beauty salon. When I said yes, they called me a Batistiana. A few of my clients may have been for Batista, but I wasn't political." She told him there was no doubt the militia came because a colorist she fired for stealing had tattled.

"Why the eggs?"

She sobbed as she described how the soldiers took from the shelf a bowl of eggs used for facials. While one held her face, the other cracked them in his hand and dripped the slime over her head and body. They broke the rest on the mirrors and windows. "The men said my shop belonged to the government, and I'd better never style another Batistiana, or they'd cut off my hair."

"Take it easy, it's over now. Let's get you relaxed." After giving her a sedative, he sat at his desk while she rested on the table. Half an hour later, when he returned to check on her, she said they needed to talk. "Sure."

"Not in here." She pulled him into the private office and closed the door.

"How's Teo?"

"Fine, I guess, but a son who ignores me and never calls." She wiped an eye. "Remember his best friend, Pedro Pedral?"

Wichi nodded. "His father telephoned the other night." She paused and tapped a finger to her lips. "Everything I say is secret information." He lifted an eyebrow. "Teo's in Miami now, part of a guerrilla force to invade Cuba and end the communist regime." Señor Pedral told her that before Eisenhower left office, he channeled thirteen million dollars to the CIA for training Cuban patriots.

"So he and the Americans will fight Castro?" She told him no. Kennedy agreed to continue with the invasion plans and supply weapons and train the exiles, but no American troops would participate. "A covert affair," he said, "just what Cuba needs to kick Fidel's butt."

Yoya began hyperventilating when she mentioned that Teo and Pedro were boys and didn't have the experience to fight. She pounded on his shoulders. "My only son—they will kill him."

Wichi clutched her icy hands. "Teo's twenty-five and a man." He gave her a cup of water. "Are they training in the US?" She shook her head and said that Pedral mentioned a remote region in Guatemala. Wichi knew ever since Teo was young he had an explosive, fearless personality. "He has the spunk to get rid of Castro."

"Can't help but worry." She rose to her feet and wobbled. "I must shampoo my hair and wash my clothes."

"What a rough day," Wichi said. "Go home, lock your door, and rest. Keep me posted."

The clock showed three-thirty, and Colonel García always appeared on time for his appointment. Wichi had thirty minutes to relax. No sooner was Yoya on her way, than Olga asked to leave early. He wondered if something was amiss. She told him nothing urgent, but her husband wanted her home. "Go on, I'm okay here." The office was quiet except for an occasional croak of the one remaining frog. The blister cell he'd seen earlier continued to captivate his imagination. Leafing through several medical journals, he found no articles to describe this finding. It might be something worthwhile to further investigate. He closed the publications after a sound at the door. The colonel and his son had arrived.

"Buenas tardes, Doctor."

Wichi shook his hand. "How are you, Albertito?"

The lad pointed to his neck. "My throat hurts."

Wichi escorted both to the examining room and questioned the father about his son's symptoms. García said he had trouble swallowing and coughed at night. He took a wooden tongue depressor and shined a light into the youngster's mouth, then examined his chest and abdomen. Wichi patted his shoulder and asked him to feed the last remaining frog. He nodded and ambled to the bathtub. He led García to his private office and informed him that Albertito needed a tonsillectomy.

"Is that dangerous because he has beta thalassemia?"

"It's riskier because of anemia and the possibility of postoperative bleeding, but without the procedure the infection may spread to the bloodstream." The colonel clutched his forehead in his hands for several moments. Wichi had not witnessed a previous display of emotion from this military man. García asked when the boy needed surgery. "It's not an emergency right now. We can get him over this episode, but future infections will be harder to combat with drug shortages." Wichi stood up and motioned for the colonel to inspect his pharmacy. The man's jaw dropped when he saw the few remaining drugs in stock, and his face paled after hearing blood banks had short supplies. Wichi placed a hand on his arm. "I will do everything in my power for your son with what medicine and supplies are available."

"Gracias, Doctor, and I likewise will do whatever it takes to give my son the best care."

The bathroom door shut. Albertito returned and tugged on his father's uniform. "Can we go home now?" He said they'd leave soon. Wichi sensed García had more to say. He knew the boy loved baseball and told him there was a sports magazine in the waiting room with an article on Minnie Minoso, the famous baseball player, called the "Cuban Comet." The youngster's eyes brightened; he smiled and stepped to the front office.

The colonel shut the door. "I didn't realize how much medical shortages are impacting your practice."

"Because of Castro's Soviet ties," Wichi said, "the US no longer ships drugs and supplies to Cuba, and my patients suffer, along with the deterioration of my personal life." He complained that his former housekeeper reported him to the Committee, saying he plotted against the government. The soldier lowered his head and remarked that Committees were necessary for the success of the Revolution. "Colonel, I'm aware you're in a tough position, sorry to unload my frustrations on you."

"We have many cases against the government," García said, "but I know you aren't counterrevolutionary." He stood and paced in front of the desk as though he debated whether to continue.

Wichi took out a handkerchief and wiped his forehead. "Colonel, you're worrying me."

"That's not my intention—to add to your aggravations," he said. "Comandante Fidel Castro has requested from us a list of physicians considered useful for the regime, and those individuals may not exit the island."

"Am I one of those people?" García nodded. "How long do I have?" The colonel wasn't sure, but they planned to enforce it soon. He emphasized the strict confidentiality of the information. The color drained from Wichi's head as he shook the colonel's hand and thanked him for the tip.

"Albertito awaits me," he said as he went to get his son, and they left the office. Wichi ran a hand through his hair, sat back, and formed a fist. First, Yoya came and said the CIA had plans for an invasion to overthrow Castro—good news. Next, Colonel García divulged he was on Castro's watch list for doctors—terrible news. When Fidel's people reached his name, he'd never leave the island, and that spelled disaster. To prevent it meant a quick decision before the window of opportunity closed.

As he passed Olga's desk, a letter from Key West caught his attention. He grabbed a pair of scissors, cut the envelope, and read.

> *Dear Doctor Barreras,*
> *It's with great joy to write these words. I am no longer married to the church but to Wong Kim. Expressions cannot convey my gratitude to you for your help in my*

time of need. My warmest regards to your precious family
and to Modesta.

Sincerely,
Bernadette Kim

The reference to Modesta drew a sneer, but the escape to Key West smacked him between the ears—God does work miracles.

THIRTY-THREE

Keep Kissing Me

Playa Neighborhood
February 24, 1961

After nine o'clock on a sunlit Friday morning, Wichi chewed the last piece of cheese in the fridge and rinsed the dish in the sink. He paced the kitchen floor, and the thought of leaving Cuba resonated in his mind. Now was the time to get off the pot since the practice had nose-dived with government regulations and drug shortages. He stepped outside and took a deep breath of the fresh tropical breeze.

Botín's whinny broke the silence. Alone for a change, the urge grabbed him to ride the horse around the neighborhood. The animal was docile and thin, a poor substitute for the high-spirited muscular stallions he relished riding, but he provided an opportunity to divert thoughts of the dismal future that brewed ahead. He walked the sluggish horse to the front yard, mounted him, and plodded across the street to the overgrown philodendron patch. Earlier in the week, the children spotted an iguana crawling there. An instant flashback of the exhilarating ride on Camagüey, years before at Pepe Fontana's farm, occurred as he glimpsed the reptile's tail. Here lay the possibility for action. He turned Botín to the left, leaned forward toward his ear, and said, "See that lizard." The horse snorted, reared his head, and trotted through the field. "Now we're moving." Botín raced to the edge of the lot, but the moment he stepped back onto the short grass, the lazy saunter resumed. He patted the horse's neck and whispered how much he'd miss him if they had to go. While meandering through several empty lots, he contemplated telling OP the disturbing news that he was on Castro's watch list—preventing doctors from leaving the island. Many uncertainties swam through his mind. He hoped for an invasion to overthrow Castro, but it may not happen, or worse, what if it weren't successful? That meant lost lives, his nephew's included.

Botín balked and indicated the ride was over, so they clumped back to the house, and the clip-clopping came to a halt at OP's space in the carport. He dismounted and tied the horse to a post. As he bent over to pick up a garden hose, he heard Mr. Crawley's voice. "Saw you riding earlier, old chap. Planned to give you a bell but couldn't wait to tell you we're going away."

"Where?"

"Miami. The dodgy circumstances in Cuba have Carina and me pigeonhearted. The jolly good times in Havana are over."

"Hate to see you go." His heart sank. Mr. Crawley was a good neighbor and a dear friend, but the Brit had seen the outside world, and it was surprising he hadn't left sooner. Cuba had sunk to the level the rats were jumping ship. "When will you leave?"

"Just waiting for the blokes at the embassy to issue exit

visas, and they know they have us by the bollocks." He paused and massaged the back of his neck. "Don't mean to poke in your affairs, but have you decided to call it quits?" Wichi interlocked his fingers, rubbed thumbs, and explained his position was more complicated. Crawley gave a reassuring pat on the shoulder. He thanked the Brit, shook hands, and stated he'd see him later. "It will jolly well work out. Cheerio."

Crawley left, and OP zoomed into the carport and stopped behind Botín. "Why's that animal tied here?"

"I rode him this morning." With a finger pointed at her, he said, "You're driving too fast, why the hurry?"

She got out of the car and stretched her back. "I'm disgusted at the incompetence of this government." He was too– –*why the dismay?* Reaching into the auto, she pulled out a paper bag and dangled it in front of him. He saw a chicken leg and bag of rice and made a face—*so what?* She narrowed her eyes. "I'll have you know, I stood in queue at the bodega for an hour in the hot sun to get these measly groceries. Vaquita was behind us in a tug-of-war with another neighbor because she had a fatter drumstick in her sack." He chuckled. Everyone knew the reputation of the "little cow" for aggressive behavior. To make things worse, OP told him there was talk of the government rationing food. It meant one pound of black beans and rice for the family every two weeks.

"That's when Castro begins his starvation program."

Her chin dropped as she shook her head in disgust. Sweat dripped onto her rumpled blouse. She begged to leave this hopelessness. He took OP by the hand, led her into the study, and shut the door. He said Castro had plans to stop him from leaving the country. "This is serious," she said as her eyes popped open. He stressed they must apply for visas as quickly as possible. She threw up her hands. "Let's hope and pray we get them. I can't take any more setbacks." She sniveled. "I need a shower." Wichi walked to the foyer and heard Botín whinny. The horse was ready to be stabled and fed.

Lizzi paced outside the bathroom before pounding on the door. "Mami, come quick, something's wrong with Sashita." She appeared with a towel in her hair and asked what the problem was. "When I removed the dirty newspaper, the bird went crazy and hit her head on the swing." Mami's voice weakened. "Now Sashita's not moving." She threw the towel on the floor and rushed into the kitchen. She lifted the canary and placed its breast to her ear.

"There's a chirp. I heard it." She pulled Lizzi closer and asked her to listen.

"No, Sashita's dead."

"She can't be." Tears raced along Mami's cheeks. "She's gone, my firstborn feathered child. What will I do?" A silence fell. Lizzi hugged her and wondered why losing a bird meant so much when she still had Rosita and them.

Wichi awakened from a short siesta and grabbed a sandwich before leaving for work. He stood at the patio door, amazed to see OP and the children gathered around stacked stones in the backyard. She knelt at the head of the altar and muttered something. *Is she loca?* Didi spotted him, came running, and asked him to join them. "What's your mother doing?" He was told Sashita died, and they were having a funeral; his eyes turned in a circle. "When the service is over, tell her I'm at the office." He kissed his daughter goodbye. *Two birds gone, and one to go.*

A few raindrops fell from the darkened sky as Wichi drove out of the neighborhood. By the time he reached Quinta Avenida, buckets of water covered the windshield. He flipped on the wipers, the right one screeched across the glass—another repair job for Rey. The wind blew hard, and the ocean churned up beside the Malecón. A massive, arching wave engulfed the car. He gripped the steering wheel and with squinted eyes tried to discern the middle line. The Coronet hydroplaned to the left. Hitting the brakes was out of the question; he might skid into the wall and flip. Best solution that came to mind was foot off the gas and ease back to the right. It worked, and the car returned to the proper lane. *Whew, not dead yet.* The turnoff to Vedado was only a block away. Heavy rain and lightning and thunderclaps still lingered when he arrived at the office. Since his umbrella was at home, he took his medical coat, threw it over his head, and made a dash to the door. Olga greeted him. "Doctor, you're soaked to the bone." She fetched a towel. He thanked her and said she didn't have to come to work today. "I'll be here until one of us leaves, but I want to inform you that my husband has applied for exit visas." He said he'd miss her but added that departing Cuba was the right thing to do.

"Is anyone on the schedule?" he asked. Olga shook her head. The afternoon appointment had canceled, and she left.

The clock showed 2:00 p.m. He strode to the private office, cleaned out his wet pockets, and laid his wallet on the desk to dry. He shed the drenched clothes, hung them on a towel bar, and put on an old pair of surgical scrubs. Many problems aggravated his life: the invasion, the watch list, food rationing, children wearing red scarves, violence, and medical shortages. He had to leave Cuba but needed connections in the US. Sitting behind the desk, he stared at the fluorescent lights. The room was quiet—too quiet, so he turned on the radio to liven the place and found a station playing his favorite songs.

The broadcaster announced, "For romantics out there, we have Pérez Prado and His Orchestra with this famous love song." The music began, and soon he hummed to the alluring tune. "Bésame . . . hmm . . . hmm . . . mucho." Then, as if a thunderbolt struck, the perfect solution came to mind. He and OP danced to that tune on December 30, 1958. Doctor Melmont from Miami invited them to the Tropicana Club. He was the vital contact needed in the States. According to Colonel García, a narrow window of time remained before Castro closed Cuba for him, but how could he reach the doctor? *Aah, Melmont gave me a business card. Where is it?* His heart fluttered as he opened each drawer in the desk—nada. *Now the lab.* He searched every nook with no luck. Beads of sweat formed on his forehead. He must find the calling card. It was a grueling task, so he sat to ponder the location. Slowly his focus shifted to the wallet on top of the desk. *It must be here.* He pulled out the clump of wet cards and began peeling them apart. A shudder seized his body when the soaked paper stuck together and obliterated the print. One by one he meticulously separated each card. His hands quivered as he lifted the last two and saw a faint RICHARD MELMONT, MD. He must now salvage the address. With a fingernail on the margin of the paper, he gently peeled away the other card. The number 5 appeared, then 4, 3, 6. Now the street number: 1 . . . 2 . . . 5 . . ., a "th" and "Str." Finally, enough information: 5436 125th Street, Miami, Florida. He kissed the card then wiped an eye on his sleeve. He reached for his favorite blue ink pen, took out a piece of paper, and wrote a letter.

> *Dear Doctor Melmont,*
>
> *I trust you and your family are well. If you recall, we met in Havana at the 1958 Hematology Meeting. The situation here worsens by the hour, and we need to leave the country as soon as we have visas. If my family and I can get to Miami, I will appreciate your helping me find a job. I look forward to seeing you again.*
>
> *Respectfully yours,*
> *Luis M. Barreras, MD*

After placing the folded letter inside the addressed and stamped envelope, he lowered it into the medical bag. A good feeling warmed his body—he'd taken the first step to vacate this godforsaken place.

The drive home along the Malecón was exhilarating. A rainbow over the water further lifted his spirits while pondering thoughts of Doctor Melmont and life in the United States. Pulling into his driveway, he saw Mr. Crawley watering purple bougainvillea bushes. The Brit motioned him over. "Cómo estás, Mr. Crawley?"

"Hunky-dory." He turned off the faucet. "Bloody good news to tell. We received our visas today and leave for Miami next Tuesday."

"That's wonderful." He placed his hand on Crawley's shoulder. "We will miss you and Carina." Just then he remembered the letter and told Crawley there was something for him. He rushed to the car, grabbed his bag, and returned.

"Hope you're not planning on giving me the needle, old chap."

Wichi tittered. "No, what I'm giving you may be an opportunity for us to live in the US."

"Do tell, what is it?"

"A letter to Doctor Richard Melmont in Miami. Hate to impose, but can you deliver it to him and do the translation?"

Crawley took the note. "Doctor Barreras, I will get this letter handed over and read to the bloke, or my name isn't Timothy Jeremiah Crawley the Third."

Wichi snickered. "So that's your name. You never told me."

"Bloody well didn't matter. You couldn't pronounce it."

Both men exploded in laughter until they had to wipe tears from their eyes. They embraced. "Toodle-pip, old man"

"Adiós, Mister Timot . . . Timoteo."

"Jolly well told you, yes?"

"Caramba, I need to brush up my English." Wichi turned and ambled home. He smiled, tossed his medical bag into the air, and caught it. Lizzi poked her head out the front door and yelled it was time to eat. He laid the bag at the door and sprinted into the kitchen. OP stood in front of the stove, stirring a pot of rice. "Looks gummy," he said and received a dirty glare. He grabbed her hand. "Let's dance."

"What? Who will cook dinner?"

"Doesn't matter. It's stuck to the pan."

He whirled her several times, dipped her, and said, "Bésame." She kissed him. "Bésame mucho." He kissed her twice.

She gazed into his eyes and squeezed his hand. "Keep kissing me, you silly fool."

THIRTY-FOUR

Never Forget Brigade 2506

CIA Trax Base, Guatemala
March 1961

Bullets whizzed above Teo's body as he crawled through the dirt on his elbows, raw by now, but he had gone halfway through the obstacle course. His partner, Pedro, behind him hollered. Barbed wire had caught the back of his shirt, and a bloodstain showed through the fatigues. "Keep your freaking head low, Pedral, here comes another round." Drenched in sweat, he managed a reverse crawl to reach his friend.

"Man, get me untangled." Teo took a knife, cut the snagged shirt, and lifted the barb out of his skin. The puncture wound was a half-inch deep, located above Pedro's shoulder blade. He pulled a bandana from his pocket and applied pressure. Just then another bullet nicked the wire above their heads. "Damn, that one nearly got us," cried Pedro. "Don't let me die here in Guatemala."

"Vamos, we have to complete this maneuver or face hell." They slithered toward the finish. Teo could tell his buddy was in excruciating pain but didn't complain since they volunteered for this mission, and no training rounds would stop them. "Come on, Pedral, keep moving. I see the end."

He helped Pedro through the last ten yards out of the barbed wire and into the clearing. He struggled to his feet before holding out a hand to help his friend. "We damn well dodged those bullets."

"Yeah, and we're not even in Cuba."

Teo put his arm around Pedro and took him to the barracks. When he told his buddy they were going to Concha infirmary, he became suspicious and questioned if Teo was a real doctor.

"What if I'm not? You're in no position to complain."

"Shit, man, I don't know if you graduated."

"Doctor Concha at your service. Now shut up and let me clean the wound." He took iodine and rubbed it hard in the gash. Pedro winced and asked if they taught bedside manners in medical school. Teo lifted the side of his mouth and winked. "Only with women." He bragged he was the top student in the class. He bandaged the injury, pointed Pedro to the upper bunk, and issued a warning not to fall on him. Teo dug into his green pouch, took out a nude Marilyn Monroe T-shirt, put it on, and patted his chest, "She can drop on me any day, boobs first." As he lay exhausted from the day's rigorous training, no matter how tough, he longed to kick Fidel's butt. The pleasant thought closed his eyes.

The sergeant's sharp bang on the metal door brought the recruits' feet to the floor at 0500, followed by a race to the latrine, dress, make the beds, and prepare for inspection. By 0530, they marched to the mess hall, chowed down bananas and mangoes, and slurped black coffee. At 0600 everyone snapped to attention. "Trainees, we will issue your Brigade 2506 patch designating this esteemed unit. We have honored the founder, Carlos Rodriguez Santana, dog tag 2506, who fell to his death while establishing Trax base."

The exiles shouted in unison, "Long live Brigade 2506."

Teo pumped his fist in the air. After being dismissed from formation, CIA Officer Nelson stopped him. "Meet me in tent number 34."

"Yes, Sir."

Pedro looked at him. "I think the principal has called you to the office."

"Yeah."

He laughed. "Man, you're always in trouble."

Teo strode into the CIA personnel hut. A dozen men sat at their stations, and a skinny guy with rimless glasses pointed him to Officer Nelson's desk. He marched there and stood at attention. Nelson offered him a seat. Behind on the wall was a board containing maps of Cuba with many red circles around military installations. He shuffled through papers in a folder bearing Teo's name. "Brigadista Concha, I see here you speak English and graduated from medical school in France. That's why we chose you as our Brigade Doctor to treat injuries during the assault."

"Sir, I'm honored."

"You are a Cuban patriot and trustworthy. Our unit needs men with your conviction. We are promoting you to the rank of captain, and you will have access to sensitive information concerning the mission." His eyes filled with an inner glow. He thanked the officer and said he'd accept the position, provided they granted him a request." Nelson nodded. Teo specified that as the brigade medic, he intended to fight alongside the other brigadistas.

"So, you're a fighter and a doctor."

"It's in my blood, Sir." Nelson accepted the proposition. Teo asked the date of the invasion. The officer said it remained classified and depended on completing the exiles' training and receiving promised air power. Teo's eyes lit when he heard of airplanes since he had flying experience. "What are we getting?" Nelson said there were fifteen B-26 bombers and several transports. President Kennedy ordered Cubans to pilot the planes, not Americans. Landing ships were the responsibility of the CIA, but the brigadistas might have to swim to shore.

The man smiled. "We'll try to get you close enough to stay ahead of the sharks."

Teo hesitated, then told him he hoped the agency knew they were up against a seasoned guerrilla fighter, and the reply was they'd done their homework. "Then you're aware we need more airplanes and equipment to defeat this bastard." Nelson said the CIA planned to have brigadistas ready and able to pull off a successful invasion. They were fortunate to have thirty-nine Cuban pilots as recruits. Teo nodded. "It won't be easy."

"You bet. Dismissed."

He gave a crisp hand salute.

The next day Teo reported to Officer Nelson for another briefing. He gasped when told that Kennedy changed the invasion site to the Bay of Pigs. The spot represented nothing but swamps and mosquitoes. A buddy had said Castro used to fish there. Located only ninety miles southeast of Havana, Fidel knew the beach well, plus the local people admired him. Lots of coral having the reputation of dog's teeth lined the bay and made amphibious landing dangerous. Nelson nodded and said, "The president won't allow intervention by American forces, so it's a risky and challenging mission. But with men of your caliber and our assistance, you will defeat Castro and claim back your country."

Teo sat for a moment and realized Kennedy's action put their butts against the wall. He doubted the president's commitment to support them. Teo stood up and stared at Nelson. "They've given us the short stick, but you can bet your ass the brigadistas will shed their last drop of blood to see Fidel gone."

"Ten-hut," the drill sergeant shouted, and Brigade 2506 came to attention.

The head CIA instructor stepped in front of the troops. "At ease, soldiers. You have completed the agency protocol training for this important mission, and we now have the long-awaited details for the invasion to move forward." Teo punched Pedro and said they were on the way. He had the bullet with Fidel's name on it. Raúl Castro was Pedro's target. The colonel continued. "Phase One—Cuban pilots take out as many of Castro's combat planes as possible. Phase Two—Bomb Fidel's remaining aircraft so there won't be any left when you hit the beaches." Teo slapped his friend, hit his own chest, and said they'd be there. "Phase Three," the instructor said, "is the invasion—Brigade 2506 will go in by sea and beat the hell out of Castro's soldiers on the ground." The men clenched their fists and vowed to free Cuba. The sergeant dismissed the troops.

Officer Nelson asked Teo to come into his office and hear the latest information. The assault set for April 17 necessitated packing up Trax base and deploying the brigadistas to Nicaragua. From there CIA ships would transport them to the landing site. Their new code name was Operation Zapata. The officer placed his hand on Teo's shoulder. "I admire your courage and patriotism, son. Good luck."

Wichi had a hard time sleeping on the morning of April 14. His thoughts focused on what his sister, Yoya, said weeks earlier. Given her information of an imminent invasion, it was disconcerting if Fidel learned of the plans. He knew Yoya had reason to worry. At half-past seven he poured an espresso, turned on the radio, and listened for breaking news. OP joined him. He'd taken a sip when the broadcaster announced a midnight fire had destroyed El Encanto. Many people were injured, and one person found dead. Four days earlier a bomb exploded and broke windows in front of the department store. OP turned pale and said that her mother may be in danger since she lived nearby. She made a quick call and came back relieved that María Teresa was okay. Mindful of the serious nature of this latest event, Wichi intended to prepare his family in case a full-scale uprising occurred along with the invasion. A water supply was necessary, so he filled the bathtubs. If planes bombed the neighborhood, they needed protection. He and OP wrangled their large mattress off the bed and into the dining room, where they shoved it beneath the table. Then he dragged the children's bedding, lined it around the table legs, and explained they may be there a while.

Luisito dove onto the mattress. "Are we going to die?"

"Don't think so, mi niño."

Lizzi grabbed her favorite pillow and covered her face. "Papi, will a bomb fall on our house?"

He shook his head. "Hope not, we're just being careful."

On the morning of April 17, Wichi awoke to the sound of explosions in the distance. OP and the children remained asleep in the shelter while he tiptoed into the kitchen. Best to let the family continue sleeping. He made coffee and contemplated what might be happening. The radio announcer said that B-26s had bombed Cuban airfields and military bases. Castro condemned these as American-led attacks and bragged they didn't destroy his air force. The disheartening news sickened Wichi, and he was sure Castro had moved the planes, but he hoped brigadistas on the ground prevailed. The drone of airplanes overhead subdued the voice of the announcer and signaled the attack he hoped for—yet dreaded. He ran back to the family.

Lizzi wriggled under the blanket. "Planes are flying over our house."

Didi covered her ears. "I don't like gunfire."

They huddled under the table. Wichi grasped the trembling girls. Luisito remained motionless in OP's arms. Planes thundered over the house, one after the other. No blasts—at

least they weren't dropping bombs. By nine o'clock the roar of
the aircraft and the shooting subsided. He told them to stay
put while he went to a window—no movement outside the
house. He cracked open the front door and poked out his head.
A creepy silence abounded in the neighborhood. Didi came up
behind and asked if they won the war. He wrapped an arm
around her shoulder. "Let's find out from the radio."

"We're sardines packed in here," said Teo. The ship filled with
brigadistas approached the Bay of Pigs. A crunch sounded on
the bottom of the boat. "Damn, knew we'd hit coral before
getting closer to shore." The CIA officer told the troops they
couldn't get nearer, and they had to leave the boat on rubber
rafts and then tread water to the beach. Teo and Pedro got out
with their weapons in the air. "Keep your rifle dry, Pedral, you
got my back." Other Cuban exiles reached the beach ahead of
them. Machine-gun fire dropped men on the sand. A plane
flew over and mowed down more of his buddies. "That's one
of Castro's planes, not our air cover!" He motioned for Pedro
to follow him to the right shoreline since gunfire was coming
from the other direction. After touching ground he glanced to
the left and saw brigadistas landing with arms extended
upward. "I'm sure as hell not surrendering; we can make it to
cover." He and Pedro hid behind the brush just as a fireball lit
up the bay. He yanked the binoculars off his belt. "Holy shit,
the American tanker's sinking like a rock. Now we don't have
aviation fuel."

Pedro's face blanched. "Look, man, they're nailing our
landing ships and supply vessels. We're doomed."

Teo shook him. "Not if I can help it."

The two slogged through the swamp, waist-deep in murky soup, swatting swarms of mosquitoes that gnawed their faces. Pedro held out a hand with at least a half dozen squashed bloodsuckers in his palm. Teo grabbed his pistol and fired a shot. The bullet zipped by Pedro's head, and he screamed, "Are you trying to kill me?" Then he pivoted to see thrashing in the bog beside him. The brown water turned red, and a tail six feet long flopped on the surface before it quit moving. "A croc—headed right for me."

"Yep."

"Guess I owe you another one."

"You buy the next round of beers."

Higher terrain allowed better maneuvering through the undergrowth. Teo stopped dead in his tracks when he spotted a soldier ahead. Lifting his rifle, he took aim and prepared to fire. The man shouted into the microphone. "This is Brigade 2506; we need air support. Enemy tanks are on the ground. Do you read?"

Teo lowered his weapon, didn't want to shoot a brigadista radio operator. He crawled along and moved closer. The noise of the rustling brush startled the soldier, and he whirled, his gun cocked. "Wait, I'm with you." The man holstered the weapon. "Did you get through to anyone?" He said it was unlikely, the battery was low. Teo smacked a hand against his head. "Castro has us by the balls."

"Even worse," the operator said, "our supply ship with ammo and supplies was sunk. We've been hung out to dry."

"The assholes knew we were coming."

The radio crackled, and the soldier on the other end

sounded an alarm. "Brigadistas, mission's finished. Americans canceled air support—retreat."

Teo scoffed as he ran into the underbrush. "It's not over; and don't forget, men—we're Brigade 2506!"

THIRTY-FIVE

Circle, Sadness, and an Empty Trailer

Havana, Cuba
July 25, 1961

"Hurry girls," Yoya said as she dabbed tears pooling in her eyes. "We have little time for the viewing." Didi answered they were coming. The sisters got out of the Coronet and darted inside her car. Wichi leaned against the sedan and asked how she was dealing with her emotions. Tía clutched the steering wheel, lowered her head, and said, "Barely making it, and I'm horrified to look at him."

Wichi consoled Yoya with a pat on the cheek. "In the meantime, I'm going to the office. See you later in the afternoon."

She drove away and wondered how to endure seeing Teo. The car slowed as it approached Fuentes funeral home, and she sobbed. "What's wrong, Tía Yoya?" Lizzi asked.

"The funeral for my husband was there and now—Teo."

"But he's not dead," Didi said.

"Sí, mi niña, but they've had him in that awful prison for three months, and who knows what Castro will do to him." As she drove toward the jail, her sadness turned to anger. Kennedy had promised air cover for the brigadistas, then at the last minute abandoned them. Her son's dreams were shattered, and after risking his life, a Cuban prison was now his home. She must face the heartbreak of trying to see him behind bars, four stories up from the parking lot. The car ahead halted, and she slammed on the brakes. Lizzi stuck her head out of the window and said that soldiers were stopping automobiles. Yoya sighed and wondered what to expect. When the vehicle in front moved on, she pulled up, and a bearded soldier lowered his rifle and glared through the window. Lizzi and Didi covered their faces. Yoya asked what he wanted.

"Checking for anti-revolutionaries."

"See any here, mister?"

"Don't get smart, lady. Move it."

Furious that these monsters stopped her, she drove ahead. If she missed seeing Teo, she'd come back and let them have it. "Tía, you disliked that soldier, didn't you?" Lizzi said.

"They're nothing but animals."

"Havana is ugly. I hate living here."

Didi leaned forward and propped her elbows on the seatback. "Tía, do you think Papi can get us out of Cuba?" She said he might surprise them. Lizzi asked how long they would keep Teo locked in jail. Yoya didn't know but was glad he wasn't in La Cabaña. Che Guevara made sure nobody there came out alive. They reached the prison, and soldiers directed them to a parking lot. A guard waved her forward. The man stood beside the car and yelled to stop and get out. Tía warned the girls to do what he said.

The soldier grabbed her purse, ransacked it, and threw it on the ground. "Gimme that sack," he said to Lizzi. She gripped it to her chest and told him it was for her cousin. "Did you bring food?" he asked and yanked the bag. "Yum, mamoncillos, haven't had any in years."

Yoya touched Lizzi's angry face, smiled, then turned to the man, her jaw tightened. "Eat them but take me to my son." The guard walked them twenty feet and stopped. A sign read: DO NOT GO BEYOND THIS POINT. Another soldier told her to stay there with the others. While they waited, men munched on the fruit.

Lizzi pulled on her arm. "They're eating Teo's mamoncillos. What are we going to do?"

"Nada, mi niña." A soldier approached and asked her son's name. "Teo Concha," she said. He picked his teeth with the blade of a pocketknife and said traitors with last names A through C soon would be called. Yoya squinted at the four-story balcony. "Can I hug him?"

"No favors for you. Your son betrayed his country."

She sobbed and held her nieces' hands. "Señor, my far vision isn't good. Por favor, let me get closer." He jerked her back and barked to bring binoculars in the future. She pounded on his chest. "He's not a criminal." The soldier shoved her to the side and warned he'd have her arrested. The girls put their arms around her. Soon a loud man's voice hollered out each detainee's name. The three moved closer to others in the crowd, held hands, and formed a ring. When they announced a loved one's name, the family proceeded to the center and waved while everyone else remained in the circle.

They blared out As and Bs and began calling the Cs.

"Coloma," the guard shouted.

A tall man ran to the middle and yelled, "Manolito, your mother and I send our love. We're praying for your release." He sobbed and returned to the edge.

Yoya held her breath for Teo's name. "Concha," the guard shouted.

Tía and the cousins hurried to the center. Didi and Lizzi twirled colorful scarves, waved, and said, "Teo, Teo, we're here."

Yoya placed one hand over her trembling lips and raised the other. Teo was far away. At that distance, she envisioned how gaunt he'd become and imagined a smile on his face. He waved his hand. *Is it quivering?* Grateful that he was still alive, she extended her arms upward, and with a cracking voice said, "I love you, Teo."

A woman tapped her shoulder. "Señora, my boy is next, please move aside." Yoya stiffened. Didi tried to pull her away, but she remained centered in the ring. The woman yelled, "Guard, remove this lady or I'll miss my son."

A soldier lifted her by the shoulder and dragged her outside the circle. "Señora, if you don't leave the premises, we'll send you to Mazorra."

A severe stomach pain ensued, and she rushed to a grassy patch and vomited. A man handed her a handkerchief. "Gracias, Señor, I'm better now." She walked toward the car and motioned for the girls to follow. A soldier gave an order to move her automobile. After this nightmare she decided not to fight these monsters anymore. Like a beaten dog, she drove away. The day was hot and wore on her body. She reached for a scarf and wiped a soaked forehead. Lizzi questioned her condition. She sobbed and then said, "I can't live without

Teo." Driving farther she sniffled. Given the opportunity, she'd shoot Fidel for ruining their lives. "Niñas," she said as she glanced back at them, "Castro made promises to make Cuba better, but he lied, and we swallowed the bait."

"What's Mazorra?" Lizzi said.

"An insane asylum."

"Are they going to take you there?"

"No way, they have to kill me first."

Wichi examined his last patient for the afternoon and then called the international visa office. A woman answered and questioned his destination—Venezuela, Panama, or Honduras? "None of those countries, señorita, I want to apply for five visas to the US."

"We're processing thousands of US visas now. You must fill out the application in person." He tidied the desk and drove to the government building. As he filled out the information, a drop of sweat fell from his brow onto the paper and smeared the ink, fortunately not his name. He finished the paperwork, then remembered something important— pick up the girls. Poor Yoya, he knew visiting Teo was tough, and he wanted to be there when they arrived at the salon. He rushed from the visa office, cranked the engine, and pulled in just ahead of her. A tear-stained face welcomed him; he took her trembling hand and helped her out of the car.

"Did you see Teo?"

"From a distance—he looked so thin." With that she broke into tears. "I'm afraid he'll die in prison." Wichi held her until she stopped crying, and he and the girls walked her upstairs to the apartment. Once she calmed down, he kissed her forehead and ushered Lizzi and Didi to the car.

On the drive back home Lizzi said, "That nasty guard at the prison ate Teo's mamoncillos." It didn't surprise him since he knew the militia lacked any feelings for the visitors.

"Papi, Tía mentioned we might leave Havana." Didi said.

"Nothing certain," he answered.

The car turned onto 194 Street, and they neared the house. Lizzi shouted that a horse trailer was in the driveway. "That's Uncle Nicolás talking to Mami," said Didi. "What's happening?" Wichi cleared his throat and said he came to get Botín. "Does it mean we're leaving Cuba?" He told her not to jump to conclusions. "But why is Botín going?"

"Because we can't get hay to feed him." He stopped the car, and the two girls dashed out, hugged their uncle, and looked inside the empty trailer. Wichi greeted Nicolás and left to get the horse. He ambled to the shed and bridled him. Botín whinnied as he patted the animal's dusty mane and fought back a tear. "I have to send you away, ole horse. Thanks for that last good ride." He led him to the front of the house. Lizzi patted Botín's nose, kissed it, and said she'd miss him.

"Me too," said Luisito. "He was my first horse."

"Give him to Baltasar," Nicolás said, "he's driving for me today." The man took the reins; the horse bucked and snorted, then broke loose and sprinted through the philoden-dron field. Wichi brought his hands to his forehead. He didn't think Botín had a gallop left in him. Nicolás shouted for the driver to chase him. He ran after the horse but returned empty-handed and gasped for air.

OP rushed out of the house. "What happened, where's Botín?" Wichi said he raced away and wanted to be free, just like the rest of them. Pita came running and said she saw their horse loose on the street with no rider. He patted her on the head and thanked her.

"Dobin is next," Wichi said to Nicolás. "You're getting him back and not going home empty-handed."

Wichi trudged into the house and brought out the mastiff. OP turned to him and sobbed. "I can't do this." He told her they couldn't afford dog food and were lucky Nicolás wanted him. She stared at her uncle. "Don't even think of putting Dobin into that hot trailer. This dog gets to ride in the truck with the windows lowered." Lizzi stroked his brown face, kissed his massive head, and rubbed his gigantic paws. OP pointed a finger at Nicolás, "Don't feed him cheap food; he's used to gnawing beef bones from la Bodega." She led the mastiff inside the truck. "Dobin, you sit beside Baltasar." The driver complained the dog was too big and may cause a wreck. "I don't care. Dobin's used to a cool tile floor."

"Wait a minute," said Nicolás, "I'm not riding in the truck bed; my El Encanto trousers will get dirty."

OP glared at him. "Yes, you are. Swallow your stupid pride." Wichi chuckled as the locos fought it out. Nicolás turned to him, threw his hands in the air, and said she was impossible. OP ruffled Dobin's ears, kissed him, and ran bawling into the house.

"Since my Chihuahuas died, do you have any other animals to give me?" Nicolás said. This was a golden opportunity, so Wichi offered Apollo and Apache. "What will Ofelia Perfecta say?"

"Nothing you'd like to hear, and you'd better get them now before she comes outside again." The boxers came when he whistled. He petted them, and liquid welled in his eyes as the males jumped into the back of the truck. "Hurry and leave, I can't take this any longer." He watched the truck drive away, pulling an empty horse trailer—with a mastiff drooling out the front window and two boxers and a crazy uncle riding behind—Wichi didn't know whether to laugh or cry.

THIRTY-SIX

Vexatious Visas

Vedado Office
August 1, 1961

Wichi walked into the office that morning with one thing on his mind—exit visas. It had been seven days since he filed the applications and received no response. He called the visa place; the phone rang forever before someone lifted the receiver. "This is Doctor Luis Barreras. I'm checking on the status of five permits to the US."

"Just a moment." The line hummed while the woman had him on hold. Thoughts turned to his beloved homeland ravaged by a sinister force and his medical practice cut off at the knees. Optimism vanished after the failed invasion. A belch of the Russian sardines from breakfast made him nauseous. Twenty minutes passed. The lady must have forgotten he called. He tapped two fingers on the desk and bit his lip. As he continued holding, he noticed two half-hidden letters. He slashed one envelope with a penknife and read.

> *Dear Doctor Barreras,*
> *We received visas two days ago and will leave tomorrow for Mexico. Muchas gracias for eleven years*

working as your secretary. There are few doctors in Havana with your caring bedside manner.

Best wishes,
Olga

He was glad to have had a great assistant, and with an office in shambles, no need to replace her. As he cut the second envelope, the receiver sounded, "Hola," said a female voice. "Are you still there?"

"For sure."

"Doctor Barreras, a medical doctor—right?"

"Sí," he said—his gut wrenched. She told him the Barreras name had a red flag on the margin prohibiting issuance of the visas. "Why is a red flag interfering with my permits?"

"There's a glitch, Doctor, we have to remove the hindrance before issuing your papers."

"Connect me with your superior—now."

"You're talking to her and don't get snippy; it takes time to handle special cases." The phone clicked. *Damn!* Wichi clenched his jaw and considered escaping on a boat to Key West. He leaned back in Olga's chair. The second letter postmarked Miami, Florida, lay under a transparent paper weight. *Why haven't I seen this sooner?* As he tore open the envelope, his heart fluttered.

Esteemed Doctor Barreras,

I hope these words find you jolly well. Doctor Melmont was easy to locate and has the information. You made an impression on the bloke. Call him soon.

Toodle-oo,
Timothy Jeremiah Crawley III

Crawley delivered—a true friend. Melmont was the needed contact. Wichi entered the private office, and thoughts raced through his mind. This visa quest reeked disappointment, necessitating a backup plan. *What if the family goes first?* The Peter Pan airlift was a way to get the children out of Cuba, but he'd never allow them to live in foster homes in the US. Since the communists wanted only him, they'd issue four visas for the family to leave, and he'd find another way to escape. Living under the tyranny of Fidel Castro wasn't acceptable.

The phone rang. *News on the permits?* His hand shook as he picked up the receiver—Colonel García was on the line. "Doctor Barreras, Albertito has a fever and a sore throat." It sounded as if the boy's tonsillitis had flared again. The father's voice hesitated. "What can I do?" Wichi told him there weren't any antibiotics in the office.

"Let me call the hospital. I'm not sure what they have." He rang the dispensary and explained the dilemma. The pharmacist was an old friend and said he'd lose his job if caught, but he could pilfer a two-week supply of the drug without being noticed. Wichi called the colonel back and told him to meet in the hospital parking lot and he'd have Albertito's medicine. He hurried to the Coronet and headed along the street. It was unfortunate the boy was sick again so soon. He gasped—the black car was behind him; didn't matter though, he promised to deliver the meds to García. He soon reached the emergency entrance, and the mystery vehicle sped onward.

He picked up the pills, thanked the druggist, and met the colonel in the lot.

"Doctor, I can't thank you enough."

"This is only a two-week supply, and you're aware Albertito needs the tonsillectomy soon."

"Yes, I know. I'm working on it."

"He's a fine boy, and he will do well after the surgery." He glanced over the colonel's shoulder.

"What is it, Doctor?"

He paused and said, "Nothing important, just a car following me and trouble getting my visas."

García nodded. "It's a way of life in Cuba these days." They shook hands and he returned to the office.

Half an hour passed; a knock sounded on the door. To his surprise when he opened it, Rey and Sarita stood there smiling. "Come in." Rey hobbled inside on crutches. "What happened?" His former mechanic held on to his leg and said they shot him during the invasion. Wichi wanted to know if he marched with Castro's army. He said he fought in the squadron but did not shoot any brigadistas.

"Fidel doesn't want wounded soldiers, so I'm free." Wichi smiled and told Rey he was a good man. "Now, here's happy news," Rey said. "Sarita, show the doctor." Gorgeous emerald eyes sparkled as she flashed her wedding ring.

"Congratulations." He shook Rey's hand and gave her a kiss. "Hmm, that necklace looks familiar." It was her Nochebuena pearl choker, and she asked if he remembered that night. Wichi wiped away a tear and said he'd never forget the evening when they brought Pepe's scrumptious lechón to his house. It had been a long time since that wonderful celebration. He rubbed his hands together. "Rey, I have an interesting story—you helped turn a nun into a bride." He looked puzzled. "Sister Bernadette has a husband and lives in Key West."

"That's great. It was an awful night in Guanabo but worthwhile getting her out of there." He waited for a moment before asking, "Who'd she marry?" Both laughed when Wichi said Wong Kim.

"No kidding, love on the high seas—an ideal plot for a romance novel."

Sarita kissed her hubby. "Rey's a hero; he risked his life for the sister."

He hobbled over to his former boss and they embraced. Wichi told him that living out in the ranch could be dangerous and required four-legged protection. Rey asked if an ulterior motive brewed. "Caramba, you guessed right. Every hard-working farmer needs a fine dog."

"Sí, that's it." He snickered. "I guess a male boxer is still at home."

"No, but Diana is the best dog for your farm." Sarita asked if he was leaving Cuba.

"Everything is contingent upon getting visas." She wished him good luck, and Rey promised to take the dog. After the couple left, he returned to the lab and smiled. *Amid oppression, love conquers.* As he passed the bathroom, the last African clawed frog sat on the edge of the tub and croaked. He didn't need her for the amphibian pregnancy test, and she seemed itching to go. The slimy toad jumped to the window; he opened it and flicked her to the ground. "Stay out of Castro's sight, and you'll be free."

At four o'clock in the afternoon, the phone rang, and he lifted the receiver. A clap of thunder made the line crackle. "Hola, who's calling?" A woman's faint voice sounded. "What do you want?" A click—disconnected—*damn.* The telephone buzzed again. He yelled, "Hola."

"Doctor Barreras," the lady said, "come by today, your visas are ready." He dropped the handset while the woman kept talking.

"The visas, I got the visas!" He hung up the phone as the storm continued. Lightning and thunder shook the office. Glad that he wrapped his medical diploma in plastic, Wichi pocketed the precious item inside his raincoat, locked the door, and hustled to the car. He turned on the wipers and stared at the office—his medical practice was now history. The visa news sounded too good to be true. *Is it a trap?* He'd take the chance since he yearned to live in freedom. The weather improved by the time he reached the visa headquarters. He parked and hurried into the building. An armed soldier pointed to a long line across the room. A short bald fellow standing ahead asked his destination. "US," Wichi replied. The man said his family had to settle for Spain. An hour passed; he made his way to the counter, and a señorita requested the name. "Doctor Luis Barreras," he answered. She thumbed through the papers once, then twice. No Barreras surname on the list. His heart sank. *What is the matter?* Desperation motivated his mind to think hard. Since they flagged him, the visas must be elsewhere. "Por favor, check again, the lady on the phone said there was a red mark by my name."

"Oh, wait here." The young girl smacked her lips, left, and

soon returned with a crimson folder. Wichi grabbed it, tore it open, and kissed the five visas. Next stop—travel office to buy airline tickets. As he drove toward Playa, CUBA SÍ, YANKEES NO filled several billboards along the way. "Fools," he muttered. "These suckers have no clue what's in store for them."

The best news in years awaited the family. He parked the car and ran panting into the house. OP stirred soup while Didi folded laundry. Lizzi and Luisito sat at the kitchen table sobbing. "Qué Pasa?"

"He's dead," Lizzi said.

"Who's dead?"

"Botín."

"What happened?"

"Someone killed him," Didi said.

Wichi gasped. "Who says so?"

"Pita found Botín's bridle in the philodendron field. Her mother said a family nearby had no food, so they shot and cooked him." Lizzi wailed and Luisito wiped away a tear. The youngster questioned why people ate horses.

"Mi niño, when people are hungry, they eat many things to stay alive."

"But Botín was our pet," Lizzi said.

"I'm sad he's gone, but I have news that will make everybody happy." Didi asked what it was. "Visas to leave Cuba. Miami here we come."

OP yelled, "Gracias a Dios," and dropped the spoon into the sink. "Children, can you believe it?" Didi threw clothes in the air, jumped on the table, and danced. Lizzi and Luisito joined her and they held hands. OP hugged Wichi. "How did you do it?"

"It was a miracle."

"Are we riding in a boat the same as Sister Bernadette?" Lizzi asked. He laughed, patted her head, and said they had five Pan Am airline tickets. Within ten days they should be gone.

"Our first plane ride," Didi said.

Luisito's eyes sparkled. "I'm going to see real cowboys and Indians."

THIRTY-SEVEN

La Última Noche

Playa Neighborhood
August 10, 1961

Nine days passed since Wichi received the visas and purchased the airline tickets. OP remained undecided what to pack; a minuscule problem because the government only allowed one small bag per person. "I can't take much," she said.

"That's the whole idea. Castro wants us to leave everything behind."

She grumbled. "Two necklaces and earrings need little room," He told her Fidel prohibited taking expensive jewelry out of the country, but they may not confiscate her wedding ring because it didn't have large diamonds. And money— forget it. Castro only allowed five dollars. "I want to take a diamond ring Mother plans to give me and turn it around on Didi's finger to resemble a trinket." He agreed that was okay since they weren't concealing it. A guy in line at the visa office said a man taped a watch in his crotch, got caught, and they arrested him. Worse, a woman tried hiding a ring up her . . .

"Don't tell me more. I get the picture," she said and bent over to pet Diana. "Her ribs are showing because she's not getting sufficient food." Wichi told her it wasn't just the dog. With

Castro's rationing the whole family barely had enough to eat. Diana was lucky being the solo pet, or she'd be skin and bones. "You should have asked me first before you let Nicolás take Apollo and Apache."

"I did what was necessary. Rey's coming to get her today, and that leaves only one bird." Curiosity prompted his asking what was to become of her final feathered friend.

"Candelaria has agreed to keep my precious Rosita." A sob, then she wiped her nose. "How can I live without my dogs and birds?" He told her to forget the pets and focus on living in a free country. "Such pain to leave them," she said, "but I'd better pack now."

The animal woes bored him, so he left and went to the kitchen. Lizzi ran in carrying a cigar box. When he asked what was in it, she presented her swim medals and wanted to carry them on the plane. Her chin dropped after he explained there wasn't enough space in the bag. "Papi, can you help dig a hole?"

"Why?" She wanted to hide the medals. "Sí, let's go to the backyard." They marked off a spot; he dug a hole two feet deep, and they buried the box. "This is our secret place," he said. She smiled and hugged him. A glass of water quenched his thirst before ambling to the bedroom. OP had placed a photo album on the bed. He told her the soldiers wouldn't allow pictures to leave the country.

"I want to take my photographs, because they tell our family story."

"Fine, but don't cry when Castro's goons destroy them."

"They better not. I want our children to remember their heritage. If we have grandchildren, they need to know us."

He laughed and said they'd wonder why she had a weird name. "You're jealous because you're plain Wichi." She narrowed her eyes and wrapped the album with her nightgown.

Didi leaned her head into the room, "Papi, you said no hidden jewelry for the trip, but can I wear Abuela's small diamond earrings underneath my long hair?" He said she could. She approached him with a puzzled look on her face. "Who will live in our house when we're gone?" He replied folks like the neighbors next door. "Did you buy our home?" He nodded. "Then why can't we sell it so we have money to take with us?"

He smiled and stroked her face. "Under Castro's communism they now own our house, and we don't get one peso when we go."

Her cheeks reddened. "That's not fair. Can't you make them pay us something?"

"No, mi niña. Fidel's soldiers have guns, and they tell us what to do."

"I understand why you want to leave." Her maturity amazed yet saddened him. He'd rather she didn't grow up so fast.

A faint knock came from the door. Wichi opened it. Pita stood there and asked for Lizzi. He called, and she came running. "Hola, I'm sorry, I can't play, we're leaving tomorrow." Pita cried and gave her a hug. The little girl said she'd miss her friend. She sniveled and ran home.

"What a nice child," Wichi said. Lizzi told him that Pita had been a good neighbor since Rosie left. Tears shimmered in her eyes as she asked if there was an amiga for her in the

US "You'll have many friends." He tickled her neck until she giggled. "Let's have a cup of mango juice in the fridge."

OP trudged into the kitchen carrying Rosita's cage. "Did you hear her sing this morning?"

"Sí, it's her swan song."

"You're awful. I'm glad Candelaria will appreciate Rosita." Next question was whether the countess planned to come get her. "No," she said, "we're dropping her off tonight when we say adiós to Mother." Tears fell on the counter while she scrubbed the sides of the cage. Rosita clung from the top bars. As she folded a clean newspaper on the bottom, he sighed. She spent more time preparing the bird's journey than getting the family ready to depart.

The mantle clock showed four-thirty in the afternoon, and Wichi told the children to stay indoors until Nicolás arrived. The plan was to stroll the city with OP on this última noche and make their last night a memorable event. "Is Baltasar coming with Tío Nicolás?" Lizzi said.

"Sí, he'll drop off your uncle, so he can take us to the airport tomorrow." How nice she remarked that he would drive them. "Yes," and then he mumbled, "since I'm giving him the car." Wichi grabbed the keys and sauntered outside. He surveyed the 1950 Coronet. It still had a new look with Rey's maintenance and TLC over the years. That car had been with him for more than a decade, and he hated to leave it. He patted the hood and then sat behind the wheel. Music played on the radio as he waited. Ten minutes later OP walked out of the house carrying the birdcage as if she were transporting the crown jewels. She arranged the canary's position in the back seat and sat in the front.

"Please drive carefully, and no sudden stops since it might upset Rosita."

"By all means since she's an endangered species." OP stared straight ahead before reminding him they must return early. He cranked the motor; they left and traveled to the end of Quinta Avenida, along the Malecón, then to Galiano and San Rafael. OP had not seen El Encanto since the fire. Wichi gaped at the charred remains of the building, and she lamented the loss of a store having the most incredible Christmas decorations in Cuba. Bedraggled people roamed the corner. "Havana has gone to hell," he said, "with lots of shady characters loitering every-where." He parked the Coronet on San Nicolás Street across from María Teresa's apartment and planned to later walk the four blocks to the Malecón. First, they had to avoid the smelly garbage in the street before reaching the front entrance. "Get your legs ready for the hike up to this so-called heavenly dwell-ing." OP gave him the cage and delivered a stern warning not to drop the darling birdie. A revelation hit him halfway to the top. "I just figured out how your mother gets up these steps—she flies on her broom."

"Stop it, show respect."

"Hope soup's in the cauldron."

"Wichi, behave—these are the last moments with Mother."

"Here we are. Hope it's worth the climb."

OP knocked, and María Teresa opened the door. "Time you arrived; our dinner is getting cold."

"See you rolled out the red carpet," he said while observing the black tablecloth.

"Put the cage in the corner. Candelaria will come get it after her nap." He eased the birdcage to its resting place. "You will have to sweep the floor if that bird messes or spills birdseed on my linoleum."

"No problem, your broom is nearby." OP elbowed him and whispered they were there to say adiós and not be snarky. The old lady slurped her soup. Wichi wasn't sure what to call it, other than not appetizing. Unfortunately, OP inherited the lack of culinary skills from her mother.

María Teresa got up, shuffled to her bedroom, and returned with a velvet bag. "Here's the ring I want you to have."

"Oh, Mother, it's beautiful." *Best to bite my tongue,* since a snowball stood a greater chance making it through hell than that piece of jewelry getting past Castro's plunderers. OP took the ring. "I'll miss you. Please come with us." Wichi gulped and hoped the answer was no.

"My place is here. I have Candelaria, and sometimes Nicolás visits." OP hugged and kissed her. She followed María Teresa as she lumbered back to the chair. She grasped the old lady's frail hand once more before telling her adiós.

He hated to break up the farewell. "So long," he said. "It's getting late."

Tears welled up in OP's eyes as she closed the door. "Never an easy task to say goodbye." He reminded her it wasn't hard for her mother, happy to remain in the snake pit. She clutched the velvet cloth. "She gave us her prized possession that belonged to Blanca."

"The sister the butler murdered?" OP nodded. "Hope she didn't palm off a cursed ring." When they reached the car, he hid the bag in the glove compartment. "This is our última noche in Havana to stroll the Malecón." They ambled along Galiano Street until reaching the concrete barrier by the sea. The crimson sun dropped into the gray water, and soon dusk gave way to a darkened sky. A full moon rose high enough to transform Havana harbor into an enchanted scene. The tips of the gentle waves glistened as they moved to the shore. Tonight the surf was more of a susurrus than a roar as it lapped over the rocks. Two lovers sat on the ledge, his arm around her waist. Their legs dangled over the edge, they smiled at each other, and they kissed. A young boy baited a small minnow on his hook and cast out the fishing line.

Wichi loved the architecture of El Morro Castle, the landmark of Havana. It dominated the entrance to the harbor and reminded him of strength, a quality he needed to embark on a journey to a country where he couldn't speak the language. A spinal chill ceased when OP caught his hand. "Remember our wedding in Havana Cathedral when I wore a long, white satin dress."

"We had many good memories in this city." He cleared his throat. They embraced, and he gazed at the harbor. "Engrave this unique landscape in your mind until we see it again someday." He stepped on the wall and peered at a large tanker that arrived bearing Soviet flags. "Caramba, look at the pollution coming from the smokestacks." She cautioned him not to fall. "I'm looking at those huge round containers on deck. Who knows what they're bringing here—rockets?" She reminded him it was getting late, and they should go home. He jumped onto the concrete walkway, and they sauntered along San Rafael. It was dark and hard to see the sidewalk.

Only a few blocks remained to reach the car when gunfire

erupted from a building across the street. Wichi yanked OP's arm, "Get low," he said. They crouched behind a dilapidated truck parked nearby. People screamed and many scrambled for cover. A woman lay bleeding in the road ten feet away. He reached her when a bomb exploded inside. Two people ran out with clothes ablaze. He dropped to his knees and checked the woman for a pulse—too late for her. He moved toward the fire victims. A young guy had doused them with water. Ambulance sirens sounded in the distance. Better to let Fidel's medics look after their needs. He had done his part attending to the healthcare of fellow Cubans, so he returned to the truck. To his horror, a tall, toothless man stood behind OP—one arm around her neck, and a knife in the other hand. She couldn't yell, and her eyes bulged. Wichi hollered at the man to release her as he ran toward them.

"Gimme money, or I'll slit her throat."

He stopped, reached into his pocket, and threw pesos on the sidewalk. "Take the money and let her go," he shouted. The man pushed her to the ground, grabbed the cash, and darted into the alley. She gasped and held her neck. "Are you okay?" She nodded, not able to speak. He lifted her, and they rushed to the car. When they arrived, he helped her onto the seat. After determining no one had followed them, he got in, and the Coronet sped away.

As they left San Rafael Street behind, OP sobbed and placed her hand on his arm. "You saved my life. Without the money in your pocket, tonight would have been my última noche."

THIRTY-EIGHT

Who's Leaving Havana?

Havana, Cuba
August 10, 1961

Wichi reached over, touched OP's cheek, and offered reassurance as she groaned and patted her skinned knees with a handkerchief. "Soon we'll be out of this wretched place." As they drove back along the Malecón toward Playa, the wind had picked up. The surf pounded against the wall and splashed onto the pavement. The wipers swished at high speed. While he gripped the steering wheel, he surveyed the road ahead, determined to make it home with no more incidents. He pointed to the glove compartment. "I'm glad the ring's in the car. If we sneak it past the soldiers, we can sell it in the US and have money to live."

"But it's Mother's . . ."

"Mothers, smothers, we only have five dollars to our name."

When they reached Quinta Avenida, she lowered the window, and the wind blew in her face. She brushed back her hair and told him she'd prefer to get a job and keep the ring. "A job sweeping streets, maybe," he said and then laughed. She took the ring out of the bag, put it on her finger, and marveled how lovely it looked. He cautioned her not to get too attached since a diamond was fodder for Fidel's soldiers. After turning the corner onto 194 Street and parking the car, he noticed the streetlights were off. OP eased out of the seat and hobbled indoors. "Be careful, the house is dark." He followed her inside and flipped on the kitchen switch—no power—another good reason to leave Havana. He tiptoed to his daughters' room. Moonlight filtered through their mosquito netting—they were sound asleep. A snorting noise in Luisito's bedroom came from Nicolás, his vibrating mouth wide open. At least the crazy uncle showed up for the drive tomorrow. Luisito snoozed, accustomed to sleeping next to the snoring boxers. Wichi wasn't sleepy. He paced the floor and ended up in the study. The comfy chair behind his desk beckoned while the moon provided enough light to enjoy a smoke. A smile settled as he inhaled the tobacco aroma that emanated on opening the drawer. One cigar remained in the box, his last H. Upmann. He bit off the tip, struck a match, placed the end of the habano above the flame, and rolled it twice before lighting it. As he drew several puffs, he watched the smoke dissipate in the moonbeams and knew the plan to leave was the right decision—Castro was killing his Cuba.

The final puff lingered, caught in the jalousie's shadow. A thought penetrated his mind—the white-bearded man's prophecy at Valencio's bar eleven years ago had unfolded just as he predicted. The name eluded him, but he'd never forget the man as they raised glasses and toasted to Cuba's future—love it or leave it. He meandered to the living room and stared at the boxes for Nicolás and at the sofa covered with a white sheet. He sprawled on it and rested his eyes for a moment.

A strong thump sounded at the door and he answered it. Without a word a bearded soldier pulled him from the house and to the curb where the mysterious black car waited. The barbudo pushed him into the back. A figure sitting in the front seat turned and sneered at him. The name tag read Modesta. She pointed her pistol at him and snarled he'd get the firing squad for letting the nun go and lying to her. She was calling the shots now and was taking him to La Cabaña. The car entered the prison gate, and it closed behind them. She cackled as they dragged him out of the vehicle, took him inside, and threw him into a dark cell. The prisoner next to him was Captain Joaquín López, who he thought was dead. The heavy cell door creaked open. Two soldiers came in; the first seized Lopez, and the second snatched him. They tied Lopez to one post and him to the other. Four soldiers with rifles stood in front of them. The executioner's face was familiar—Che Guevara. He raised his hand and yelled, "READY, AIM, FIRE."

A sound jolted him. He clutched his chest; his shirt was soaked—blood—no, sweat.

Another loud noise. "Let me in."

He stumbled to the door. "Nicolás, you're outdoors in the middle of the night."

"It's six o'clock, and a splendid morning for a walk. Someone locked the house."

Wichi shrugged, slogged toward the sofa, and pinched himself to make sure what he'd been through was a nightmare. His head pounded; he was beat, and a momentous day still lay ahead.

Nicolás rested in the lounger and brushed back his receding hair. The bags under his eyes moved as he wiped the sweat on his face and fanned himself with a newspaper.

"Hope Miami has decent weather," he said. "Your big day, huh? Think you can handle it?"

"Bet your sweet ass." He sprang to his feet and left to take a shower.

OP paused combing her hair when he entered the room and questioned why he didn't come to bed last night. "I fell asleep on the sofa." While waiting for the water to get hot, he watched two lizards parade above the tub and inflate their pink throats. The warm liquid soothed his aching head. Leaving this rat's nest was a comforting thought, but long-term plans after their arrival in Miami were disconcerting. The uncle who lived near Homestead, Florida, had invited him to stay there; however, he said the house was small and the wife had dementia. He guessed it was a polite way of evoking the three-day-visit rule. So much depended on Doctor Melmont getting him a job and a place to stay. He took a towel and watched the reptiles. "Okay, geckos, the shower is yours, compliments of Fidel Castro." A few articles of clothing on the bed demanded his scrutiny. A short deliberation followed, and he selected a white shirt and dark pants, trying to achieve a professional look. Underwear cloaked the prized possession—his medical diploma at the bottom of the bag. Without this document he'd have to clean toilets. Five American dollars lay on the dresser—his mustard seeds. After a final scan of the bedroom, and with a half-smile, he squared his shoulders, grabbed his meager belongings, and sauntered to the front door. "Four o'clock and time to go. Everybody, grab your bags."

OP wept as she glanced at a blooming red hibiscus. "I'll miss my yard." He plucked a flower and slipped the stem behind her ear. She touched the petal, smiled, and dried her face. Now a part of her garden was leaving with her. Lizzi held on to her doll and cried while Didi fidgeted with the diamond ring. Luisito grabbed his bag and announced he was ready to see the Wild West.

"Where are you, Nicolás?" Wichi said as he tapped his foot on the front steps.

"In here," he yelled, "just turning off the stove."

Wichi arranged the luggage in the trunk while the children climbed into the back seat. Nicolás opened the passenger door for OP and sat beside her. Wichi cranked the engine and stared at the uncle. "I busted my rear to buy this car, so don't wreck it." He nodded and enumerated his driving skills. Wichi backed the car onto the street and faced the house. His voice cracked. "Children, no matter what happens, 194 Street remains your home. Adiós."

Silence with intermittent sniffles prevailed as they left the neighborhood. The sky darkened, raindrops hit the windshield, and a strong north wind bent the palm branches while approaching Rancho Boyeros for the five o'clock flight. At the airport armed militia waved the Coronet to the departure terminal. Wichi's stomach twisted while reading the sign: VUELOS PARA GUSANOS, Flight for Worms. "That's us—creatures wriggling our way to freedom." The storm had worsened by the time he stopped the car and gave the keys to Nicolás. Rain poured; the wind howled and jerked the umbrella when he stepped onto the pavement. He popped open the trunk and handed everyone their bags. OP hugged Nicolás and ordered him to take care of her mother. "Make a run for it," he said. She and the children dashed through the pelting raindrops to the terminal awning. He stuck his head through the window and said goodbye to Nicolás and his car. The Coronet lurched a few times before it sped away. A flashback of the day he bought the car lingered in his mind until he realized water had seeped into his shoes. *Dammit, quit dreaming and get out of the rain.*

"Gusanos, follow me this way," shouted a soldier. Wichi and his family marched behind the man toward the departing lounge—La Pecera, the fishbowl.

Lizzi tugged at her father's shirt. She reminded him that Rosie had to sit there. "Nothing has changed," he said. "We aren't just worms but goldfish in a glass prison." He then offered her a smile of encouragement. As they walked, he slipped a piece of paper into OP's hand. She turned and gave him a startled look. "I've written Dr. Melmont's address and phone number. If I can't leave Havana, you contact . . ."

"Wichi, you don't mean that?" Her mouth fell open.

"You heard me. Get the children out of here." The thick glass enclosure was straight ahead. Two families in front waited. Wichi recognized the first man, a doctor from Pinar del Río he'd met years ago. The guard pulled the physician out of the queue but made his family move into the lounge. He calculated he was next, so he leaned to OP and spoke in her ear. "Keep moving and don't act surprised when I walk away. Promise to meet up with you later."

OP's chest constricted after he disappeared into the crowd. Lizzi asked why her father left, and OP said he went to the restroom. As they entered the fishbowl, her heart throbbed, and soon sweat drenched her body. She didn't want to continue this journey without him. Families ahead lined up in rows for questioning.

"Barreras," shouted the bearded soldier rummaging through her luggage. "What's this?" He laughed, held up the album, and said she wouldn't need this anymore.

When he flipped open a lighter, she grabbed his wrist. "Señor, for the love of God, don't destroy these pictures, I beg you."

She screamed while he flicked the wheel and brought the flame toward the photo collection. A sergeant came over and pulled back the guy's arm. "What's the commotion?" he growled.

"The gusana wants to take photographs out of Cuba."

"Pictures of my family and my dogs," she said. The sergeant grabbed the album and asked what breed. "Boxers and a mastiff." She showed him the dog photos after he told her he raised boxers.

"Let her take the album." He motioned them ahead.

Her confidence waned while suffering through this ordeal alone, but she had to shake it off and be brave for the children.

Thumps sounded as passengers tossed their possessions in large containers scattered around the room. "What are you hiding inside that doll?" a guard said to Lizzi. Nothing, she told him. "Throw the ugly thing in the tub."

"My doll's not ugly, she's wearing my school uniform." He snapped at her and said toss it. While she sobbed, OP took off the clothes she had made for the doll and then lowered it into the bin. This was unbearable. *Where is Wichi?* A little girl wailed when a soldier snatched her teddy bear and hurled it into the barrel. The pinging sound from a metal bucket got louder as they neared the table where guards searched for jewelry.

The man grabbed Didi's hand from her pocket. "What do we have here?" He yanked at her ring finger and told her to remove the diamond. OP slapped his arm, and his eyes glared as he gripped his pistol. She gasped, realizing what she'd done, then with a calm voice said it was a family heirloom. When he pulled out his gun, Didi pleaded for him not to hurt her mother. The soldier put the weapon back in the holster and shook his fist. "Señora, next time, I'll lock you behind bars." He scowled at Didi. "Give me the ring, or I'll cut off your finger." She wept, and OP removed the ring and tossed it into the bucket—another ping in the room. Didi continued to cry. OP pressed her close in a hug. Luisito wanted to know where Papi was, and she whispered he'd be there soon. A quick backward gaze revealed the soldier had reached inside the container and pocketed something. Disgust sickened her—he took Abuela's ring. She paced the filthy floor and looked through the dingy glass for Wichi, suspecting they detained him, *but for what reason?*

"Atención, form a line for the final pat-down. Rápido."

She grunted. "Vamos niños, we have to endure this part."

Lizzi pulled on her arm and said they must wait for Papi. OP covered her mouth and whispered to be quiet. A greasy-haired guard inspected the male passengers. "Arrest this worm," he said. "He tried to smuggle a ring in his underwear." The soldiers came, and the trembling man yelped as they beat him and dragged the poor soul away. Lizzi whined. OP had to push her and the other two ahead for a grubby female soldier with dirty fingernails to frisk them.

"Gusanos with cleared passports continue to the tarmac," shouted a guard.

OP grabbed Luisito's hand. "Let's go, there's the airplane."

Rain poured on the taxiway as they hurried to the Pan Am. By the time they reached the top of the stairs, water soaked them. They entered midway into the cabin, and a stewardess directed them left and to their seats in the forward section near the cockpit.

Lizzi turned to OP. "Where's Papi? We can't leave without him."

She squeezed her hand and nodded. "He'll be here." Her voice broke. Passengers boarded and soon filled most of the seats. As she wiped a hand on her dress, she felt her arms tingle and stomach churn. No plausible reason existed why Wichi wasn't there. He had a visa, and they planned to leave Havana together. Reaching into her pocket, she pulled out the paper with Doctor Melmont's information. *Did he give me this at the last minute, knowing he couldn't come with us?* If so, she'd never have boarded the plane. Her chin trembled.

"Mami, your eyes are red," Lizzi said.

Didi told her something was wrong. "Where is Papi?"

"I'm not sure," OP said as she cupped her mouth.

A stewardess announced that the DC-7 was ready for takeoff, and the passengers must fasten their seat belts. The plane taxied to the runway. A bolt of lightning struck nearby. Rain poured in sheets obscuring everything outside the window. "May I have your attention please," boomed a man's voice over the speaker. "Because of the severe weather, the tower has instructed us to stay here until ready for departure." The sky was black, and torrential rain continued. The feeling was unbearable that Wichi was not aboard. After waiting thirty minutes, passengers clamored to leave Cuba.

"Let's get moving," shouted a man three seats away.

A woman said, "I want out of this rathole."

"This is your captain; we are cleared for takeoff. Make sure your seatbelts are securely fastened." People cheered.

"We can't go to the US without Papi." Lizzi said.

OP couldn't help but to cover her face and cry. *What is life without him?* She regained her composure and turned to the girls. "Your father told me we must go, and he'll join us later." Lizzi asked how he planned to leave. "I don't know," she said.

The engines roared, and the DC-7 rolled along the runway, faster and faster until it was airborne. "Stop this plane," Didi yelled. OP shushed her. She stared at Wichi's empty seat while the girls bawled.

"Tell Luisito to come sit with me."

"He's not behind us," Lizzi said.

"Where is he?"

"I don't know. Didi and I watched the lightning, not him."

OP's heart sank—first Wichi and now Luisito. She screamed for the stewardess. The woman finished announcing that passengers may remove their seatbelts. She rushed the refreshment cart to OP's seat. "My son's disappeared," she said. "You must find him."

"I'll look for him as I head to the tail section, and the other attendant will check the front."

The stewardess hurried toward the back and was knocked aside as a man climbed over the cart and yelled, "Estoy aquí, I'm here!"

Lizzi turned around and pointed to him. "It's Papi!"

"I can't believe he's on the plane," Didi said. They both

jumped out of their seats, pushed people apart, and scurried to meet him. He opened his arms, and they tumbled into his embrace.

"Mis niñas." He kissed each one.

He saw OP standing, both hands grasped her head. Passengers moved out of the way as he rushed along the aisle, then climbed over two rows of seats to reach her. They embraced. "Where's Luisito?" he said. Tears filled her eyes.

"I don't know. He disappeared, and we have to locate him." Wichi ran toward the cockpit and noticed the attendant clutching his son's hand. She directed Luisito to him, and he came running.

"Papi, I knew I'd find you, but I got locked in the bathroom." He lifted and squeezed him. "Sí, mi niño, you found me." Tears poured across his cheeks. The stewardess assisted them to their places.

OP stroked his wet shirt, then grabbed his ears. "You gave me a scare. How did you get on this plane?" When he said through the door, she slapped him on the shoulder. "Why didn't we see you?"

"You sat in the front section, and we were in the rear."

"What do you mean, 'we'?"

"Give me a minute, and you'll hear the story." Wichi gathered the family—Luisito sitting on his lap and the girls standing next to him. He began the saga. "It was Colonel García—he's the one who released me from jail, got our visas, and had the black car protect us. His men took me from the terminal to the tarmac where he and his son waited inside a parked van."

"This is crazy," OP said. "He works for Castro."

"Sí, but he risked his life to sneak Albertito out of Cuba." She gave him another puzzled look. He told her the lad needed surgery, and the colonel's boss refused to let Albertito leave. "García planned the boy's escape with our departure so I could be on the plane with him to Miami. His aunt is waiting for him to arrive."

"Where is he?"

"In the rear section. He's a brave boy, and the stewardess is looking out for him. The terrible weather made it easier to conceal the youngster and get him on the plane. We boarded from a truck and a ladder just before takeoff. They rushed us to the back, and that's why you didn't see me until they turned off the seatbelt sign." He caught his breath. The emotion inside him erupted, and he roared, "My family and I left Cuba together." He ruffled Luisito's hair, clenched the girls' hands, and kissed their cheeks. Travelers applauded. The stewardess congratulated them and ushered the children to their seats.

"Good evening—this is your captain speaking. It won't be long before we land in Miami. Welcome to the United States of America."

Passengers cried as they sang the Cuban national anthem. After they settled back, OP gripped Wichi's hand and smiled. She reclined, took a deep breath, and her eyes closed. Exhaustion overwhelmed her.

A ruddy, white-bearded man seated in front of them stood up, shifted around, and said, "Hola, Wichi Barreras."

He nearly fell out of the seat. He knew this man. *What was his name?* Eli—something. Then it hit him. "Elías Verdadero, I've thought of you often since 1949. Everything you told me has come true."

"Yes, my friend, and I'm ready for another toast." He handed Wichi a beverage. "This drink is to better times ahead." He raised the bottle. "To the future—may you and your family live it in freedom."

They toasted and shook hands. "Ladies and gentlemen," came the man's voice from the cockpit, "we've encountered unexpected turbulence. Please fasten your seatbelts." Elías turned and sat. The plane quaked and the cabin darkened. Muted cries echoed along the aisle. The storm lasted about fifteen minutes, and soon the ride smoothed. Wichi was glad OP remained asleep; her ordeal merited a good rest. He got up and checked the children seated behind. The girls were talking, and Luisito thought the bumps were fun. He returned and saw no one occupying the seat in front. *Caramba*— he called the stewardess and asked the whereabouts of the gentleman seated there.

"Sorry, Señor, you must be mistaken, this seat is empty."

He slumped back onto the cushion, stared upward, and muttered. OP reached over and held his arm. "Wichi, what are you saying?"

"Elías Verdadero—he's gone."

The End

ACKNOWLEDGMENTS

First and foremost, praise and thanks to God for His guidance during the years composing this novel. We have been blessed. This book would not have happened without my coauthor husband of fifty years, whose wit and excellent command of the English language assisted in augmenting true personalities of the family and fictional characters. He believed in the story from the onset and was determined to see the project to completion.

Our son, Doctor Louie Meier, helped overcome the initial dilemma on where to end the book—in Cuba or continue life in the US. We took his advice that Cuba during the fifties intrigues readers. He also picked the correct sample cover and pointed us toward an appropriate title.

The editing skill and patience of Marsha Cornelius was vital for new writers. She served as our coach and cheerleader. Thanks, couldn't have done it without you, Marsha. After completion of the manuscript, the next step was finding an exterior designer. Since a book is often judged by its cover, we were fortunate to find Pamela Trush, who hit a home run with the 1949 Coronet, the crab, and a little blood. Kudos to Delaney Designs.

To our dear Texas friends, Celia and her husband, who both love Cuba, muchas gracias for being our first beta readers. The Bookies, the coauthor's book club in Dawsonville, Georgia, got things started by whetting her interest in writing. Because she was Cuban, they invited her to discuss *The Cuban Affair* by Nelson DeMille. Inspiration followed, and shortly thereafter work on our book began.

Ronnie Fox, a friend and author, gave us needed advice and encouragement in the beginning of the long writing journey, and for that we are grateful. Best wishes for your new book, *Beyond My Strength*.

The Atlanta Writers Club is fortunate to have George Weinstein as president. This award-winning author goes above and beyond the call of duty to help and inspire countless writers including us. We're honored to know him.

We needed advice on the airplane chapters, and our good friend for many years, Jim Hunt, a former captain and pilot in the USAF, helped us greatly. We appreciate the assistance, and any aviation errors are ours.

Firsthand information is the best, and our buena Cuban amiga who recently immigrated offered valuable information concerning Castro's educational indoctrination. We're thankful she's in the US.

Lizzi's brother, Luisito, Doctor Luis Ramon Barreras, helped us understand the relationship between Wichi and Dr. Melmont, particularly his laboratory experiments. Thanks. It added tremendous perspective to this important character.

Few people are blessed to have a relative and friend as Tom Chorey, who gave us legal help and advice. He's a Virginia gentleman and an outstanding fisherman.

A NOTE TO READERS

For us, writing a historical fiction novel carried a burden not borne by authors of solely fictional work. Many of our characters on various occasions participate in actual political and cultural situations. The sources of information for the book came firsthand from the coauthor, her parents, and family. She lived in Cuba from 1949 to 1961. Her father had many friends, patients, and a keen interest in Cuban politics. He continued to follow and discuss events pertaining to Cuba after immigrating and becoming a US citizen. Her cousin was a brigadista in the Bay of Pigs, jailed by Castro, released, and lived with the family for a while. He shared many unforgettable stories, especially experiences concerning the invasion. Ofelia Perfecta's photo album remains a priceless resource for authenticity.

SPECIAL RECOGNITION

A major objective of *Killing My Cuba* is to present a factual over-view of Cuban history during the 1950s in an informal manner using real and fictional characters and events. While verifying our information, we happened upon a blog: *Cuba1952-1959.blogspot.com* that is ideal for readers who wish to delve fur-ther into accurate Cuban history. The interactive timeline for-mat is ideal to readily obtain desired material. This wealth of information is derived from a historical book by Dr. Manuel Marquez-Sterling, Professor Emeritus of history at Plymouth State University, titled *Cuba 1952–1959: The True Story of Castro's Rise to Power*. The blog was created by R.R. Aranda and Professor Marquez-Sterling. These two men deserve recogni-tion and praise for providing easily accessible facts pertaining to a crucial segment of Cuban history.

Havana Suburbs

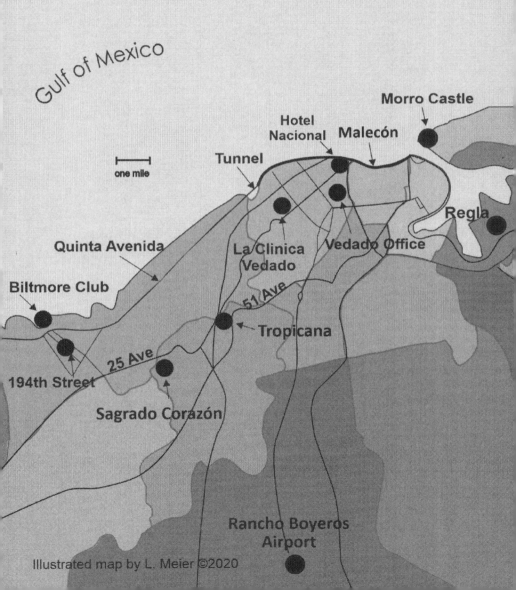

Gulf of Mexico

one mile

Morro Castle

Hotel
Nacional   Malecón

Tunnel

Regla

Quinta Avenida

La Clinica
Vedado

Vedado Office

Biltmore Club

51 Ave

Tropicana

25 Ave

194th Street

Sagrado Corazón

Rancho Boyeros
Airport

Illustrated map by L. Meier ©2020

Vedado, Centro Havana Old Havana

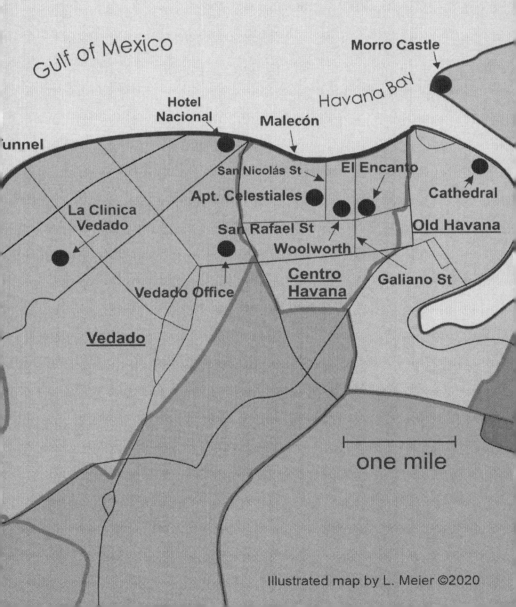

Gulf of Mexico

Morro Castle

Havana Bay

Hotel Nacional

Malecón

Tunnel

San Nicolás St

El Encanto

Cathedral

Apt. Celestiales

La Clinica Vedado

Old Havana

San Rafael St

Woolworth

Centro Havana

Vedado Office

Galiano St

Vedado

one mile

Illustrated map by L. Meier ©2020

ABOUT THE AUTHORS

The Meiers live in Georgia and enjoy grandparenting, fishing, boating, hiking, reading, and taking care of Sandi, their almost fourteen-year-old lab.

The photo below shows them seated on the Malecón with Morro Castle in the background, taken during the first of two trips to Cuba. Lizzi had the surreal experience of seeing the home at 194 Street she left in 1961. The owner invited her inside.

Visit us at our website at KillingMyCuba.com
or
Email us at KillingMyCuba@gmail.com

Made in the USA
Columbia, SC
14 September 2021